"Fast, fascinating, and funny, *Gotham Diaries* exposes a world of high-end New York real estate, conniving socialites—gay and straight, trophy wives, corporate shenanigans, social climbers, and one woman's struggle to not only stay sane and scrupulous, but triumph. This book will have you giggling, gasping, ~~and~~ ~~~~ ~~~~."
—Jill Nelson, author of the ~~~~ ~~~~

"*Gotham Diaries* is a poignant and deeply ~~~~ ~~~~ ~~~~ ~~~~ ~~~~acy, race and class within the African-American ~~~~ ~~~~ ~~~~ ~~~~ury."
— Henry Lou~~~~

"The Lee/Anthony team is the Edith Wharton of new black money…
vicious, funny, juicy." —*Publishers Weekly*

"Ambition, Betrayal, and Class are the ABCs of this millennium tale of Edith Wharton proportion. *Gotham Diaries* is a thrill ride that keeps us wondering as to when just deserts will be served and whose claws will be used to eat them."
— Brian Keith Jackson, author of *The Queen of Harlem*

"A decadent romp that's sure to entertain while reminding readers that money isn't everything . . ." —*People*

"Lee and Anthony bring their intimate knowledge of the glittery New York scene to this delicious novel."
—*Booklist*

"This titillating debut novel is irresistible; a richly absorbing tale of Manhattan's upper crust packed with sex, lies, and backstabbing, and a heroine you're truly rooting for. *Gotham Diaries* is written with heart and intensity, and describes a luxurious world few ever have the opportunity to glimpse."
— E. Lynn Harris

GOTHAM DIARIES

GOTHAM DIARIES

TONYA LEWIS LEE

CRYSTAL McCRARY ANTHONY

HYPERION NEW YORK

Poetry on p. vii, from THE COLLECTED POEMS OF LANGSTON HUGHES by Langston Hughes, copyright © 1994 by The Estate of Langston Hughes. Used by permission of Alfred A. Knopf, a division of Random House, Inc.

TRADE PAPERBACK ISBN: 1-4013-0802-3

Hyperion books are available for special promotions and premiums. For details, contact Michael Rentas, Manager, Inventory and Premium Sales, Hyperion, 77 West 66th Street, 11th floor, New York, New York 10023, or call 212-456-0133.

Book design by Lisa Stokes

First Trade Paperback Edition

10 9 8 7 6 5 4 3 2 1

To Spike, for all of your love and inspiration.

—T.L.L.

To my angels, Cole Hinton and Ella Ann—your smiles alone give me reason to wake each morning. Thelma and Magellan McCrary—my parents, my rocks, my sources of strength—no two people take greater pride in their children, a legacy I hope to continue.

—C.M.A.

The rhythm of life
Is a jazz rhythm
Honey.
The gods are laughing at us . . .

—*Langston Hughes*

GOTHAM DIARIES

Looking good had become a way of life for Manny Marks. His outward appearance was vital to his existence. Whenever he stepped out of his Harlem brownstone, he made sure to put forth the best image money and connections could buy. In the fiercely competitive Manhattan real estate business, perception could easily become reality. And Manny's immediate reality was that he was trying to impress his new clients, even if he was tired of selling real estate.

Today Manny Marks was decked out in his finest summer's threads: khaki linen slacks, crisp white shirt open at the collar with an Etro rust-and-navy-checked sport coat. The jacket accentuated his suntanned cocoa-brown skin and chemically whitened teeth. He had been told over the years that he had a great smile, so he took care of that asset almost as carefully as he maintained his thirty-six-year-old lean, muscular physique. The Hermès handkerchief in his left pocket was an extra touch; Manny hoped it would signal to the world that he was a man of refinement.

The first stop of the day would be a scenic walk with his new clients, the Joneses, before their first appointment at 515 Park Avenue, a condominium building friendly to new black money. Normally he would have greeted his current patrons with car and driver at their hotel if they were out-of-towners, like the Joneses—or at their homes, if they were city inhabitants, which he preferred. Occasionally clients met him at the property he was showing. But today was the first time in August that the temperature had dropped below 90 degrees, and the Manhattan air was breathable for a change. It even seemed free from the exaggerated summer scents—burning pretzels, peanuts, sour mustard, gyros, and onions. A crispness descended upon Manhattan near the end of the summer.

Then there were the Joneses. Even if they were Tandy Brooks's friends, Eric and Tamara Jones were Midwest imports and required handholding, something Manny had grown weary of unless the people were special contacts worthy of cultivation. The Joneses were anything but special in Manny's eyes; the "barely" millionaires no longer intrigued him. The real bother, however, wasn't their lack of large funds. Rather, he found them dull. They both were so ordinary in their drab, midlevel designer wear, and they lacked sophistication. But Tandy had hand-delivered them and expected him to take care of them. And that was an order Manny dared not disobey.

Manny reminded himself that a commission from anyone was money in the bank. Despite the Joneses' shortcomings, Manny still needed to make sure the young African-American couple from Flossmoor, Illinois, trusted him enough to buy a three-million-dollar apartment from him. The broker's image had a significant impact on potential buyers, a concept Manny had learned early in his career, and he had set up the showing to underscore that he was the real deal. His firm's solid reputation came from strategic planning carefully managed over the course of many years. As the trio navigated the array of fashionable shoppers striding down Madison Avenue, Manny tried to imagine Tamara Jones fitting in with the throngs of chic people. Manhattan could either excite and stimulate newcomers—giving them the opportunity to live their lives to the richest and fullest of their imaginations—or chew them up and spit them out, breaking them in the process. Manny didn't see Tamara's dream in these streets.

"Good afternoon, Mr. Marks," the portly black doorman from Hermès called out to Manny as they passed the posh store filled with women begging to spend six thousand on a Birkin bag.

"Hello!" Manny returned, noting out of the corner of his eye the Joneses watching the exchange. Impressing upon them his familiarity with the neighborhood and its inhabitants was crucial. They had to feel that Madison Avenue was accessible to Manny and to them. The high-priced boutiques often intimidated newcomers, the snooty salespeople making them feel unworthy. Manny was certain that despite their lack of savoir faire, the midwestern couple knew the significance of Madison Avenue. Each passing acknowledgment from the neighborhood regulars heightened Manny's image. His familiarity with this world, where the city's natives stepped in and out of jewelry stores, spoke into their cells while carrying bags from Barneys, or hailed taxis with the ease of dancers, would hopefully demystify the surroundings for his clients.

As they waited at the corner of Sixty-fourth and Madison waiting for the light to change, looking toward the Krizia boutique, Fifi Pennywhistle stepped out of her chauffeur-driven Rolls-Royce, undoubtedly for a day of running up her credit cards. Manny could not have scripted the scene any better as Fifi leaned in to him, air-kissing both cheeks as if he were her long-lost stepson.

"How aah you, dahling?" she asked. Fifi was a rail-thin Upper East Side staple with a penchant for Chanel suits and oversize round glasses. He had met her when he worked at Tiffany, before opening his own real estate firm. Fifi tipped along in her Ferragamos, gesticulating with her hands; the sun glinted off her assortment of large rings, adornments that overpowered her frail physique—beauty long gone but baubles remaining like artifacts from a better era.

Manny responded mock-humbly, a technique Tandy had taught him. "Fine, dear, just earning my keep."

"I'd say you've earned your keep quite well." Fifi winked at Manny. "So, when are you going to the Vineyard?"

Manny was pleased that she had mentioned his vacationing at the Vineyard in front of the Joneses. He exaggerated his southern drawl, which northerners like Fifi found charming. "You think all I do is vacation? Some of us do have to work." Fifi giggled, looking charmed by her exchange with Manny. She should be happy. His last Tiffany "deal" for her had been a 15 percent discount on the seventy-five sterling-silver charm bracelets she bought as shower gifts for her daughter's wedding.

"You are so adorable. Isn't he adorable?" she asked, patting his cheek and glancing in the direction of the Joneses, though not expecting a response. She continued on her mission. In Fifi's eyes, no one was really important outside of her enclave, least of all the Joneses, but her acknowledgment of Manny was invaluable.

"Who was that?" Tamara asked.

"Fifi Pennywhistle. She was one of my former bosses' clients. Very wealthy. I think her father had a steel company or something." Manny purposefully neglected his days as a jewelry salesman.

"She looks like steel money." Tamara ogled as if she had come in contact with Queen Elizabeth. Fifi had that effect; she may have clinched the deal for him. At last Tamara was truly impressed. She actually smiled. Before witnessing the small grin that spread across her face, Manny hadn't thought she was physically able to lift her heavy jowls into a smile.

Manny was feeling full of himself by this time. This was the high he experienced every time he felt like an insider—a true New Yorker. He was prepared to sell the Joneses all of Central Park. As they continued up Madison, his clients seemed to relax, seeming to realize they were in good hands. Manny was their safari guide through the jungle of Manhattan. He picked up his stride, confident in looking every bit the part of an Upper East Sider, even though he hailed from Alabama.

Times had changed a lot for Manny since that day, over seventeen years before, when he'd shown up at his cousin Tommy's fourth-floor walk-up in Brooklyn. He'd been carrying his footlocker turned suitcase and wearing the ill-fitting Brooks Brothers suit he had gotten as a high school graduation present from his grandparents. Manny sat on the dry, cracked wood floor of Tommy's hallway all night, waiting for his cousin to return. The smell of fried fish seeped out of another apartment, making Manny's stomach growl. But even that didn't bother him, because he had finally arrived in New York City. If he had stayed one more day in Birmingham, he would have blown his brains out. He never would have survived working for his father's construction company, and his mother would have spun in her grave if he had taken a job at the Haley department store selling cutlery—his only other prospect. Instead, he took the money his grandparents had given him—another graduation gift—and bought a one-way ticket to New York.

When he arrived, he sat falling asleep outside Tommy's door, waiting for his cousin to get home from his job as a bartender in a place called the Village. But Manny was so excited he didn't mind the smell or the discomfort in the dimly lit stairwell. He was ready to start a new life. As a gay black young boy, he had never fit in in Alabama. Not that he had ever told anyone he didn't much like girls. He simply never dated one, except at prom, to which he took Lucille Pritkins, who had sat next to him in typing class their senior year. Truth be told, she didn't have much interest in boys.

Tommy's voice woke Manny from his nodding: "What you doin' down there on the floor with your country ass?"

As soon as Manny looked up at Tommy's towering physique, high-top curly fade, catlike green eyes, and tight, tight blue jeans—tighter than Manny had ever dared to wear—he knew he had made the right decision. He stood up to properly greet his older cousin like his mother had taught him. He could not stop smiling.

"What you so damn happy about?" Tommy said as he unlocked what seemed to Manny a Fort Knox of bolts before opening his door. Manny followed behind his worldly older cousin like a puppy dog.

When they entered the one-room apartment, Manny's eyes roamed over the tie-dyed sheets hanging from the ceilings. His gaze lingered on the cozy space, a bed in the middle of the room covered with an assortment of colorful velvet pillows. Manny wondered what it would feel like to lie in such an indulgent bed. It seemed so plush. Tommy must have been reading his mind as he said, "You get the couch."

Manny felt tongue-tied and silently nodded. He hoped he hadn't done something wrong already. Tommy pulled back a black velvet curtain, exposing a small yellowing refrigerator. He opened the freezer compartment and pulled out a plastic bag filled with a brown weedy-looking substance. He pulled out some papers and rolled the stuff into something resembling a cigarette. Manny watched in amazement at this new world, where his own family member seemed so self-assured, so at ease with himself, as if he didn't give a damn what anyone else thought of him. After lighting the cigarette that didn't smell like a regular cigarette, Tommy finally seemed to notice Manny again. "Let me look at you. Take that tired-ass jacket off, looks like yo' daddy's coat."

Tommy's eyes felt like ray guns. Manny was frozen.

"I'm not going to bite you, I'm just checking you out. You turned into a good-looking kid. A little skinny, but we'll buff you up. The boys will love you here."

Manny's face was on fire. How did Tommy know? Was it that obvious, or did Manny simply remind Tommy of himself when he arrived in New York ready to "find himself"?

"You need some new clothes, though. You got some money?"

"Yeah."

"Good, we'll go to SoHo and get you some new stuff. You also have to pay me rent."

"I know, Daddy told me."

"Good. Then we understand each other. We'll have . . . we'll have—" Tommy stammered as he began to cough uncontrollably. Probably from the stinky cigarette, Manny thought. "We'll have fun. Right now I need—some sleep," Tommy said, still not gathering himself from the coughing spell. "We'll go out, eat, shop, do the town when I get up."

Manny excitedly sat on the small covered sofa, unable to go to sleep, he was so thrilled. Tommy's nap turned into a six-hour fitful sleep filled with

grunts, groans, coughs, and whispering. But when he woke, he took a shower, put on black leather jeans and a white T-shirt, and looked like he'd slept all night and was ready to party again.

That day Manny fell in love with Tommy and New York City. Tommy took him all over the Village, which was nothing like the village Manny had envisioned. Manny bought the tightest jeans he could wiggle his little butt into, size 27. And then Tommy opened up to him the New York he had dreamed of, filled with dancing, clubs, drinking, partying, and men. Manny lost his virginity in New York at the health club where he started working out with Tommy. Life was idyllic for the two of them, until that morning Tommy didn't get out of bed and something called AIDS was the culprit. Then the tough times began. Tommy withered and died. Manny was out of money, and there was no way he would go back to Alabama.

Continuing their walk, Manny was pumped up by the thought that even though he lived in Harlem, he truly was an Upper East Side staple. He had become a member of Manhattan's society, albeit a junior member. With Tandy Brooks, a living legend in New York society, and It Girl Lauren Thomas as his biggest fans, he had been propelled to near-star status as a real estate broker to the African-American elite. Still, a mere real estate broker would never be a major player—a thought that was weighing on his mind more and more these days. He had yet to make the transaction that would put him over the top, give him some fuck-you money and social respect. Despite the fact that he owned and operated the most profitable African-American real estate firm in Manhattan, to many, he was only a highly paid salesman.

"You know the neighborhood quite well, I see," Eric Jones, a light-skinned classic pretty boy who had eaten one too many cookies, remarked in what Manny interpreted as an appraisal.

"Fifteen years in the business will do that."

"Fifteen years in New York?"

Manny proudly nodded as they walked past Daniel, currently the best

restaurant in New York City, housed in one of Donald Trump's many converted condominiums.

"What about the accent?" Eric asked. Manny was immediately suspicious of the question. Eric was from the Midwest, a place where plenty of black southerners had migrated. A southern drawl wouldn't be deemed charming in Flossmoor, Illinois, like it was in New York.

Manny gave what had become his "story" once he started working at Tiffany: "I'm originally from Birmingham, Alabama, but I moved to New York for college." Everyone seemed to respect a student who worked part-time to make ends meet.

"Oh?" Eric said, perking up. His wife continued to walk silently beside him. Manny almost felt bad for her. The raw energy of the city streets seemed to stifle her. He could see how things would probably go once they relocated. Eric would have many late nights, going to working dinners and fund-raisers. At first he would invite his wife. She would go once, maybe twice, and be intimidated by the high-octane crowd. She would stop accompanying him to social and business outings, preferring to stay home alone. He would stop inviting her. Then Manny would start running into Eric around town, surrounded by plenty of company. Manny did not envision the two of them lasting. Attractive, aggressive men like Eric always seemed to need a little extra attention once they started believing the hype the city fed them.

Eric continued, "Where'd you do your undergraduate work?"

Manny felt a gnawing prick. He did not appreciate Eric prying into his personal business. What difference should it make where he went to school, thought Manny, feeling slightly inadequate. Eric Jones would be the type to ask where someone did his undergraduate work with the implication that he had an advanced degree as well.

"I went to New York University," Manny said, then quickly changed the subject, reaching into his thin brown leather briefcase and removing the day's itinerary. "The first apartment we're seeing today is in estate condition, with about twenty-five hundred square feet of space, three wood-burning

fireplaces, an eat-in kitchen, and good light." He hoped these country clients understood that in New York, a deteriorated apartment could cost millions just because of its location. Famed agent Barbara Corcoran had put her seal of approval on estate-condition property when, early in her career, she offered one of New York's prominent families a "thirty-two-million-dollar fixer-upper." Manny looked at Tamara and Eric to read their faces. The first sell on the first day was always the most difficult.

"And how much is this one?" Tamara asked, with an edge Manny had not heard from her.

Manny glanced at the price on the itinerary, even though he already knew the answer. He hated this part with people like the Joneses. "The asking price is three million."

"For twenty-five hundred square feet?" Tamara's voice rose an octave.

Manny stopped himself from showing any emotion as he silently wished that out-of-towners buying property would first bone up on Manhattan real estate values. Taking a deep breath, he tried to muster as much sympathy as possible before answering. All he could bring himself to say was "Apartments with that much space in this area command a lot of money." He stopped short of calling her "honey."

Manny knew he sounded a bit short, but his patience was running thin. He was tired of coaxing people out of their sticker shock, especially people who had the money but didn't know how to spend it. Whiners. Yes, Manhattan real estate was pricey. Either get with the program or go to New Jersey. Manny hated having to convince people of the value of the city. If they didn't understand that the convenience and style of living in the world's royal city had a huge price tag, then Manny didn't want to deal with them. In any case, these two were not his first choice in clientele. True, Eric Jones was a successful Chicago businessman and on the rise in New York City. But he had no style. If Tandy had not referred them, Manny probably would have been at Martha's Vineyard for Lauren's last summer weekend at the house.

"Why don't we go inside and get a good idea of how the space lays out.

Twenty-five hundred square feet can be very spacious. And you can always move walls to make whatever rooms you want."

"Hmph." Tamara seemed to be growing more comfortable. "That's about the size of my guest wing."

Manny refrained from saying, "Then stay the hell in Flossmoor!" He suggested they go upstairs and take a look. He then reassured them that they had only just begun their search, and there was plenty on the market for them to see. The sticker-shock virus had just begun, and so had Manny's headaches.

As she entered the grand dining room of the Pierre Hotel, elegantly set for an illustrious crowd's luncheon, Tandy Brooks reflected on the many gatherings that she had organized for charitable events in New York, stopping short of becoming nostalgic. No need for that right now. Today she was here as an honored guest for all of her work in helping to raise millions of dollars for Manhattan's most prestigious charities. However, her mood was not joyful. She was preoccupied, thinking, planning how to make sure this event would not be her last hurrah.

At fifty-one, Tandy could rival any woman from thirty on up. Her cocoa-brown skin was flawless, barely a wrinkle in sight, thanks to many facials and expensive creams. Her dark brown hair, perfectly styled in her weekly visits to the salon, hung just above her shoulders. Finishing her sophisticated look was her vintage beige Chanel suit with gold buttons. She had purchased the outfit fifteen years ago, when she bought new couture every season before it hit the stores. Her weight stayed consistent, at 122, though at five feet six, maintaining her size had become occasionally painful. But pain was something Tandy thrived on. She had been through so much, yet still she seemed to hold it together.

She looked down at the ecru card with gold calligraphy that she had received upon checking in, to see where she would be seated. As she began to make her way toward the front of the room, Lisa, a petite blond woman, rushed up to give Tandy a kiss on each cheek.

"Tandy, you look great, as always. You're sitting at table two, right next to the stage."

"Thank you, Lisa. Everything looks lovely. You did a remarkable job," Tandy said.

"You are so kind. I learned from the best. Are you going to help me on the foster-care event next year? We really missed you this time around. It wasn't the same without you."

"I don't know. I still feel like it might be too soon. I'll let you know, though," Tandy answered, looking deeply into Lisa's eyes, making sure the young woman could feel her hesitancy.

"I understand. No pressure. But you are irreplaceable."

"Thank you." Tandy smiled humbly and continued on to her table.

Already milling about the orchid-filled table was the other honoree of the day, Jennifer Walters. Jennifer was a philanthropic wonder. Her parents were wealthy, having made their money in the rail industry. She had married well, of course, to a man whose fortune came from his parents' multimedia empire, though he also had a grand career as a lawyer. Jennifer, a smart woman with a good heart and a large pocketbook, had given millions over the years to New York arts organizations, children's groups, the homeless, and HIV awareness. Next to her Tandy felt a little small; not that she was intimidated, but she realized that her recent troubles were going to push her further and further away from this important scene that she had worked so hard to crack. Even in death, her husband's weakness would plague her.

Tandy's journey to this day had been hard-fought. As a young girl, Tandy had always known that she would live among the most important

2 percent of the population. She dreamed of dining with the rich and rubbing elbows with the famous. For black people in Chicago, her parents were well off. Her father owned a funeral home, and her mother took care of the house and of Tandy and her younger brother. Tandy was the classic overachiever, always vying for approval from her father, who rarely gave it. Thus Tandy worked harder. Her brother, on the other hand, felt that their father never expected anything out of him, so he didn't want to disappoint. At twenty-two, he died from a drug overdose, though Tandy and her parents preferred to call it a suicide. Around the time of her brother's death, Tandy met Phil Brooks. She was in law school at Boston University. He was finishing his JD/MBA at Harvard. Phil was smart and knew all the right people, white as well as African-American. She saw him as her chance at the life she had dreamed of. And for a while they lived that fairy tale.

Phil would do anything for Tandy. When she wanted a new home with a better address, he provided it, even though he felt they couldn't afford it. When she wanted expensive clothes, he never told her no. When she insisted they send their daughter, Deja, to the most expensive school in New York, he pulled it off. Not that Phil wasn't making a lot of money. He was a partner in one of the biggest law firms in New York. He was well respected and well liked among his peers. He worked hard and was compensated accordingly. But living in Manhattan was expensive, especially with a wife who had a social agenda. The annual two-hundred-thousand-dollar charitable contributions were just the beginning of a lifestyle that could bankrupt even the most highly paid workingman.

"Tandy! This is so exciting." Carol Wharton beamed and hugged Tandy forcefully. "You know this year is so special for me. I am so happy to award *you*, someone I have grown with over the last ten years. Isn't it something? We have truly come a long way, baby." Carol and Tandy laughed and reminisced about turning a small idea into a large, important New York City organization.

Indeed, Tandy had given a lot to MotherLove, the brainchild of Carol Wharton. Carol's husband, Mathew, and Phil had gone to Harvard together. They remained friends after school and inevitably ran into each other over business dealings. Carol and Tandy had hit it off immediately. Carol had attended Harvard Law School a couple of years behind her husband. She worked for about five years, three more than Tandy, then became a housewife/socialite.

Bored with being simply a lady who lunched, Carol came up with MotherLove, an organization designed to help homeless mothers get back on their feet. She enlisted Tandy from the very beginning. Tandy was happy to get involved. She knew helping Carol would put Tandy in the company of some very well-connected people. Carol and her husband were both lifetime New Yorkers. They knew everyone of importance. Anything on which Carol put her stamp eventually became a darling of New York. In just ten short years, MotherLove grew from a small living room operation to a multimillion-dollar nonprofit organization supported by corporations, foundations, and celebrities nationwide. Tandy was being honored today for her help in propelling MotherLove, and for her work in the various other charities in which she had gotten involved.

Today should have been exciting for Tandy. She had worked so hard to be a part of this world, and she had succeeded. But she was concerned about the next thirty years. She was supposed to be secure for the rest of her life. But not only was she in a position where sustaining her annual contributions would, embarrassingly, have to stop; she would also have to figure out how to make ends meet, a situation she had never been in before. Still, she would persevere. Though it might take some time, Tandy was working on a plan to dig herself out of the huge hole in which her husband had left her.

Lunch was served: mesclun salad followed by poached salmon with dill sauce. As chocolate cake with raspberry sauce was being placed before the ladies, the program began. Lisa stood at the podium, thanking everyone for attending and contributing to the lunch, which had netted five hundred thousand dollars. The crowd gave a thunderous applause for all of their donations. Lisa then introduced Carol Wharton, who would be handing out the awards to her honored guests. The first award would be given to

Jennifer. Her contributions, though large, had come only in the last few years, though she was being recognized for the many other organizations that her golden touch had graced. She accepted her award, going on about herself and how she had become involved in community outreach as a child because her parents made her and her siblings serve Thanksgiving and Christmas dinners to the poor. She learned then that what seemed like a little gesture could make a huge difference in one person's world. She closed her lengthy speech by congratulating Tandy as well.

Carol explained that the next award was so special to her because Tandy had supported her from the very beginning of MotherLove. "Were it not for Tandy's efforts, and I truly mean this, MotherLove would not be the organization it is today. Tandy is one of the hardest-working, most dedicated people I know. I could call Tandy at any hour of the day or night, and she always had time to listen to me and help me figure out a plan. She gave to us her time, her money, and her spirit. New York is better because of her. On behalf of MotherLove and the numerous other charities in New York that have consistently depended on Tandy Brooks for her never-ending energy and devotion, we thank you. Tandy, come on up and get your award." The crowd stood in ovation as Tandy gracefully moved to the podium. Her work was well known throughout New York, thanks to the publicity she procured for every bit of labor she put out. And though Phil had died a year ago, Tandy made sure the publicity reminded everyone of the tragedy and how she still mourned.

As Tandy reached the podium, she kissed Carol's cheek and claimed the crystal statue of a nude woman with wings holding a baby. She weighed the heavy sculpture in her right hand and gathered herself to say a few words of appreciation.

She began without any notes. "Thank you all. Carol, you are so kind. MotherLove has had and will always have a special place in my heart. The women I worked with in this organization are strong and smart and committed to more than themselves. I have learned so much from them. I have been given perspective and strength from the women we have served, the homeless mothers, through their strength and their stories of perseverance and faith. As you know, I lost my husband a year ago. Philip Brooks was a man of wisdom and integrity, someone who guided me, someone whom I respected." Tandy paused for effect. "He supported all of my endeavors. Without him, my service for MotherLove and everything else would have been so small. So Phil, this is for you."

With that, she kissed the award and shoved it up toward the heavens. "Thank you," she said into the microphone and stepped to the side for a photo op with Carol. The crowd roared with applause again. Tandy briefly wondered in which publication these shots would appear. She could feel the warm glow of empathy gushing from the room toward her. She had learned that playing it humble to the public was the classiest route to go. No one liked a braggart. That was better left to people like her personal publicist, Roxy Nixon, or the suck-ups who worshiped Tandy. And she always played her husband up, even if she thought he'd been an asshole. No woman looked good trashing her man. Even the feminists couldn't argue with her for loving her husband, as long as she got the credit for her work.

Gathering her belongings from the table, Tandy pushed back a gnawing feeling of dread in her stomach. As much as she wanted to enjoy the moment, she couldn't help but feel that she had just participated in her own funeral. All of the accolades had made her queasy, since she knew that as things stood now, she would not be able to keep up with her track record of the last ten years. The shame of poverty would hurt, but not as much as the thought of being a social outcast.

Bidding the socialites farewell, Tandy stepped out into the warm fall air and took in a deep breath. Walking toward her co-op, she rationalized that while things may have been bad, she was still in New York, living on Fifth Avenue. Somehow, some way, she would make sure that today's honoree would remain the toast of the town.

THREE

L AUREN Thomas watched from her enormous walk-in closet as her husband, Ed, stood in front of his bathroom vanity mirror with a towel wrapped around his waist, slowly shaving the five o'clock shadow from his chin. For Lauren, it was hard to remember that Ed was twenty years her senior. Six feet tall, he had beautiful skin and kept his body in great shape. At fifty-five, Ed still had a six-pack. He was one fine-looking man, she thought to herself.

"Lauren, come on. You need to hurry up. If we don't leave in twenty minutes, we are going to be late. You don't look even close to ready," Ed admonished her.

"I was just admiring my fine husband. You are so handsome. I'll be ready in a minute. I don't know why we have to arrive exactly on time," she pouted.

"You know I have to leave early to get to San Francisco. I'd like to be able to stay long enough to pay my respects to the museum. I'm a board member, and they're counting on me. Besides, the Museum of Harlem is a great organization for you to start getting involved in. You could take over my seat, and that would be one less thing on my list to do."

Oh, great, he was telling her again what she needed to do with her life, Lauren thought. She turned herself to face the mess that her closet had become over the last hour. Shoes and handbags were strewn all over the floor. Three gowns, each a different color and style, hung along the closet racks.

Lauren had been in the process of getting dressed for the last ninety minutes, yet her naturally curly, shoulder-length chestnut hair was still in a messy upsweep, and her makeup looked as though someone had thrown paint on her face. She was not usually so discombobulated, but this black-tie gala benefiting the Museum of Harlem made her uncomfortable. The barons of black society would be in attendance, along with well-to-do cultured white patrons of the arts. The stature of the attendees did not make Lauren miserable; she knew most of them from growing up with them in Westchester. More frustrating for her were the condescending glances and stage-whispered comments coming from people envious of her union with Ed. Throughout the four years of her marriage, Lauren had learned that most of the people in the crowd—even some of her mother's friends—felt she was not equipped to be married to such a powerful man. People would knock into her or push her over to get to Ed. They were rude and disrespectful. Women flirted with Ed in front of her as if she weren't standing there holding his hand. And when they did acknowledge her, they would say, "Oh, you're Ed Thomas's wife. Lucky girl." When Lauren complained to Ed, his only comment was "Why do you care what those people think of you?"

Lauren knew that tonight would be much easier to endure if Ed were more empathetic. Lauren was feeling a subtle chill from her husband—something unclear, unsettling. She could not articulate her feelings, certainly not to him. There was no tangible issue to discuss. Still, her instincts were on alert to a potential problem in their relationship.

As she put the finishing touches on her face and hair, Ed lovingly placed his chin on her shoulder. "You have so much going for you. Make to-night fun. Your friends will be there, and I know for a fact the people from the museum are anxious to talk with you about any ideas you might have on your vision of the museum. I've been telling them about you."

"Why, why do we have to do these things? Can't we stay home tonight and watch a movie like we used to? Do you have to go out of town again?" Lauren pleaded, suddenly feeling proprietary. She wanted to forgo the event and have Ed all to herself, as in the early days of their relationship. For an instant she fondly thought of the times he declared that he never wanted to share her with anyone. She was the one feeling that way now.

Ed jerked his head away from Lauren's shoulder and responded in a sharp tone, "You know we can't do that. Get dressed, and let's go."

Looking up at Ed, so handsome in his tailor-made tuxedo, Lauren felt a twinge of sadness. Their quality time and carefree living were becoming obsolete. With a touch of melancholy, she couldn't help thinking of what had propelled her into love with him in the first place. Fresh out of Wharton business school and excited about her blossoming career, Lauren had reconnected with Ed when she landed a job as a marketing executive at Thomas Industries. She had been a great student, was highly sought after by many companies, and was thrilled to be offered the position at Ed's company. She had followed his career for many years since first meeting him years before on Martha's Vineyard, at her parents' barbecue, when she was just a high school student. He was a self-made man, and most of America was fascinated by him, especially black America.

Ed's business had started as a small bottling company with a contract from a big soda company in the Midwest. Ed and one other investor then bought a small midwestern beverage company, which they quickly sold to a larger conglomerate, resulting in substantial gains. With the money Ed made on that deal, he bought a regional consumer-products company that specialized in the snack market. With hard work and a talented marketing team, he turned this venture into a nationally recognized brand that began giving Frito-Lay big competition. PepsiCo eventually bought that company. Ed's largest deal came with a leveraged buyout of another beverage company that manufactured and marketed flavored iced tea.

At the time, Wall Street analysts had predicted that this company was near bankruptcy, and that Ed's purchase would surely be the death of his success. After only one year, Ed turned the company around with new management and marketing, brought it back to profitability, and made his iced tea one of the most recognized worldwide. The next year he sold that beverage company for a billion dollars, the largest sale for a company of its kind and the biggest deal any black man had pulled off. He was on the cover of every business magazine. Ed Thomas had become a true legend. In twenty years he had built himself a billion-dollar fortune. Soon afterward, his first wife divorced him, citing years of neglect and grown children who didn't need their parents to stay together. At fifty, Ed found himself very rich and very eligible. And Lauren, who worked in his marketing department, had wanted nothing to do with him personally.

However, Ed pursued the elegant and beautiful Lauren until he wore down her resistance. Her caution was fueled by her fear of Ed using her for the moment and then casting her out of his life, and out of his office, when he had grown tired of her. Lauren was serious if not passionate about her career. She hoped to move to the top of her field and to own her own company eventually. But the more she held back, the more Ed poured on his affections. She declined, explaining her desire for him to continue taking her seriously at Thomas Industries. She thought he had gotten the message. But a few months later, a corporate retreat was planned in Geneva, Switzerland, for the marketing department, along with high-ranking executives. It was during those five days that Ed made himself irresistible to her.

Later he would explain that he had devised the entire trip to get Lauren's attention. On the first night after dinner, unbeknownst to her, Ed had the hotel change the lock on Lauren's room so that her key card would not work and she would have to go to the front desk to get another. He waited for her in the lobby and convinced her to have a drink with him in the cozy lounge. They settled themselves in front of the roaring fire, nestled among oversize goose-down pillows. The whole experience felt surreal to Lauren. She and Ed shared stories of their upbringings. Lauren, hailing from Westchester, was a fourth-generation college graduate. Ed, from Durham, North Carolina, was the first in his family to go to college. Lauren respected Ed's ability to pull himself up by the bootstraps and become one of the country's leading businessmen. He was fascinated by her privileged upbringing and her ability to remain so unaffected by it all. They hailed from two distinct worlds, yet they were here together, yearning to learn more about each other—each wondering where this night might lead. Finally, after several hours of talking and comfortable silences, Lauren floated back to her room alone and intrigued; this time with a key that worked.

The next day Ed sought to impress her on the slopes, keeping an eye out for her at all times on the hills. That night he had the hotel call Lauren to say that the plans had changed and that dinner was to be served in the hotel's private dining room instead of at the restaurant, as specified on the company-wide agenda.

When Lauren arrived at the dining room, she saw an ornate table set for two with candlelight and sprays of baby roses everywhere. The view was of the Alps they had skied earlier in the day. Ed immediately apologized for tricking her and begged her not to be angry with him. "I understand if you don't ever want to have dinner with me again, but please give me the pleasure of your company in this beautiful setting tonight so I will at least have the memory of how your eyes glow in the light." Although they kept their relationship a secret for several months, Lauren and Ed became inseparable from that night on.

He continued to hold her interest tenaciously for the next year. He took her around the world in his private jet. He sent flowers. He sent handwritten poetry. He introduced her to Portuguese jazz and Senegalese rhythm. He dazzled her with rare wines, fine art, and culture. At the end of that wild year, they married.

Ed interrupted her reverie with a brusque "Your hair is perfect. Put on your dress, and let's get out of here."

After stepping into her size-four black jersey gown that fit her like a glove, Lauren opened the safe in her walk-in closet, large enough to be a master bedroom in most mansions. She pulled out a ruby and diamond bracelet and matching earrings that Ed had given her one Valentine's Day. Putting the earrings through her lobes, Lauren couldn't help but think that perhaps all of those folks who thought she was in over her head were right. Being married to a billionaire had taken getting used to. She knew most people would say, "Let me try dealing with the problems of being wealthy." But she understood all too well that while having money was wonderful, not having control of her own life was unsettling. She didn't know exactly, but she figured the earrings and bracelet had to be worth half a million dollars. And that was just the beginning of what she didn't know.

She had no idea where all of her husband's billion dollars were invested. It could be in money markets, the stock market, bonds, Treasury notes. And she never saw a bill. Every month accountants paid their bills, though Ed signed the checks. Lauren could also sign a check but never needed to. She had her own bank account, with a huge monthly allowance, more money than she could ever spend. What she didn't spend she put in her own savings account or money markets. She also had a reserve, two million dollars in the trust her parents had set up for her. But the big money and whatever property Ed might own all over the world, she had no way of knowing about. And if she wanted to find out, she would have to go through so many accountants and assistants and extraneous people that it was too daunting even to try.

In order to gain control of something in her life, Lauren had decided to go back to work. Ed had made her leave Thomas Industries once they were married. His other employees wouldn't think it fair, he had explained. She had always been creative, directing undergraduate theater, and wanted to make films and television shows. Her parents had steered her to business school so she would be able to support herself. They'd urged her to never depend on the trust fund. After her marriage and with Ed's initial support, she had decided to pursue her dream career as a documentary filmmaker, which allowed her to delve into underrepresented issues and to fulfill her creative spirit.

Passing through the hallways of her grand apartment, with the museum-quality art on the walls, only made Lauren more cognizant of her lack of power over her own life. There was so much pressure to be socially involved in the New York philanthropic world, though she really was not interested in everyone else's agenda. Lauren craved a simpler lifestyle. Sometimes she fantasized about running away with Ed, back to that quiet retreat in the Alps, and never returning to New York.

FOUR

THE flash of the paparazzi's cameras nearly blinded Manny as he and Tandy sauntered down the red carpet to the Museum of Harlem's annual gala, held at the Metropolitan Club. Manny lived for such events, especially this one, which was the signature African-American social gathering of the year in New York City. Not only was he getting more attention than he had ever received at any fete in the past, but he was with the queen.

"Tandy! Tandy! Over here!" an elderly German photographer whom Manny recognized from the *Daily News* hollered out as they neared the entrance. Manny marveled at Tandy. She was a pro. She pretended to be preoccupied with trying to reach the front door, but Manny knew better. He could tell she was profiling her face to accent her best angles without appearing to be posing for the camera. Not that Tandy had a bad angle. Her features were perfect: high chiseled cheekbones, deep-set almond-shaped brown eyes, caramel skin, jet-black shoulder-length hair softly layered, framing her heart-shaped face. Graceful and elegant in her burgundy one-shoulder vintage Valentino gown, Tandy glided through the crowd.

Even though she was regularly written up in *W, Vanity Fair, Town &*

Country, and *The New York Times* as a socialite and a model of style, she rarely stopped to pose for pictures, always telling Manny that it was gauche to mill about waiting for some photographer to find you. "Pathetic and desperate," she would say. She was photographed only on her terms. So now she continued along on her mission to enter the gathering that she was cochairing. But damn, Manny wished she would at least agree to a couple of posed photos. He didn't get many opportunities like this, and he sure wouldn't mind showing up in any one of the publications she spurned as she sped by the clicking lenses and style-page reporters waving spiral pads, waiting to get quotes. This was the sort of publicity Manny had waited years to get, but he reminded himself not to be too eager or pushy with Tandy. Those were traits she despised. He should be grateful simply to accompany her. Still, he wanted more.

In the past, Manny had come to the Museum of Harlem event solo. He hadn't had a prominent table, let alone paparazzi trying to snap shots of him. Attending the gala with Tandy was a coup. Not only would he be ensured a highly visible seat, but her acceptance of him would also signify to the African-American bourgeois that he was one of them, or at least firmly on his way. True, he and Lauren were closer friends—she had welcomed him into her inner sanctum—but she was not a member of the old guard, like Tandy. She was also still working her way out of the stigma attached to being Ed Thomas's younger second wife. And the fact that Ed's first wife was so well regarded did not help Lauren's position. Hell, Lauren's own mother had been an acquaintance of the first Mrs. Thomas. Tandy's more established stamp of approval of Manny carried greater weight. Manny was reminded of Tandy's clout by the crowd, craning their necks to see what she was wearing or trying to get a few seconds of her time. Manny had been one of those people on the outside looking in not so long ago. Even though his mother had been excluded by groups such as this one, she had primed him his whole life to be accepted by the elite African-American circles.

Near the arched stone doorways, the crowd thickened almost to a standstill. Manny wanted to keep moving, to get the evening started. He wanted to take full advantage of this night with Tandy on his arm. He felt like a kid at Magic Kingdom, not knowing whether to ride on Dumbo the Flying Elephant or Space Mountain or to meet Mickey Mouse first. Manny became increasingly hyped as he glanced around at all of the faces he recognized, nodding their heads, anxious to greet Tandy. The barons of black society had turned out for this gathering: Robert Johnson and Debra Lee, the CEO and COO of Black Entertainment Television; Kenneth Chenault, CEO of American Express, and his wife, attorney Kathryn; Richard Parsons, CEO of AOL Time Warner; Earl Graves, publisher of *Black Enterprise* magazine; Ed Lewis, CEO of Essence Communications; and Vernon Jordan—groups Manny was still trying to infiltrate. Soberly, he realized that feat would take more than being Tandy's date. He needed to operate on their level, not merely service them. He'd been living commission check to commission check, though he wanted to make a mark in their world.

Right beside the entrance, Manny spotted Lauren and Ed Thomas posing for pictures and being interviewed by Elise McNeil from the *New York Journal* style section. Tandy seemed to hesitate, but Lauren noticed them and gave a huge grin, motioning for them to join her and Ed. Manny was ready to take part in the photo op, but Tandy waved and kept moving. Not prepared to rock the boat with Tandy, Manny mouthed to Lauren that he would meet her inside. That is, until Lauren gave him and Tandy an SOS look, letting them know she needed them to bail her out. Apparently, the backup on the red carpet had been caused by the slew of reporters and photographers waiting to get photos of Lauren and Ed. After all, Ed was one of only half a handful of African-American billionaires, and his wife hailed from a rather prominent family herself. As the press vultures hovered, Ed wore a proud expression; the flashbulbs continuously went off, and the photographers called out to Lauren: "Mrs. Thomas, over here!" "Lauren, who are you wearing tonight?" "Lauren, when is the Museum of Harlem going to become more accessible to children?" "Mrs. Thomas, is that couture?"

Obviously, Lauren had not taken lessons from Tandy on the proper way to enter an event. She was letting all of the photographers take pictures, even posing, showing off the simple black strapless Armani Manny had helped her select at the Bryant Park Fashion Show. Lauren was so stunning she needed to wear simple clothes, otherwise her beauty would collide with her wardrobe.

"Manny!" Tandy began as she glanced around at the crowd rather distastefully. "Are you coming?"

Manny caught Lauren's exasperation. She appeared to be pleading with him and Tandy. "I think Lauren needs us to rescue her."

"Rescue her? She's perfectly fine, Manny. Her husband can take care of her," Tandy remarked with a bit of an edge.

Manny looked at Lauren longingly once again, feeling a bit like a child whose mother had just forbidden him to go to the playground. But before Manny could respond, the very boisterous Cynthia Westerly, wearing a gown resembling a rainbow-colored parachute, accosted Tandy.

"My goodness, Tandy, when are you all going to move this gala to a venue that can properly accommodate the guests? This is ridiculous. I've been waiting a half hour just to get inside. It's like a college party." Cynthia was the sort of woman who believed the money she and her father had made as owners of Cadillac dealerships throughout Stamford, Greenwich, and Westchester gave her the right to say whatever was on her mind. Manny understood why no one had ever married her. But he knew no matter how much someone like Cynthia complained, she wouldn't miss the Museum of Harlem gala for her own daddy's funeral. He got the impression she was still hoping to meet the man of her dreams, and what better place than here, where all of the eligible African-American men in the Tri-State area were in attendance?

As Cynthia sidled up to Tandy, Manny took the momentary reprieve as his opportunity to at least go and say hello to Lauren. He also knew she would drag him into a few pictures.

"Smile for the camera, darling," Lauren said. Ed nodded his usual greeting. Even when Manny had been their broker, Ed had very little to say to Manny unless it was a specific question. He was a direct man who seemed to dislike idle chitchat.

As Manny cheesed for a few pictures with Lauren, he was determined not to let Ed's standoffishness spoil the moment for him. Ed did not have to be his friend. He and Lauren were hanging buddies. When Ed was out of town, Manny filled an increasing void for Lauren.

"Oh no, you didn't leave Tandy there with Cynthia," Lauren said, looking over in Tandy's direction.

"I better get back on duty."

"I'll see you inside."

Manny hurried back to Tandy and placed his hand on her elbow to steer her away from Cynthia, who would have undoubtedly gone on talking all night. Tandy seemed a bit agitated as they entered the lobby, filled with an even larger crowd dressed in their finest evening apparel. Now they were moving about an inch a minute, but Manny didn't really mind. He was enjoying the people-watching, although he dared not let Tandy catch him gawking. Manny could sense her body stiffening. He was not used to seeing her in such a state. She was usually totally composed. He wondered if she was feeling unwell, or if the crowd was bothering her. Then it hit him. This time last year, Tandy would have been arriving with Phil. Maybe she was getting nostalgic and holding it inside, Manny thought to himself. Tandy was not the type of person to share her emotions, and Manny was not the type to pry—especially not on a night like tonight.

Tandy felt nauseated. She needed to get a grip on herself before she passed out. This was not the place to be laid out flat, but she felt like her world was spinning out of control. Tandy had felt sick from the moment her stilettos hit the pavement. Nothing felt right tonight. The problems started when she could not afford a suitable new dress. The gowns her publicist had brought over were from last season—a total slap in the face by the designers. In the past, Tandy had been given first dibs on the latest couture gowns for all of the events she chaired; the designers and boutiques were fully aware that she would ensure great visibility. For this year's affair, she had been forced to wear one of her vintage gowns and try to pull it off as a retro look.

Tandy knew she needed to conquer her fear before the facade she fostered crumbled. She did not intend to be found out a fraud. The immediate injury was that Elise McNeil was foaming at the mouth over Lauren Thomas. Normally, Tandy would have been the person Elise handpicked to interview. After all, she was on the museum's board and this was her signature event. But for some reason, Elise had barely noticed her tonight. Sure, the third-rate paparazzi had hounded her for a quote, but they didn't matter. They weren't *Town & Country* or *Vanity Fair* or *The New York Times*. Tandy was not of the belief that any publicity was good publicity. Such matters needed to be carefully orchestrated. All of the publications of social importance were jockeying to get shots and quotes from Lauren. And the sick part was that Lauren didn't even care about or need the publicity. It was a joke to her, something for her to shrug at or laugh about over lunch with Manny and Tandy. Lauren was becoming a media darling and did not care. Tandy had slaved for years to be in the position Lauren had fallen into just because she had married a billionaire and happened to be stunningly beautiful. Well, so was she, Tandy thought; or she used to be, until Mother Time had started chipping away at the one weapon she'd counted on over the years. Despite the fact that she once had been that rare bird—a female African-American junior partner in a prominent New York law firm—she had relied on her appearance to give her the extra edge. Sadly, she thought, since she had not practiced law in twenty years, her fading looks might be all she had left.

"May I check your wrap for you?" Manny asked as they neared the coat check.

"You're a doll," Tandy told Manny, who she thought rather resembled a little chipmunk, scurrying about kissing the ass of everyone he thought might buy property. She wondered if he'd be so eager to run every one of her errands, including taking her fabric to the upholsterer, if he knew she was damn near bankrupt. She doubted it, but that did not stop her from using him for every favor he was willing to give. Despite his charm, he was transparent to her. But he had Lauren fooled. Hell, if Lauren weren't married to Ed Thomas, if she lived in a Chelsea rent-controlled apartment, Manny Marks wouldn't fit her in to an interview for his assistant's job. The way he sucked up to Lauren was disgusting, running over to her and Ed to kiss their rings as if they were royalty. Lauren disgusted Tandy. She wasn't royalty. She had simply married a king—the one Tandy should have snagged when she had the opportunity all those years ago. She and Ed had shared something special. She was still trying to determine whether or not that opportunity was lost for good. Now here Lauren was, a little girl playing dress-up, giggling all the time, eyes wide like she was so damn innocent. Tandy was the real royalty, only Ed had not realized it. Their timing had been wrong. They both had spouses when they had several romantic trysts over the course of a hot, humid Martha's Vineyard summer. Tandy was the one who had earned the right, the respect, the title. Her problem was the lack of cash. But that would be changing soon. She was determined of that, even if she had to marry a troll.

Tandy maneuvered through the crowd, stopping every couple of feet to say a few words to an acquaintance. She always smiled, always wore a pleasant expression. She could be on her last dime, but she'd sooner move into the YWCA than let the people here know about her predicament. The room was filled with a sea of African-American art patrons, some of them old guard, some of them new, and some of them plain nouveau riche. And tacky, she thought, careful not to let the distaste show on her face. *Times are a-changing*, she thought as she watched Coffee and Darryl Raye, the most outrageous new-money couple in New York City, saunter through the crowd with an entourage big enough to make up a football team—people who had no business at an affair such as the Museum of Harlem gala. The Rayes could bend the rules because they were entertainment types, but they were a disgrace, walking in with their posse, as loud and boisterous as if at the racetrack. And Coffee had the audacity to be dressed in a white leather strapless dress with a matching collar resembling something more appropriate for a dog. Darryl was even worse, with his plaid sport coat, T-shirt, and Bermuda

Tandy glanced around the crowded room. People were intertwined like an overgrown forest, all of them competing for social and alcoholic nourishment. The most densely populated area was the bar. It would take twenty minutes just to get a drink. How had this party gotten so out of control? There was no way it could be held here next year. The board would have to find a new location or cut the guest list in half. Could the times really have changed that much in only twelve months? The number of invitations had swelled to include a growing group of possible patrons. The African-American philanthropic crowd loved showering attention—and, most importantly, money—on the Museum of Harlem. Tandy no longer felt like socializing. She realized that, like the gala crowd, her life had spiraled out of control.

"Let's go to the table, I'll have a drink there," Tandy told Manny, ignoring the disappointment on his face. She knew he wouldn't want to miss out on the hobnobbing. Tough for him. She'd be damned if she walked to her seat without an escort.

"Uh, do you mind if I say hello to the Rayes first? They're my clients."

"Oh, Manny, where has your taste gone?" Tandy asked, doubting her decision to bring him tonight. Apparently, her referrals were not enough. He had to go and attach himself to the lewdest, wealthiest people he could find. Manny could be such a fly, flitting about, landing on any available scrap of food. "Just go on," Tandy told him, and turned toward the ballroom. She no longer felt like dealing with Manny.

"I'll be right behind you, Tandy. Oh, and we're at table twelve."

Tandy froze in her tracks. Things were worse than she'd thought. But maybe Manny had made a mistake. "What was that table number again?" It was supposed to be two. Tandy had made sure of that herself earlier in the day, when she came by the Metropolitan Club to check on the final arrangements.

Manny glanced down at the small square linen card and said, "Twelve. I'll see you in a moment."

Now her head throbbed. Twelve was not where she had put herself. She and her guest were supposed to be at table two, front and center. True, she had not bought a whole table this year, but twenty-five thousand dollars was more than she could afford. Still, Tandy never imagined someone would move her without the common courtesy of notifying her. The table was still respectable, but it was not her normal spot. Sadly, nothing was normal anymore.

BLACK Label oozed from Manny's pores by the time he made it home from the gala at midnight, but he could hold his liquor. He easily could have stayed at the event until the last person left, but Tandy insisted they leave just as the dancing was about to begin, and he dared not risk angering her by suggesting they remain any longer. It was well enough, though, he thought, anticipating getting a little lovin' at home. But as Manny opened the door to his renovated brownstone on Striver's Row, the prospect of getting his groove on quickly changed to annoyance. The first floor of his house looked like a gang of teenagers had had a block party there.

The impeccably decorated narrow living room was a mess. Copies of *Vibe*, *SLAM*, and *The Source* were thrown across his camel Ultrasuede sofa, and his pony-hair pillows were flattened and tossed on the floor like discarded newspaper. A Lucky Charms cereal box was turned on its side atop his leather coffee table, along with a half-empty bowl of milk, not a marshmallow charm left in sight. Empty Now and Later candy wrappers were strewn in his Hermès ashtray. And the worst part was that his entertainment center had been tampered with. A damn Play Station was connected to his Sony flat-screen television, with so many wires protruding it looked like a black-and-gray tarantula had landed on his Aubusson rug. To top it all off, every light in the house was turned on.

Irritated beyond words, Manny began tidying before he even removed his tuxedo jacket. He thought about leaving the room like he'd found it, but realized Trenton wouldn't straighten up the mess, either. Manny had created a monster. If Manny did not do the work himself, his house would look like a tornado had hit it until the housekeeper arrived on Wednesday. After a quick cleanup, he headed upstairs. Getting laid was now the last thing on his mind; a hot shower and Egyptian-cotton pajamas and sheets seemed the better option. But the second Manny entered the bedroom, that calming thought left his mind. He stared at the empty Dolce & Gabbana and Gucci shopping bags thrown across the bed. No Trenton in sight. Manny was pissed! Not only had that basic Negro fucked up his house and run up the credit cards that Manny paid for, but he had the nerve to be out, probably at a damn club. This was not the homecoming Manny had envisioned.

Manny started picking up the bags, cursing under his breath. He put up with so much shit from Trenton. Yes, he was fine as a motherfucker, and he was the best lover Manny had ever had, but he couldn't help getting the feeling that Trenton was starting to take him for granted. As he folded up the last bag, Manny glanced up at the black-and-white Calvin Klein underwear shots of Trenton Duncan framed above the dresser. His twenty-four-year-old body was a work of art, and his sculpted ebony features resembled those of an African prince. Every morning they lay in bed together, Manny marveled at Trenton's beauty and considered himself a lucky man to have someone so gorgeous to share a life and home with. Manny also had to admit to himself, he loved parading Trenton around on his arm at the appropriate functions. Trenton never would have fit in at the event tonight, nor would he have had any desire to attend a ball. But on those occasions when Manny convinced Trenton to go to the gay bars in the Village, Manny may as well have been Don Corleone. Not only was Trenton better-looking than most men, but he had a bit of celebrity, a lethal combination in a city like New York.

Walking into the black granite and stainless-steel master bath, Manny wondered where Trenton was shaking his ass tonight. He was undoubtedly at a hip-hop party that some rapper or baller was throwing. Trenton didn't like the typical gay clubs and went only when Manny bribed him. He preferred the trade in straight clubs. After all, that was how they had met: Manny had accompanied Lauren to a party thrown by a promoter friend of hers. Trenton had been shaking his tight butt with some of his male and female model friends in the VIP area. And even though he had been dressed rather butch, Manny knew by the look in his eyes that he was in the family. Manny immediately sent over a magnum of Cristal for Trenton and his group.

That had been enough of a calling card for the studly brother from Albany, New York. When he approached Manny to personally thank him, the deal was done. Manny was smitten. He had to have him, at whatever price. And the price had been steadily increasing, since Trenton had not worked in the past six months on anything other than his abs. He had been a fairly successful model—a few runway shows but mostly print work, catalog, in fact. That is, until he started showing up late all the time, and his booker stopped sending him out for jobs. Manny partly blamed himself for Trenton's tardiness. They had been in the honeymoon stage of their relationship, and things were hot and heavy. Manny had been eager to keep his new man and was playing the big-shot older-boyfriend role. He basically told Trenton he didn't need to work, that he could be a kept man. Once Manny gave him the gold American Express, Trenton was only too happy to comply.

Manny ripped off his custom-made white tuxedo shirt and quickly washed his face, too pissed to do his exfoliation. His skin would be angry with him in the morning. But even as mad and drunk as he was, he wouldn't skip his teeth-whitening treatment. He flung open the medicine cabinet and pulled out his silicone tooth moldings and began searching for the last tube of whitening gel but couldn't find it. "Dammit! Where the hell are you?" Manny hollered into the cabinet.

"Is that any way to greet your boo?"

Manny turned. Trenton filled the whole bathroom doorway with his solid six-four frame. Manny's breath caught. Even after two years, every time Manny saw Trenton, he was taken with how gorgeous he was. But he gathered himself, determined not to let Trenton talk his way out of the latest mess.

"Do you know where my teeth-whitening gel is?"

"Why the attitude? I was only kickin' it, too, while you were out."

"No attitude, do you know where my gel is?"

"I think it's in the garbage."

"Why would it be in the garbage, Trenton?"

"'Cause I used it."

"But you don't even have any trays. What, did you just rub the shit straight on your teeth?" Manny couldn't believe this boy.

"Yeah." Trenton smiled, walking into the bathroom to look at himself in the mirror. "Don't my teeth look whiter?" He leaned over the sink, closer to the mirror, so Manny could get a good look.

Manny wanted to say, "No, but your ass sure looks good in those leather pants." But he stopped himself and just stared at Trenton in disbelief.

"Come on, man, why you trippin'? I was all geeked to get home and see you tonight."

"So that's how you show me you want to see me, leave the house a wreck and go out shopping and then go to some club and come home smelling like smoke and cheap wine?"

Manny pushed past him and went through the bedroom to the walk-in closet. Trenton was on his heels.

"You the one always going to some high-class somethin'-or-other and don't never invite me. You act like you ashamed to bring me around your uppity-ass friends."

"Oh, so now you're trying to turn this around on me."

"It's true," Trenton said, sounding like a child.

"Trenton, please. Even if I did ask you to go to some of these events, you wouldn't. Don't even try to act like you wanna be bothered with my friends. You should hang out with us sometime. They would love for you to be around," Manny said, looking Trenton dead in the eye. He even had to crack a smile. Trenton would no sooner want to be bothered by Tandy Brooks and Lauren Thomas than Manny would want to go to one of Trenton's hard-core hip-hop basement parties in Brooklyn. Besides, Trenton didn't think the people Manny hung around were real. He viewed them as snobby, pretentious folks he'd rather not be bothered with. Of course, Trenton never complained about any of Tandy or Lauren's referrals if they translated into a higher limit on Manny's credit card.

Manny slipped out of his pants and felt some of the anger subside. It was amazing how that happened, just having his man at home. Suddenly, despite their differences, he was grateful to have a man in his life whom he loved. He felt himself getting aroused and decided to skip the pajamas. Still, he wanted Trenton to grovel. Manny left him in the closet and headed straight for the bed, wearing only his boxers. If nothing else, they had an amazing sex life. Manny knew Trenton felt the same way.

Trenton stood at the foot of the bed. Manny placed his hands behind his head and stared up at him before saying, "So, are you ready to make it up to me?"

"Make it up to you? You the one jumping down my throat."

"You ready to get back on my good side?"

"On *your* good side?"

Manny nodded, pleased that Trenton was ready to play, removing his shirt, revealing rock-hard pecs and an eight-pack stomach.

"That's a start," Manny nearly groaned as Trenton unbuttoned his pants and turned around to peel them down to his ankles. Manny was in agony now, but that would soon turn to ecstasy as Trenton crawled to the head of the bed and sat on Manny's face.

SIX

TANDY had been coming to the J. Sisters salon at least ten years for her bimonthly Brazilian bikini waxes from Renata. She loved Renata's quality wax and mother wit, which was why she continued patronizing the salon, despite the fact that she inevitably ran into people she knew on the way to one of the most private of her personal services. But it was one of the premier spas in the city, and she couldn't expect to have the whole place to herself.

"Tandy? Oh my God, is that you?" a loud voice from behind her called. Tandy turned and looked over her dark sunglasses to find a very excited-looking Dana Trip smiling brightly in her face while getting a simultaneous manicure and pedicure. Dana, a tall, thin, fair-skinned strawberry blonde, was one of Tandy's holdovers from college, someone she had avoided for the past year. Dana's fortunes had been on the rise while Tandy's spiraled down. Tandy resented Dana for the ease with which she'd stumbled into her life.

Fresh from Omaha, Nebraska, Dana had not been looking for a husband, let alone a filthy-rich one. She had simply been trying to adjust to the fast pace of the East Coast. When she and Tandy were freshmen at Boston

University, they lived across the hall from each other in the dorm. Dana had been a fairly quiet girl, attractive in a clean and wholesome way, as if she had been living in the fields among the cornstalks—rosy cheeks, clear baby-blue eyes, and shiny hair. She had been dull during their college years unless she was surrounded by boys, and then she affected a loud, grating laugh. When Dana moved to New York City after graduating at the bottom of the class, she took a position as an advertising assistant and married soon after. Women like her married well very easily, Tandy realized. Dana was tall, white, blond, buxom, and educated. It had not been difficult for her to snatch the multimillionaire Charlie Trip from his second wife. Dana had the unaffected persona down to a science: the sort of aloof demeanor that made a man chase her all the more.

"Dana, it has been too long. You look radiant!" Tandy never gave a compliment she didn't mean. Dana, who had lost some of her bloom after marrying, really did appear healthier. Maybe she had given up smoking.

"Thank you. I am feeling wonderful, too. I've been involved with Shuram Alita, who is an amazing guru. Have you heard of Stonemark Forum?" Tandy nodded. She had heard people talking about it here and there. "Well, I've been working with them for the last year and a half. Shuram Alita is the founder, and he's taken me under his wing. He has been a lifesaver to me. But listen, I could go on forever. Pull out your Palm Pilot, I know you have it with you, and let's make a date for lunch."

Feeling a little hesitant but unable to think of an excuse quickly enough, Tandy reached into her handbag, a medium-sized chocolate Birkin she had purchased long ago. Dana was always a little nutty, even in school. She was into tarot cards and astrology and even went through a phase of trying to learn white witchcraft. Tandy did not feel like wasting any of her time listening to Dana ramble on about her encounters with a guru who was probably going to take her for all of her husband's money. But then again, one never knew; maybe Dana could figure a way to help Tandy out of her misery. Maybe, Tandy thought, she could come up with a project that Dana and her husband could finance and support that would pay Tandy a salary or some kind of financial bonus. She would be ready to pitch an idea by the time their lunch arrived.

After setting up the date, Tandy proceeded toward the very back corner of the shop to let the bikini-wax assistant know she was here to see Renata. "How are you, Tandy?" the assistant greeted her, with a sweet smile and a Portuguese lilt. "Go on in. She will be right there." Tandy always showed up for a wax first thing in the morning, as soon as the salon opened. Coming in early assured that she would not have to wait and usually would not run into anyone she didn't want to see. She also got Renata at her freshest.

The small room reminded Tandy of a doctor's examining room. She placed her purse on the floor and stepped out of her mules. After sliding off her panties and pants at the same time, she hung them on the hook by the door, careful to hide her underwear. Saddling up onto the table, covered in clean white paper, she did her normal glance around the stark white room to see if anything had changed. Everything remained the same. The photo of Renata's granddaughter, the name plate engraved with Renata's name, and the various products that helped heal and manage the waxing, such as Tend Skin, were perched in their assigned places. While the world changed, this room and Renata seemed to remain exactly the way they had been from the first day Tandy stepped in the door. Sitting naked from the waist down, with her arms wrapped around her legs, hugging them close, Tandy thought it was a relief to know that somewhere things remained the same.

"Goood morning, Tandy!" Renata said with a bright smile as she flung open the door. Renata was about five feet tall and always wore white to highlight her natural skin color, which looked consistently tanned. Her thick black hair was pulled back in a bushy ponytail that bobbed from side to side as she spoke. "How are you? Things are good with you?" Her thick accent revealed her heritage, reminding her clients that they were receiving an authentic Brazilian bikini wax. Never mind that the Brazilian wax was not really Brazilian but an ode to *Playboy* magazine. But Renata was a consummate professional, and her waxing sessions were more than mere hair removal. They were also therapy sessions for her clients. Renata not only listened, she also offered advice through wonderful stories of the struggles of her family, her adolescence, of being a single mother after divorce, of being a grandmother. She had many clients, and most of them were VIP. Renata's little room, filled with the scent of beeswax, was a place where worlds collided. Ironically, while Renata was discreet, she still liked for everyone to know with whom she worked, that they were part of a special crowd. She also liked to make connections, and she knew who knew whom.

"You saw Dana Trip when you came in?" Tandy and Dana had both been clients for a long time, and Renata had seen them in the salon together in the past.

Tandy lay back on the table with her sweater pulled above her belly button to avoid getting talc on her clothes. "Yes . . ." she answered as Renata angled her right leg, like that of a ballerina getting ready to make a pirouette.

Renata dipped the wooden spatula into the hot wax and gently blew on it. "She told you about the Forum?" Renata spread the wax along the right side of Tandy's groin. "She looks very good, don't you think?"

"She does," Tandy agreed, wincing from the sting as Renata ripped the muslin from her skin.

"She is so happy. She said she is living life like never before." Renata continued applying the wax to the left side of Tandy's groin.

"Good for her," Tandy managed, wishing that Renata could talk about something other than Dana's new fad. Once again Renata ripped the muslin, smarting the tender skin. Now Renata tapped Tandy's right leg, indicating that it was time for Tandy to lift it. Tandy placed the leg against the curve of Renata's waist so that her small frame held Tandy's thigh. It was this position that Tandy hated the most. She always felt so exposed, with her legs spread-eagled and her femininity open to all the world. Thank God no one ever walked in.

Renata delicately handled the lips of Tandy's vagina as she covered them in wax. "She said the Forum made her realize that it was time for her to leave her husband. She was not happy in her marriage and is ready to live life her way instead of the way he wanted."

Oh, the pain of the hairs tearing out of this soft spot on Tandy's body made her eyes tear every time. Thank God Renata snatched the muslin quickly. "I hope she knows what she's doing," Tandy thought out loud.

The cynic in Tandy figured that Dana had probably decided she would be better off single and rich than married to an overbearing man. Face it, most women dreamed of being free of their marriage at some point. And the possibility of being wealthy and single versus wealthy and married could poise the neglected women—or those at the opposite end of the spectrum, the micromanaged—to flee during that down moment in the cycle of matrimony. But sometimes, when the fantasy became the reality, life could get much harder. Tandy knew that sad fact all too well.

During their marriage, Phil had handled all of the major financial affairs. He paid the mortgage, managed the portfolio, and kept all of the large items in check, or so Tandy thought. She paid the credit-card bills and everything related to the day-to-day management of the house and their charitable contributions. When Phil died, Tandy was ready to handle the big business of her life. She knew there was some debt but figured the worst-case scenario would result in the sale of her apartment. But even that wouldn't be so bad, since the apartment had increased in value so much since they'd bought it twelve years before. She would still have enough, including the insurance, to be comfortable for the rest of her life. The insurance policy was something that Tandy had been adamant about. She had insisted that Phil increase his coverage from two million to six million the year before he died. She had pestered him, and finally, he had taken care of it. Tandy had reasoned that Phil's need to be reminded about the policy was an unwillingness to accept his own mortality. He figured he would be around forever. But Phil had high blood pressure and high cholesterol. He was about forty pounds overweight, did not exercise, and worked very very hard. Tandy did not want to take any chances. With his enormous love for her, Phil had to acquiesce. That was what he told her. He said he wanted to be sure she was well taken care of in case something happened to him.

As Tandy continued to delve deeper into her thoughts and Renata applied more wax to her bottom, she got angrier. Phil had been so weak and untrustworthy. The day she went to their accountant's office for the reading of the will and the explanation of the disbursement of the estate, Tandy had been optimistic. She knew she was going to be a wealthy woman. With their daughter set to enter college in a year, Tandy would be free. Instead, she discovered that her bastard of a husband had not known how to manage shit and had left her in debt to the tune of millions. Over the years he had run up horrendous debt that left her exposed to the realities of life. The first big blow came when Tandy asked about the insurance policy. The accountant was aware that Phil had investigated executing a new policy; but, he told Tandy, her husband never got around to actually signing it or paying anything on it.

"What? He did what? You mean he never executed the insurance policy that he told me he got a year ago?" Tandy pushed her chair back, stood up, and began pacing the large conference room. "Okay, then. What did that stupid ass leave me? Will someone get me a drink? I know there's some Scotch around here somewhere." She felt a rage well up inside of her that she had never known before. "What about the apartment? If I sell that, I should be fine."

"Well, actually, Tandy," the heavyset, oily-skinned accountant continued, "Phil had taken out a second credit line against the apartment. As you probably remember, there is a lien from the government because of back taxes still owed from last year. If you sell the apartment now, you will probably be able to cover the lien and repay one of the loans, but you won't have much, if anything, left over."

Tandy sat back down at the head of the table as someone ushered a bottle of Johnnie Walker Black and a Baccarat tumbler her way. After taking a deep swallow of the liquor, she began grabbing at straws, hoping for some relief. "What about the 401(k)?" she demanded.

"That is at about five hundred thousand, but given some of the loans, you may be in a position where you have to use that money to pay them off. I suspect we can take some of it for general living expenses, but it will be tight. So that you know, your daughter's trust is in good shape. Phil made sure to contribute to her trust, so that stands at two million dollars, which no one can touch. When Deja turns twenty-one, she gets full control of the trust. Until then, Phil instructed me to be the trustee, covering her school expenses and other pertinent costs."

Tandy cocked her head to the side as if trying to really hear what the man was telling her. "You mean Phil made sure her trust stands at two million dollars, which I cannot touch, and I am in debt? How am I supposed to live? What am I supposed to do?" Tandy shouted at the room. She was irate. The thought of how Phil had pretended to be so in love with her, always trying to be intimate with her, when he was such a lousy lover! His smelly breath and thick spit had kept her from ever wanting to kiss him on the lips. The way he had feigned undying love for her but in the end treated her like trash, leaving her near destitute while he made their daughter rich!

Hell, all those years she served as PTA president and attended countless meetings; all those years she pretended that Deja's awkward, overweight ass made her a fine ballerina at her painful recitals, when she was really the clumsiest girl onstage. Tandy had toiled for years, volunteering at Deja's various schools, being on block duty in the dead of winter, chaperoning the class on boring field trips. She had even painstakingly coached Deja when she wanted to try out for the tenth-grade play. The poor thing had not been able to act worth a damn, but still, Tandy worked with her on posture and enunciation. Tandy was a good mother, and this was how Phil repaid her? If she could, she would dig him up and beat the living hell out him. Since then, in fact, she often had dreams that Phil was still alive. They would be walking along the beach hand in hand; she would turn and look up into his face, and then she would start beating him, punching him, and clawing at his droopy eyes. He would be too weak to fight back. She would see the blood on her hands and wake up.

"Oooh . . ." Tandy winced again as the final tug of muslin pulled the remaining hair from the crack of her behind.

Renata said, "So, Dana says she is going to be very smart about how she leaves her husband. She plans to sell property and even jewelry before she tells him. She definitely has a plan."

"I hope it works the way she plans." Tandy didn't care what happened to Dana. She would most certainly end up better than Tandy had.

"All done," Renata singsonged as she sprayed a disinfectant that stung Tandy's bikini area as if it were an open cut. The pain reminded her that she had better come up with an idea to get out of her own situation quickly, otherwise this would be the last sixty-dollar bikini wax from J. Sisters.

SEVEN

"I TOLD you there would be some cuties at the gym this morning. See what you've been missing by not coming with me?" Manny teased Lauren as they entered her apartment building.

"There were some hotties, but I couldn't work out at the Harlem gym every day. I'd be distracted and feel like I would have to look good while I sweated. I'm better off in the fuddy-duddy gym over here on the Upper East Side, where the only eye candy is the occasional good-looking trainer." Lauren laughed.

"Suit yourself, but all you need to do is put on some spandex and pull that hair back, and you look better than any of the women in there. We had the best bodies in there this morning, and you know I'm telling the truth." Manny always liked to let Lauren know that he appreciated how attractive she was.

"Aren't you sweet."

"I'm just telling the truth."

The warm scent of something delicious tickled their noses as Lauren and Manny stepped off the elevator and directly into Lauren and Ed's foyer.

"Mmm. Smells like Mr. Francis has already gotten started. I told him to make us some egg-white omelettes, fruit salad, waffles, and mimosas."

"Oooh, that sounds so good after that workout. But check out the treat I brought for us. We should hit this before we have brunch." Manny removed a thick joint from his sport pack. Lauren hesitated and looked around the soaring octagonal foyer with multiple doors as if she thought Mr. Francis might pop out of any one of them. She and Manny had smoked pot together in the past, although not in the middle of the day.

"How about we save that for a more festive occasion," Lauren started, with her voice lowered. "I need to get some work done before tomorrow morning."

"Well, you keep it and think of me when you take that long drag," Manny suggested as he pressed the joint into Lauren's hand. He was sorry they wouldn't indulge this afternoon. But by now Manny had discovered that occasionally, Lauren had a difficult time loosening up. She had to be in the right mood, and it had to be on her terms. But he figured she could enjoy the reefer when the spirit hit her.

"Listen, Manny, I need to take a shower real quick. I'm getting itchy from the sweat. Why don't you wait for me in the library and check out the papers. See who made the style page. I'll only be a minute."

"Okay, Lauren, but hurry up. I don't want to be down here by myself for long."

"Don't worry, I'll be quick," Lauren said, bounding up the stairs two at a time.

Manny noted to himself, surveying the palatial digs that overlooked Wollman Skating Rink in Central Park, that when she and Ed decided to sell, he would make a huge commission. The place had to be worth twenty million today, and more than that in a couple of years. Sometimes he still couldn't believe that he was so intimate with one of the world's wealthiest people. Who could have known when he was growing up that this was where he would be?

Clarice Marks would have been so proud if she had lived to see him hanging out with the rich and famous, Manny thought. His mother always wanted to be around people like this, she just never knew how to fit in. Poor thing always tried too hard. His mother was the sort of woman Tandy would have ripped to shreds for her overeagerness. Sadly, Birmingham's equivalent of Tandy Brooks had spent years alienating Manny's mother from every social group the small Alabama city had to offer black folks. Even though Clarice had memorized Emily Post's book of etiquette from cover to cover and had a husband who made a respectable living for his family, she never mastered the art of social graces. Her efforts were overbearing and clumsy, usually resulting in scaring off or insulting would-be important social acquaintances. In short, she was gauche and desperate for acceptance. Manny had watched his mother's pained attempts at social climbing and promised himself that he would not make the same mistakes on his own carefully charted ascent.

Manny sat down on the small leather sofa in the library, a dark salon encased in oak paneling and bookshelves. One small window faced the street, but the black wooden blinds and dark olive drapes hid the view. As Manny began rifling through the Sunday papers that sat on the wooden coffee table, Mr. Francis eased in without him realizing. "Hello, Mr. Marks."

Manny jumped nearly out of his skin. "Oh, oh. Mr. Francis. I didn't realize you were there. You startled me. How are you?"

"Fine, Mr. Marks. Can I get you something to drink? Coffee, orange juice, a mimosa?" Mr. Francis was an older African-American gentleman with salt-and-pepper hair. Today he was dressed in a gray sweater vest with a white oxford shirt, black chino pants, and classic black leather loafers. To Manny he looked like he belonged in another era, perhaps as a butler in an old black-and-white movie. When he spoke, he overenunciated each word, the way black people were taught to speak in the segregated schools they grew up in during the days before integration.

"I'll have a mimosa, thank you."

"Certainly," said Mr. Francis as he turned and left the room. Manny found the style section. He did not want to tell Lauren, but he almost never read the Sunday papers unless he suspected his name would appear somewhere. He found them so boring: so many pages, so many words, and nothing really interesting going on. When he did check out the newspapers, he read only the gossip and astrology pages and, in the case of the Sunday *Times,* the style section. He turned to his favorite part, the paparazzi page. To Manny, looking at photographs of the New York social scene was business. What parties took place where, for which charities, and who was there were always good conversation for any client. And any print time for himself was good marketing. If he was seen rubbing elbows with the important people, that always translated into an increase in inquiries on his listings.

He spread the pages out on the coffee table in front of him. Much to his pleasure, they held photographs from the Museum of Harlem event. He glanced over each picture, his heart beating hard against his chest. Would he, could he, be on this page with Tandy? And then he saw it. There he was. In black and white, every tooth showing in his full smile. Granted, he was in partial profile, but he looked good. Next to him stood Lauren and Ed. What an awesome opportunity. Mr. Francis interrupted his moment of joy by bringing Manny his mimosa. "Mr. Marks."

"Thank you." Manny accepted his drink without taking his eyes off the page.

"Oh, Manny, I feel so much better. So sorry to keep you waiting." Lauren entered the room smelling of lavender. She looked relaxed in her sweatpants and wifebeater. "Do you mind if we eat now, Mr. Francis?" With that, the butler once again turned to leave the room.

"Lauren. Look at this. You look stunning!" Manny uttered with a big grin on his face, shoving the paper into her hands.

"Uh-huh. But you know and I know you weren't looking at me. You were looking at yourself. You do look good," Lauren teased. "What does the caption say?" Manny looked down, essentially admitting that he hadn't read the caption. "Do you read anything ever?" Lauren scolded with humor in her tone. "Let's see. Number three." Lauren scanned down the page. "Here we go. Lauren and Ed Thomas . . . Oh well."

"Wait. Is that really what it says? You're teasing me. I'm not mentioned at all?" Manny grabbed for the paper, hoping she was wrong. How could they publish his photo and not credit his name? That kind of thing was such a dismissal. It might have been better if he weren't in the picture at all. Now he was Nameless Man. "Oh my God. But that's okay. At least my face is there with you and Ed. Tandy isn't even in here. I know she's going to be mad." They giggled a bit. While Manny and Lauren both adored Tandy, they knew that her social standing was eminently important to her.

Still hogging the paper, Manny began going over the page meticulously. "Let's see who else made the cut." He read out the names, then paused. "Ooh, look, Lauren, Darryl and Coffee Raye. What is she wearing?"

Lauren leaned over Manny's shoulder, trying to get a closer view. "What is *he* wearing is more the question. What is that? A sweatshirt? Somebody help that brother."

"But Miss Thing looks a mess with all that white on. You would think people with money would have better taste. Who is this pretty girl in the photo by herself? It says she's a dancer."

Lauren eyed the photo. "Alyssia Banks. Oh yes, she is the new dancer who moved here to join the City Dance Company. Ed sits on their board. I've seen her dance. She is very talented."

"She's cute." Manny knew that if this woman was a dancer with a company Ed had some dealings with, it might be a sore subject for Lauren. No matter how secure the relationship, no female liked the idea of another good-looking woman around her man when she wasn't. "But she looks kind of cheap and tawdry."

"Manny, you are so bad. How can you see that from a simple black-and-white photograph?" Lauren may have brushed off the comment, but Manny knew it told her he was in her corner. With those few strategic little words, he let her know "I've got your back, sister," and she heard him loud and clear.

"Who is this white woman? Do you know her?" Manny would go over every name of every person in the photos from the Museum of Harlem event. He wanted to know exactly whom he had been rubbing elbows with.

"I don't know. I've never seen her before." Tandy would have known, Manny thought. Tandy knew who everyone was. Lauren took little to no interest unless the person was someone really special to her. For Tandy, everyone had value, especially if they had some money or power.

Lauren went on, "That is so strange, though, that Tandy's picture didn't end up in the *Times*. She was a co-chair. I know she is going to go off on somebody. She lives for her well-deserved glory. I hope when I'm her age, I look as good as she does and carry myself with her regal charm. She's been through so much, and yet she gets better and better. I remember being a little girl, watching Tandy and my mom head out to their fancy dinners on their girls' nights out. Tandy always seemed to be so much cooler than everybody else. She appeared to float when she walked, and her voice was sultry. And she always had time for me. But even as a kid, I knew that being on Tandy's bad side was not a good place to be."

Manny knew Lauren was right. Tandy was the ultimate diva. He'd seen she was the real deal the moment he met her. Lauren and Manny had been in Hermès on Madison Avenue three years ago. Manny had been trying to pick out a new wallet when Tandy approached Lauren, turning her back to Manny. He recognized her dismissal as a power move, letting him know he was not important in her world. Manny continued viewing the wallets, not wanting to interrupt the conversation between Tandy and Lauren. He knew all too well who Tandy was and respected her right to ignore him. She was a legend, and he knew his place. He would not make the same mistakes his mother had made. He was barely worthy to be in the same room. As if sensing his deference, Tandy had chosen to speak to him, admonishing him not to buy the wallet he was holding because it would cause a bulge in the pocket of his pants—which, she later informed him, were too tight. But Manny was thrilled. Tandy had noticed him and acknowledged his presence. From that time on, Manny had become a useful friend to Tandy. His role had increased in the year since Phil's death. Manny enjoyed being her walker.

"I wonder if she's going to be mad at me since my picture is in there and hers isn't." As Manny said the words, he knew Tandy had no reason to be upset with him. It was not his fault that the *Times* had printed the picture of Ed and Lauren with Manny "coincidentally" standing beside them. And it wasn't his fault that he'd happened to say hello to one of his best friends while Tandy made pleasantries with her fans, ignoring him. Besides, his name wasn't even mentioned. But still, a slightly guilty feeling crept over him.

"She knows that you had nothing to do with getting your picture in the style section and her being left out. There is no way you could have planned that. I'm sure her picture will show up somewhere else, like *Town and Country,* or *Avenue* or even *Jet*." Lauren and Manny chuckled. "We are being so silly. This whole conversation sounds stupid. Let's go eat. I'm starved." Lauren edged her way to the dining room.

"Me, too," said Manny as he followed Lauren into the gracious space.

Bagels, cream cheese, fruit salad, coffee, a pitcher of orange juice, and a pitcher of mimosas lined the buffet. The antique Beidermeier table, which would comfortably sit fourteen, was set for two. After filling his plate—Waterford bone-white china with platinum trim—with fruit and bagels, Manny took the seat to the left of the head chair. Mr. Francis appeared again, asking Manny what he wanted in his omelette. In a few minutes, fresh-cut mini portobello mushrooms, green peppers, and flawless creamy light yellow egg formed a palette on the plate the butler placed before him.

"Do you want to go to a book signing tonight? It's for my friend E. Lynn Harris. You've met him," Manny offered, enjoying the flow of the day, wishing to keep it going. Also, any opportunity to show off his friendship with Lauren was money in the bank. Since Manny had met Lauren—four years ago, when she was looking for an apartment to replace the one Ed had lived in with his ex-wife—his business had literally doubled.

"I can't tonight. Ed is back in town. I want to be home when he gets here." Lauren looked forlorn. "I miss him when he's gone."

"Oh, please, Lauren, you've got the best situation. His schedule allows you to do what you need without him being all in your hair. Can you imagine if he were around all of the time? He would drive you crazy."

Lauren talks out of both sides of her mouth, Manny thought. *She was just looking at the brothers in the gym and mentioning how uptight Ed is, and then she turns around and says she wants to sit up under that tired old man. Who does she think she's fooling?* But he continued smiling, allowing her to whine on about her empty home.

"I know, but sometimes it can get lonely being in this big old apartment with just me and Mr. Francis around. And you may think Ed is old, since he is over fifty, but I like sleeping with my husband. It's the best sex I've ever had."

Manny didn't want to hear about Lauren's sex life, but he knew she was lonely. That was how he had infiltrated her life. She didn't have many friends. As she had explained it to Manny, once she and Ed got together, some of her good friends couldn't handle it. They were envious, or else they expected that she and Ed would finance all of their dreams. The new people she met were either much too old and boring for her, or they were too opportunistic. Manny was neither—at least that was the image he presented to Lauren. He made sure to pay for lunch whenever they went out, and to call a car service to drive them around. However he could, he made himself useful, not needy. Manny also knew how to have a good time, something Lauren had seemed to be desperately missing when he came on the scene. She had a couple of friends who liked to party, but apparently, Ed was averse to Lauren hanging out with them. Manny, gay and professional, became the perfect ticket out for Lauren, as far as her husband was concerned. Ed didn't say much to Manny, but he obviously didn't mind Manny looking out for Lauren when he wasn't around. And Manny always made himself scarce when Ed was in town and wanted to be with his wife. Manny found himself in the perfect role of being a good friend to Lauren while taking nothing from her and offering her a good time. In return, he looked richer by association, went to swankier parties, met more powerful people, and made more money. And if the Thomases ever decided to sell their fabulous apartment, Manny was poised to seize that commission. He was also prepared to use her friendship to ascend to the next social level.

He said, "I'm sure the apartment can get lonely, but I don't want to hear about what you and Ed do and how great it is. That is too much information for me. Enjoy your evening with your man." Manny meant what he said. He very rarely sulked at rejection from this friend. With every rejection, there would be another opportunity. Besides, he needed to get home and be with Trenton tonight.

"Maybe the next time Ed goes out of town, we can go out to have some real fun. It's been awhile. I don't want to do anything respectable." Lauren seemed sincerely excited about the idea of going out to hang.

"Okay, Miss Lauren. Let me know when that day comes. I'll get the car and driver."

"Sounds like a plan," said Lauren, and with that, she took a bite into the largest, reddest strawberry Manny had ever seen.

EIGHT

JOHN Coltrane wailed *My Favorite Things* in the background as Lauren sat in the oversized library chair, staring at the books on the paneled shelves. The forty-two-inch plasma screen remained dark; the *In the Heat of the Night* DVD sat idle on the coffee table in front of her. Lauren had expected Ed home three hours ago. He had called two and a half hours before to say that he was running late—some business colleague was in from out of town, they were having a quick drink—but he expected to be home in time to watch a movie before bed. That was the last she'd heard from him. She had tried his cell phone, but it kept going directly into voice mail.

Lauren felt sick. When they first got together, Ed was always available to her. Even a few months ago, he'd been as attentive as in their early days. Something had changed recently. She feared the worst but wanted desperately to believe in the man who had captured her heart. Laying her head on the arm of the chair, Lauren allowed herself to reminisce about the good old days.

. . . .

Ed had cautiously invited Lauren to take a short vacation with him. They had been secretly dating—not telling friends or business associates about their relationship, which was quickly becoming serious to them both—for eight months. He wanted to take a week in the South of France. It was summer, time to rejuvenate his soul, he said, and he needed Lauren by his side to truly relax. He was careful with his request because he did not want Lauren to feel that he was being too presumptuous. They had spent a significant amount of time together, albeit in private. Taking a trip to the Mediterranean might be the beginning of a public relationship. They would be recognized by people, and others were likely to talk. He hoped Lauren was ready to take that step.

As a young woman, Lauren had been exposed to many things—she grew up never wanting for anything; she went to the best private schools, and her parents paid for college and graduate school; she lived in Europe for a year to find herself; her parents bought her a BMW for her sixteenth birthday— but she had never experienced the lifestyle of the truly wealthy. Lauren's parents lived well, debt-free, always with an eye toward conserving and saving. Thus, Lauren was not used to unwarranted extravagance, as her grandmother would have referred to such opulent living, even if one could afford it.

During her days at Thomas Industries, Lauren had become accustomed to the sense of wealth and power emanating from the halls of the office building. She had also been to Ed's luxurious, well-appointed apartment, which was clearly the home of a very wealthy man. But Lauren had never traveled as his guest. Eventually, she consented to accompany him to Europe, never imagining how impressed she would be by the lifestyle he led.

On the morning they were to leave, Ed picked her up at her one-bedroom Central Park South apartment. The driver carried her bags and placed them in the Rolls-Royce as Ed handed Lauren a cup of coffee. They rode to Teterboro Airport in the back of the car, hand in hand.

The G-5 waited on the Tarmac, door open, steps to the ground, inviting them in. The interior of the jet was all comfort. The cream-colored overstuffed leather chairs accented with golden wood paneling, the leather sofa, and the plush shag carpeting made the plane feel more like a living room than an aircraft. The staff of three was polite and friendly as they welcomed Lauren on board.

They settled into their comfortable seats, and the ride was pleasant. Ed was attentive. He made sure Lauren was familiar with the plane, as though showing her around her new home. They then settled into a long conversation about life and the pursuit of happiness. It always amazed Lauren that they never had a shortage of subjects to discuss, whether it was politics, the arts, spirituality, or their numerous common goals. Both of them wanted to have as few regrets as possible. They also both agreed that exploring their relationship to the deepest level was important. And when there was a lull, they filled the moments with kisses, laughter, and sweet glances. The entire eight hours to Nice could have been a shuttle flight to D.C., they passed so quickly.

When the limousine pulled up in front of the marina, Lauren was pleasantly surprised. She'd assumed that Ed had rented a house. She had no idea that he had arranged to have his hundred-foot Hatteras sent down to the Riviera so they could sail the Mediterranean for the week. Lauren had been on a yacht of that size only when she attended a boat show with her parents as a child. She was mindful of the beautiful lines and the pristine luxury.

Lauren climbed on board thinking, *Wow,* but saying to Ed, "This is so beautiful." His reply was, "Now she truly is, with you on board." Lauren smiled, bright-eyed. She was overwhelmed by the trappings of Ed's wealth. But he was also kind, and he doted on her. He made her feel very, very special.

They traveled along the Mediterranean coast from St. Tropez to Monaco. They took day trips, driven in an Aston Martin along the curving hills of the Riviera, famous for the car racing. They dined in small, quaint restaurants that dated back to the early eighteenth century, tucked away on tiny cobblestoned streets. They stuffed themselves with foie gras, venison, exquisite cheeses, and rare St. Emilion wines. She spoke French, and Ed beamed with pride as her mastery of the language affirmed what he already knew. "Beautiful lady, and speaks so well," the locals commented. He would nod with a confident smile. They attended a party hosted by one of his European colleagues at the very glamorous Hôtel du Cap. They danced until sunrise and returned to the yacht drenched in sweat, eager to satisfy the urges that their bumping and grinding had conjured.

On the last night of their trip, after a day of skinny-dipping in the sea, Lauren and Ed had a dinner of grilled lobster, fresh vegetables, and two bottles of Cristal. Full from their feast and the love that had grown stronger over the week, they went out to the deck to lie in each other's arms in a reclining chaise, gazing at the stars.

That evening Ed pulled from his pocket a tiny copy of Khalil Gibran's *The Prophet*. Lauren was astonished. *The Prophet* had been a favorite of hers in college whenever she felt the need for poetic guidance. Ed read to her from the passage about love, reminding her of Gibran's caution that in love one must experience pain to truly appreciate the pleasure. He expressed his deep feelings for her, telling her that he wanted her to always be by his side. Lauren sensed that he was talking about marriage, but Ed had more to say before he began his earnest proposal.

"It is important to me that you know about me from me," Ed said. "There has been a lot of talk about the antics of my first marriage, and with shame, I admit that many of them are true." Lauren felt a nervousness inside and a slight compassion for a man with so much power who could admit his shortcomings.

Ed looked deeply into her eyes. "Claudia and I were married very young. We were both extremely ambitious. As time went on and we had our sons and the business began to grow, I needed to go where the work was. I traveled a lot, and Claudia had to stay home to take care of the kids and the house. After so many nights apart, we drifted from each other. I take the blame. I sacrificed the marriage for the business. I realize that now. And as much as I love my boys, I do not want to have kids when

I marry again. Call me selfish, but I would like to have my wife all to myself." Lauren listened intently and believed that he was sincere in his self-assessment.

Ed stared at her and asked her what she thought of his admission. Lauren stared back, feeling as if fate and all of her ancestors had placed her in this very moment. She loved him, and she knew he loved her. Deep in her soul, she knew they were meant to be together. Still, he was asking a lot for her to forgo having children. Aside from her feelings on the matter, she would be depriving her parents of grandchildren. But she respected his honesty. There were a lot of men who had children and did not want them. At least Ed was in touch with what he truly wanted out of life. Lauren had gone down the path of the lying, immature boyfriend too many times, and she had no desire to experience that again. Fortunately, Ed was a mature man.

Lauren gazed at him, adoring him all the more. His admissions made him more vulnerable and made her feel closer to him. "I think you're a strong, sensitive man. It seems that you have really taken the time for self-exploration. I believe your past mistakes make you a better man today. And I appreciate your honesty." She smiled, trying to assure him that she understood his history and would not hold it against him.

"I love you, Lauren. I love your beauty, I love your heart, I love your mind." Ed kissed her face, her neck, her hands as he spoke. "You make me so happy. I didn't know I could feel this way."

"I love you, too," Lauren said softly. Her heart was full. "This, us, it feels so right."

"I'm glad to hear you say that." Ed stammered as he went on. "Because, I, I want to ask you something."

Filled with nervous excitement, Lauren sensed what his question would be.

"I know we haven't been dating long, but I know when something is right. I've made it my business to know a good thing right away." He laughed. Suddenly, Ed wasn't as eloquent as he had been before. "What I'm trying to say is that I want to spend the rest of my life with you. Will you marry me?"

Even though she had been expecting the question, Lauren was not prepared for the level of emotion that welled up inside of her. This romance had been a whirlwind. Initially, she was uncertain of Ed's intentions. She didn't want to fuck her boss only to be fired when he tired of her. Over the course of their short courtship, she'd found herself falling in love with him. He said all of the right things. He was sensitive and attentive. She had never felt so secure with a man.

Ed broke the silence. "Please say something. You're scaring me."

"I'm sorry. I'm just thinking about how quickly our entire relationship has moved. Marriage?" Lauren was still trying to get her mind adjusted to the idea that he had actually proposed. She wanted to yell "Yes, I'll marry you!" and throw her arms around his neck, but questions remained. Was he really serious about not wanting children, or did he just feel that way now? She loved children; other people's children. She could not say with certainty that she wanted children of her own, but she also could not say that she did *not* want children. She sat up on the chaise and stared at him face-on. He looked so open, so hopeful, so full of love. Maybe he would change his mind about children later. But even if he did not, did she want to risk losing the love of her life by demanding something she was unclear about herself? She did not think so. Ed was what truly mattered. They could spend their lives loving, pleasing, and spoiling each other. Lauren repeated, "Marriage?" then asked, "When?"

"Soon, though I hope I'm not pushing you too fast. You are my heart. I don't think I've ever felt happier. I know you are happy, too. We belong together, Lauren. You and me. Fate expects us to live out our providence." Ed's eyes continued to bore into her as he spoke. Lauren, too, had felt on numerous occasions that fate had played a hand in bringing them together. She believed in destiny, and she believed in Ed Thomas.

"I'll marry you," she finally said that balmy evening, with true love in her heart.

"You have made me very, very happy," Ed said. "I promise I'll do everything in my power to make sure you always feel as happy as you do today." He kissed her lovingly. Remaining on the deck, they made passionate love that ached with tenderness, desire, and the promise of dreams yet to be fulfilled.

The ringing phone brought Lauren out of her reflections.

"Lauren, were you asleep? You sound groggy," came her mother's voice, sounding terse and proper.

"No, Mom. Just sitting here reading," Lauren lied. "What's up?" That sinking feeling, cropping up more and more often these days, lingered in her stomach. In the past, she had always been able to reach Ed. He never completely turned off his phone; he put it on vibrate or silent in important meetings so he would know when Lauren called. He might not answer right away, but he usually returned her call within a few minutes. All Lauren could do was sit by the phone and wait. Unfortunately, the only call she had received was from her mother.

"I was calling because I wanted to invite you and Ed up to the house for Sunday brunch in the next couple of weeks. What's your schedule like?" Grace Martin was all business.

"Mom, I have to check with Ed, but I know I'm free." Ed's schedule had become a sore spot for Lauren of late. He had begun traveling often, leaving Lauren at home—so she could focus on her work, he had said. The first couple years of their marriage, he'd insisted that she accompany him on almost all of his business trips.

"You don't know whether Ed will be in town the next couple of Sundays?" Grace asked, sounding slightly accusatory. Given the unenthused response of Grace and Earl Martin when Ed had asked permission to marry their only daughter, it had been clear to Lauren that her parents did not trust her intended. After all, Ed's philandering ways in his first marriage were well known in Grace and Earl's social circles. Grace had immediately implied to Lauren that Ed was probably not capable of a faithful marriage.

Earl had simply told her to tell Ed to kiss her ass every once in a while for good measure. Clearly, the Martins had hoped to defuse their daughter's plans of marriage.

"No, Mom, I don't know exactly when Ed will be home. He isn't Daddy. He doesn't leave his printed itinerary by my bedside every week," Lauren responded, dripping with sarcasm.

Grace quickly changed her tone. "I know it must be difficult dealing with all of Ed's comings and goings. You just let me know when you're available, because I'm going to invite Daddy's buddy Tim Johnson and his wife, Cara; the judge and his wife, Jenny; and the Wrights, who would love to see you. Daddy and the guys may play golf in the morning and then come back in time for brunch. And if Ed can't make it, that's fine. I'm really just interested in spending time with my precious only child."

"Okay, Mom," Lauren answered heavily. Despite her concerns, she could never confess to her mother her feelings about Ed's absence. While she and her mother spoke almost daily now, Lauren had never told her mom about her boyfriends. As an adolescent, she always sensed her mother's reluctance to view her daughter as a young woman with a life out-side of her parents. As a married adult, Lauren didn't trust the critical eye of Grace not to cast further judgment on Ed. She didn't want any unsolicited advice or admonishings about having made a bad decision.

"You go back to your reading," Grace coddled. "And I'll talk to you later."

After Lauren hung up the phone, she remained in the library chair. Loneliness in her marriage was not supposed to be her fate. She stared into the air, focusing on the various scenarios of Ed's evening that danced in her head. What was he doing out in the street when he was supposed to be home watching a movie with her? She hated to think of it.

NINE

MANNY counted the parade of people as they filed out of the stretch SUV—Coffee and Darryl Raye, their nine-month-old daughter, Coco, their Filipino nanny, Darryl's personal assistant, their publicist, a photographer, and Niche, the feng shui specialist. He had been accompanying Coffee and Darryl on all of their showings to assess whether or not the places had good chi. Today's locale was the Olympic Tower on Central Park West. The apartment was half hotel, half residence, but all extravagance. Celebrities regularly stayed on the hotel side of the building, and out-of-town actors and directors filming in New York occasionally leased one of the apartments, starting at the small fee of fifteen thousand a month.

Darryl and Coffee already owned a thirty-acre estate in East Hampton and a loft in Tribeca, but with the birth of their daughter, they were ready for more conveniences. Hotel-style living appealed to them, but a place like the Pierre was too stuffy for their hip-hop style. Manny had shown them a few co-ops, though they probably would be rejected by all of the desirable ones. Hell, if Mariah Carey and Madonna had been passed over by the nouveau-riche Upper West Side co-ops, the Rayes would be run out of New York if they set foot in front of any respectable board.

They were royal pains in the ass and had a habit of running late. Even more unbearable, Darryl had commissioned a documentary on himself and was constantly surrounded by camera crews and photographers. Manny envisioned the finished product as a real-life version of Don King's *Only in America*. The Raye family and posse were almost impossible to deal with, other than the ten million dollars they were willing to spend. So Manny wearily assumed the suck-up role he had mastered during his years in New York. He also went into broker mode, prepared to dazzle them with his knowledge about the new construction they were about to view.

Coffee Raye gathered her willowy self in front of him, all six feet ensconced in hip-hugging vintage Levi's and a mustard chiffon Gothic blouse with sleeves that swept the concrete. Manny knew she was expecting a compliment on her suntan and new canary diamond pendant the size of a quarter. He immediately obliged, careful to add how fabulous she looked—which she did, with her graceful neck, smooth chocolate skin, and short curly Afro. She reminded Manny of what Foxy Brown might look like in the new millennium. Discreet Coffee was not; nor was her husband, with his matching mustard sweater, blue jeans, and bright yellow boating shoes. As a couple, they wanted not only their every accomplishment chronicled in the press but every marker of their existence to be acknowledged. Public adoration seemed to be the fuel that drove them. And amassing a quarter-billion-dollar fortune in textiles and then the music industry afforded them plenty of adoration.

The Rayes certainly had a down payment on Manny's commitment. Now all they needed to do was cross the threshold and buy, Manny thought as he ushered the cattle through the lobby. Suddenly, the serenity of the all-white marble entry felt more like a Barnum and Bailey convention: The photographer was snapping pictures of Coffee and Darryl "looking natural" as they checked out the minimalist lobby decor and pretended to make meaningful commentary. The concierges clad in their black shirts and black sport coats didn't seem to notice, as if they were used to this sort of activity; or maybe they were simply accustomed to Coffee and Darryl sightings all over the New York papers and magazines.

"We need some green in this space," Niche said with a sneer, moving his hands in the air like a conductor.

Manny pretended not to hear their feng shui man, whose olive-colored parachute pants and white silk blouse resembled those of an MC Hammer backup dancer rather than some house organizer from the East. Even though Manny was used to Niche's zany inspection routine by now, he was tired of the man vetoing every apartment they visited with claims that the space did not have good chi, whatever the hell that meant. Manny simply wanted them to hurry up and purchase something so he could stop dealing with their excess baggage and excessive personalities. But as much as he wanted to collect his commission, he knew enough not to rush them or to appear pressed. Some of his colleagues might not have the patience for their procrastination. That sort of pressure was a real turnoff for a buyer and could translate into a deal-breaker. But Manny was sure that the Rayes would buy eventually. The key for him was to appear aloof yet caring about their concerns. He needed to give them the impression that he wanted them to have the right home. Even if it took them five years, he would be there, faithfully ushering them around New York City.

In reality, Manny was already counting the quarter-to-half-million-dollar commission he could be collecting, depending on whether or not they bought a co-brokered apartment or one of his exclusive properties, as was the case today. Not only did he plan on beginning the renovations on the third floor of his house, which would complete his study and en suite guest room, but Trenton was also pressuring him about buying a vacation home in Miami. He had been complaining to Manny about not getting down to South Beach as much as he had when he regularly modeled.

As they filed into the smoky mirrored elevator, Manny pressed PH, which was a duplex occupying the forty-eighth and -ninth floors.

"I like the elevators, though, the smoky mirrors are very metaphorical, you know," Niche said, glancing around.

"Me, too," Coffee announced, sounding eager to please Niche. Manny got the impression that everything Niche said was gospel. He wondered what "in" person had insisted that Coffee and Darryl hire Niche. He could not imagine them acting without first clearing it with their social counsel, whomever that might be.

On the warp-speed ride up to the top floor, Darryl's two-way pager started playing the song "So Fresh, So Clean" by OutKast. The nervous bespectacled assistant took out a voice recorder/Palm Pilot/cell phone, prepared to receive an order. Darryl opened the two-way and read the message aloud to the ever-waiting assistant: "Quarter got the car, but the rims ain't twenty-inch. Holla back." However annoying these exchanges were, Manny had gotten accustomed to them and acted as if he had heard nothing. He concentrated on the fact that they would not be his clients forever and their money would help put the finishing touches on his home. The elevator opened onto a long corridor with beige damask walls and sturdy but stylish tan carpeting.

"There's more than one apartment on this floor?" Darryl asked, sounding annoyed.

Manny was prepared for this question. "Yes, but the other one is personally owned by Maxwell Wax and rarely used." Manny knew owning an apartment across the hall from the real estate mogul Maxwell Wax would impress the Rayes. They were the type who might buy it just so they could tell their friends he was their neighbor. What Manny had neglected to inform them was that Wax never used the apartment himself and occasionally rented out the space for outrageous sums to wealthy friends.

"Is his apartment a duplex also?" Coffee asked just as Coco started to cry.

"No, his is only half the floor. The one we're seeing occupies half of the forty-ninth floor and all of the forty-eighth floor."

"So the one you're showing us is bigger than Maxwell Wax's?" Coffee asked, eyes wide.

"That it is, my dear," Manny told her as he unlocked the front door to the increasing screams of the baby and an eager photographer's camera in their faces.

The palatial apartment was impressive even by Manny's standards: It had a twenty-by-twenty mocha granite foyer and domed entry ceiling with faux marble painting. All of the public rooms were on the top floor: gourmet eat-in kitchen, fourteen-foot-ceiling living room and family room, leather paneled library with teak floors, dining room overlooking Central Park, three thousand square feet of bluestone terrace space with a view of the Hudson River, and five bedrooms plus two maid's rooms on the lower level. Even Coco's cries did not seem quite so loud as the entourage took in the airy apartment.

The nanny tentatively approached Manny. "Sir, sir. I must change baby diaper."

"Of course." Manny was only too happy to oblige as he noticed the pleasant expressions on Coffee's and Darryl's faces but, more importantly, on Niche's. Manny said to the nanny, "Is the kitchen counter okay, since there's no furniture?" He was almost ready to ask if she needed some help steadying the baby on the slick counter until he smelled that Coco had let out more than a pee-pee.

Manny dared not ask them what they thought, but he silently continued to read their body language. Coffee wanted to check out the master-bedroom closets once again; they were bigger than most New York City studio apartments. After the group surveyed the apartment two more times, Manny was convinced they were sold.

But just to make sure, he told them, "You know, they're going to be opening a Haku here in the spring." He was letting them know that the chicest Japanese restaurant was coming uptown. He knew they loved sushi. He also knew they loved the star-studded crowds who frequented the Tribeca Haku.

"In this building?" Coffee was indeed impressed.

Manny nodded. They lingered in the foyer looking satisfied, as if they had just finished a good meal—a sign that the showing had gone well. Even Niche was uncharacteristically quiet. The silence was broken by the happy gurgles of the baby, fresh from getting cleaned up by the nanny.

"Sir, what to do with this? I no see garbage." The nanny held up the stinky diaper. Coffee and Darryl did not even look her way. Apparently, their baby's shitty diaper was not their problem.

"Why don't you leave it in the kitchen, dear, and I'll toss it after I clear things up," Manny managed to say with a smile despite the stench.

"All right, man, we'll talk to you later," Darryl said, reaching out to shake Manny's hand. "Definitely, this was nice."

"Yes, we'll want to come back," Coffee chimed in, then checked with Niche to see if he approved.

"We will come back," Niche said, sounding as if he were issuing a decree.

Manny felt relief.

Niche added, "But we will bring Judy Miller."

"Oooh, yes, yes, we should," Coffee and Darryl said in unison as the assistant pulled out the recorder again and whispered the order into the mic.

"Is she a relative?" Manny wondered aloud.

Niche was deadpan as he said, "No, she's a psychic. She'll give us the final assessment."

Manny thought he was joking, but to judge by all of their faces, Niche was serious. "Allrighty, well, just call me when you want to come back, even if it's short notice. Since the apartment is vacant, it's easy to get in." He ushered them all to the elevator, his enthusiasm waning as he contemplated the next loony person whose approval they wanted before committing. Manny held his head high, though, as he walked back to the apartment to turn off all the lights.

After shutting off what seemed like a hundred switches, Manny headed for the front door. As he was about to exit, he remembered the diaper fuming on the floor. Holding his breath, Manny leaned down and clamped the thing between his thumb and forefinger. He quickly headed out of the apartment to the incinerator, which was located around the corner from the elevators.

Just as he was about to open the steel door to the garbage chute, he heard footsteps in the hall. He briefly wondered if the Raye party had forgotten something in the apartment, but that thought vanished when he heard an angry female voice.

"It's hard not knowing what the future will bring. I work hard. I'm never late for rehearsals. I've been working since I was six years old. And what will I have to show for it? I mean, what happens when you decide to toss me out? Then where will I be? Living with three roommates in a four-story walk-up?"

"That won't happen," a deep male voice responded tenderly.

"How do you know? I need security, and we need our own place for real."

"Aren't these accommodations suitable?"

"They're not mine. Nothing here is mine. They're not my pictures on the wall, my furniture, my sheets. Nothing. I don't even have my own towels here," the woman whined.

"Well, what do you propose we do?"

"Only what you promised when I was still in San Francisco," she said, like a little girl trying to get her way.

"Would that make you happy, baby?" the man asked, sounding patriarchal, but Manny doubted he was the woman's father.

"To get my own place?" the girl asked excitedly.

"Yes."

"You wanna know how happy it would make me?"

"How happy?" the man asked seductively. Manny sincerely hoped they were not about to start making out in the hallway, because he was tired of standing in the garbage room. The smell was beginning to nauseate him.

"Real, real happy," she said. Then there was silence.

Manny waited a few more minutes before he figured the coast was clear. But when he rounded the corner, he realized his mistake. The couple was still in front of the elevator, locked in a passionate kiss, like two teenagers. When they heard him, they pulled apart, and Manny saw that the man looked an awful lot like Ed Thomas. And then their eyes met.

Ed straightened his tie and adjusted his suit jacket as he glanced at Manny. The woman merely looked at Manny like an underling who had interrupted them. Manny had never seen Ed look so disheveled. Here he was, one of the most prominent African-American men in the world, and he'd been flat-cold busted with his lover by one of his wife's closest friends.

"Hello, Manny," Ed mumbled.

"Ed," Manny said uncomfortably. He had every intention of ignoring the young woman and returning to the apartment for his briefcase, but she shoved her hand at him, not going to be overlooked.

"Alyssia Banks," she informed him, even though Manny had become well versed with the ballerina's bio after seeing her picture in the *Times* style section. Whenever there was a new face of color on the scene, Manny made a point of getting on the Internet and finding out everything that was public record. Alyssia hadn't trained formally as a ballerina until the age of fourteen, when she was plucked off the streets of Compton, California, to dance at a prominent school. She was considered a prodigy and had quickly risen to the top, then had been invited to join the City Dance Company as a principal dancer.

Manny shook her hand. "Manny Marks." Her small hands grabbed hard as she willed him to look her in the eyes. She was a feisty little thing. Clearly, Ed had not trained her. She was behaving so indiscreetly, introducing herself. The mistress? Manny knew she was a world-class ballerina, but there was something so crass about her; she looked so base in her form-fitting black Lycra pants and black halter top with brass studs around the collar. She was tacky. True, she was beautiful and talented, but she was an inexperienced girl from the hood. And there was a roughness to her, like an unsanded and unpolished flawed gem. Lauren could run circles around this child.

The three of them stood in silence, frozen until Ed said, "Manny is a real estate broker."

"Ohh, really?" Alyssia began with an exaggerated smile. "What a coincidence. Well, we might be giving you a call. Do you have a card?"

"I'm fresh out," Manny lied as he patted his coat pockets. He never ran out of business cards.

"I'll look you up, then," she promised with a piano-key smile. Manny believed she would track him down. Something about her told him that much. There was a darkness to her. Manny recognized the look. He had learned to cover it in himself over the years.

TEN

Today had been a good day, Lauren thought as she hurriedly began to change her clothes. She had finished preinterviewing the last of the men for her Style Channel documentary on the challenges of black male models. This was her first gig in the industry, and working as a freelance producer with television professionals made Lauren feel connected to the real world. When she was with them, she was not the wife of Ed Thomas; she was a producer with a vision. She knew she had a lot to learn, so she listened and watched. She was also mindful that her long-term goal as a documentary filmmaker was to expose more social injustices, particularly those inflicted upon women of color. But as a newcomer in the field, she was grateful to get her foot in the door. Subsequently, she took the opportunities that came her way.

Lauren had been thrilled when Rhonda, a business school colleague, had suggested she pitch an idea to the development staff at Style Channel. Rhonda was not a development person—she worked in acquisitions—but she made the necessary connections for her friend. It was the first pitch Lauren had ever made in her life. Rhonda had informed her that they were looking for something sexy and edgy. Lauren worked hard at clarifying the story she wanted to tell and practiced the pitch over and over. While her nervousness made her stumble a few times, the hard work paid off. Style Channel loved the idea. They claimed they could pay her only scale, which would amount to nothing after expenses, but that was okay with Lauren. She was not trying to get rich from this segment; she was looking to gain knowledge. She would have done the work for free.

Feeling like a working girl once again, Lauren had dashed home to change from her jeans and T-shirt to something more appropriate for the dinner that Ed expected her to attend with him later that evening. They were dining at Le Cirque with Thomas Industries' four top managers and their spouses to celebrate the third-quarter earnings. Ed always made sure to reward his soldiers and show them his gratitude. He made it clear to Lauren that these dinners were mandatory. He expected her to perform as sort of a senior spouse. He took her leadership of the wives seriously and let her know that she could be a great asset in making his subordinates feel as though they were part of a family. Though Lauren wanted to please him, she always dreaded taking on the role of the supportive corporate wife.

Lauren had witnessed her mother live the life of the perfect housewife despite accomplishments in advanced education. Lauren did not want Ed placing her in that box. She wanted to support him but did not want to be absorbed by him, something she had been thinking about more often lately. His amped-up schedule gave Lauren more time and space to consider her own goals, personally and professionally. Work was a priority. Keeping busy helped keep her mind off her loneliness. Previously, her schedule had revolved around Ed's. Now it seemed as if he called upon her only to fulfill her official duties as Mrs. Ed Thomas, like tonight. Despite his shortness with her, she still held up her end of the bargain. This evening's duty: hosting the "women."

During these social gatherings, Lauren did not have difficulty finding something to talk about. The wives were friendly enough, probably because they felt they had to be. But they reminded Lauren of the cliquish teenage girls from the social club Jack and Jill that her mother made her participate in, who were afraid Lauren would steal their boyfriends. They were too polite—unctuous—and she felt the slap of snootiness beneath the veneer.

The woman Lauren related to most easily was Toni, the wife of a marketing director for the Thomas bottled-water division. Toni was the youngest of the corporate wives Lauren had met thus far. The few times they had socialized, conversation revolved around Toni's adolescent children, her husband's annual fishing trip, and the tribulations she faced during her days on the golf course. Though shy around Lauren, Toni always claimed that being a part of Thomas Industries was a joy and privilege. Another wife, an uptight editor at *The New York Times,* took herself too seriously. She condescended to Lauren, speaking to her as if she were a child. The other wife who would be at dinner liked to talk about her achievements as a painter and her travels with her women friends. Not one woman ever asked Lauren about her life, yet they all seemed to get along with one another really well. They had known one another for at least a decade. Perhaps they resented Lauren for marrying Ed, since they had been friends with his first wife.

Whatever the case, Lauren was becoming increasingly stressed, thinking about the evening that lay before her. She was feeling antsy and unsure of herself as she walked into her closet and knelt on the floor. She pulled out a shoe box from a stack of many others and removed the top. The joint Manny had given her lay between the tan suede loafers. She contemplated lighting it up. She thought about how it might have a soothing effect, as on the first time she had smoked pot—the first time she had tried to be a part of a world that was not quite sure how to deal with her.

As a junior at one of the most prestigious private all-girls' schools in Westchester County, Lauren had become friends with Margy Stevens, an heiress whose father had made his multimillions by inheriting his father's car-engine-parts company. Most automobiles made in America possessed a Stevens engine. The business wasn't glamorous, but it paid the Stevenses big-time. Margy and her older brother lived with their parents in a mansion that encompassed about twenty thousand square feet of indoor space; the grounds included acres and acres of woodlands. Their parents traveled frequently for business and pleasure. Sarah, their Jamaican nanny, ran the house, along with a bevy of other staff who had watched over Margy and Michael since they were babies. But at sixteen and seventeen, Margy and Michael now lived their own lives.

Margy had embraced Lauren, who was lonely, snubbed by many of the other girls. There had been only two African-American students in Lauren's age group since grade school, and Lauren had spent much of her childhood feeling isolated. Lauren and Margy were in advanced-placement classes together. At lunch hour, they would go to the student lounge for a smoke, a privilege extended only to juniors and seniors. The friendship made Lauren feel cool. Margy was a revolutionary wanting to help the underdog, since she had grown up so privileged. Her place among their peers was secure. She was rich, blond, thin, and liked to party. Yet she extended her hand to Lauren.

Margy and her brother were close. He went to Lauren and Margy's "brother school." The siblings liked to socialize together, and they enjoyed the collective crowd at home after school. When Lauren went over to Margy's house, she felt like she was at a party. There were always people lounging around with little or no supervision. Sarah would make sure everyone had snacks. She did not lurk over the teenagers but let them do as they pleased. Lauren guessed Margy and Michael's parents must have given the nanny these orders to assuage guilty feelings over never being home.

One lovely spring afternoon Lauren went home with Margy, lying to her mother about a study session. As usual, a couple of Margy's other friends from school came with them. Michael was already there with a few of his buddies. Kids were drinking beer and mixing liquor into fruit juice, all the while eating pizza and chips that Sarah had laid out. Of course she had no idea that the kids were drinking, though she probably didn't care. Music was pumping, and some kids were playing Atari; Pac-Man was all the rage. Margy took Lauren aside and told her she wanted to show her something.

Curious, Lauren followed Margy up one side of the marble double staircase to Michael's room, where a very good-looking chocolate-brown boy was bobbing his head to the Sugarhill Gang, blasting from the speakers on Michael's desk.

"Yeah, see, man. I told you this shit was good," the brother was yelling over the record, with a wide grin that accentuated the dimples in his cheeks.

"Yeah . . ." was all Michael said. He was also bobbing his head. "Margy, close the door. I don't want anyone coming up here, seeing what we've got."

As always, Margy jumped to do what her brother had asked. To Lauren she said, "Michael said of all of my friends, you were the coolest, so he said I could bring you up here. But Lauren, you have to promise not to tell anyone else."

The compliment made Lauren feel ten stories high. She knew she was fun to be around, but it felt so good to be validated by this hip senior who always seemed to be on the cutting edge. And Margy had said it in front of this good-looking black guy as well.

"Lauren, this is my buddy Foster. Watch out for him. He's smart as shit, and chicks love him." Michael had again made Lauren feel like she was the new member of a very exclusive club.

"Hey," Lauren offered, tossing her hair behind her ear, trying to live up to the image the Stevens siblings had painted. At that moment she was glad she had gotten up half an hour early to make sure her Farah Fawcett do was perfectly in place, with the right amount of sheen and bounce.

"Hey, mama. How are you doing? Don't just stand there, come on in. Get comfortable. We've got a treat for you girls." Foster was the definition of cool, with his high-top fade, zigzag hair design, and trace of a mustache. He was confident and obviously not concerned with what these white people thought of him. Lauren liked him instantly.

Michael pulled out a plastic bag that revealed a greenish herb. Marijuana, Lauren assumed. He cleared the books and trash off the top of his desk and dumped some of the herb onto the table. He then took out a piece of white paper and began rolling it into a cigarette.

"This shit smells good," Michael said. "I figured you girls would get yourselves into this eventually, so you should do it here, see how it feels, and then know what the high is like so no limp-dick assholes try to take advantage of you when you get high and we're not around."

"How do I know you won't take advantage of me now?" Lauren flirted.

"Because you're my little sister's friend," Michael deadpanned.

"I'm totally trustworthy." Foster grinned, showing his dimples again, as he brought the cigarette to his lips. "Now, ladies, watch how I do this." He took a long drag on the joint, holding the smoke in his lungs. Exhaling, he began to cough. "Woooo. That is some quality bud. Mike, you've got a badass connection."

Michael laughed and took the joint from Foster, having his turn. He then handed it in the direction of the girls. They exchanged glances, tentative about trying drugs. Finally, Lauren, anxious to maintain the impression that she was cool, grabbed the joint and inhaled. She instantly felt a burning sensation in her throat. "Aahh. Aahhh" was all she could muster as she handed the cigarette to her friend. As the burning sensation in her throat began to ease, she waited for the unknown.

"So, did you like that?" Foster asked her.

"I think so, but I'm not sure I'm feeling anything."

"You will. Give it a sec. And take one more hit."

Lauren took another drag and coughed a bit more. The drug began to take effect. She turned to watch Foster, who was now bobbing his head to Led Zeppelin. Michael was playing the Atari game set up on the television. Then Lauren realized that she was beautiful and strong, and that she never again had to feel isolated. The room came alive with color and texture. So many thoughts were coming to her mind. She felt clever and witty, as if she were making observations that no one ever had before. Turning her attention to Foster, she was ready to converse.

"So, Foster. Where are you from?"

"I'm from the bad part of New Rochelle. My parents aren't rich like yours," he said with a smile.

"My parents aren't rich. What makes you say that?"

"Oh, Michael and Margy told me about you. You might not be rich-like-Stevens rich, but you know your daddy got bank. I know you live in a big old house."

"When I look around here, my house looks like it should be the garden shed." They laughed and talked for hours nonstop.

That evening Lauren stayed at Margy's until eleven o'clock, bargaining on the phone with her mom, claiming that they were studying for a big test the next day. For Lauren, the day had been monumental. She had gained acceptance from Margy's big brother and his cool friend Foster, who would remain a lifelong friend. She had also learned that marijuana had the glorious effect of relaxing her when she needed it.

"Mrs. Thomas, here are your . . ." Mr. Francis interrupted her thoughts. He was carrying Lauren's dry cleaning, standing in the entrance to her closet. "Oh, excuse me," he said, looking around the spacious area and then down at the open shoe box. "I was just bringing in your cleaning. I knew you were on your way out."

Lauren quickly returned the lid to the box and spoke fast. "Oh, Mr. Francis. You startled me. Could you leave those things in the chair or on the bed? I need to get dressed. I'm going to meet Mr. Thomas and will be out of your way in a couple of seconds."

"Of course, Mrs. Thomas," he said deferentially. She doubted he had seen the single joint between the shoes, but still, she was tired of him sneaking around their home. He always seemed to pop up when she least expected him. He had been with Ed since his divorce, and she knew his loyalty was not with her.

After Mr. Francis left, Lauren dejectedly pushed the box back in place, no longer in the mood to smoke. She was not in high school anymore. Getting high before her husband's company dinner might put her at ease, but it would not make anybody want to be around her.

ELEVEN

"WHAT is the problem?" Tandy demanded of her longtime friend and publicist, Roxy Nixon. Roxy was seated at Tandy's kitchen table, drinking hot tea and munching the little sandwiches Tandy had set out for their visit. With money as tight as it was, she no longer had a housekeeper/cook to prepare snacks for her visitors. "Where is my coverage on the Museum of Harlem gala and on that damn MotherLove award?" Tandy raged as she held up copies of the *New York Times* Sunday style section, *Town & Country, Avenue, W,* and *New York,* which she then threw on the table in front of Roxy. It had been a few weeks, long enough for the press to print pictures of Tandy at her various social gatherings. Usually, Tandy could expect to find her image at least in one of the trades. She should have been featured somewhere, since she was a cochair of the Museum of Harlem event.

"The MotherLove lunch should have registered in *Avenue,* but Tandy, you know how New York is. There are fifty lunches a day honoring at least one hundred people. I didn't expect much for you on that, but it was a great honor for you, and your picture was on their website," Roxy said, trying to make her feel better.

Tandy cut her eyes at Roxy. "Their website? Is that a joke? I'm not laughing."

"No, I think there is a lot more value in Internet publicity than ever before. Anyway . . ." Roxy squirmed visibly. "As far as coverage on the museum gala goes, I think the problem was timing."

"I don't understand." Tandy sat down across from Roxy and waited for an answer.

"Well, you came in just a few minutes after Lauren and Ed Thomas. The press seems to have become enamored with her. And once they were through shooting there, the press line broke apart and began shooting pickup photos at the dinner."

"Lauren?" Tandy stood up again. She rolled the name Lauren over in her mind. The pain of being pushed out by youth registered in her heart. Ed had chosen his second wife well, she thought. Tandy had known Ed for at least twenty years and had known Lauren practically since she was born. When Tandy had learned that Ed and Lauren were getting married, she felt a mix of anger and sadness. Despite her intimate history with Ed, she should have guessed he would not marry her, though she would have dumped Phil in a minute if she thought there was a chance. However, she was too old, and he had been too close to Phil. But for Ed to marry such a young girl was as if Ed were saying to the world that a woman Tandy's age was not good enough. The thought now haunted Tandy. She always commanded attention because of her beauty and her style. With age, fading beauty, and the lack of funds making it difficult for her to keep up with the trends, Tandy would be replaced in society by a neophyte who was clueless about her own power and the business that was going on around her.

The melodic tone of the door phone broke Tandy's thoughts. She looked at her watch, wondering about the interruption. The man from the consignment shop was not scheduled for another hour and a half, and she was not expecting any deliveries.

The doorman informed her that the consignment guy had arrived. The man was early because he'd been called out to Columbia County for the afternoon. He would review her items now. All he needed was for her to point him in the direction of the things she wanted to sell. Against her judgment, Tandy decided to let him come in. She needed to unload some of her furniture for cash. Roxy could stay in the kitchen and would never see the man. The last thing Tandy wanted was Roxy going around town with her big mouth, telling everyone her client was selling her belongings. That would definitely send out the message that she was desperate. The thought of her circle of friends getting a whiff of her dire predicament made her shudder.

Tandy opened her door and extended her hand toward the six-foot-tall graying white man with a fat gut. He shook her hand with a limp damp grip, looking around the room instead of directly at Tandy. Instantly, she regretted letting him in. Her instincts told her he would not be pleasant to deal with. But since he was here, she decided to show him into her large living room, decked out with antiques and classic furniture she and Phil had collected over the years. She then told him he should also review Phil's den. She showed him how to use the intercom, then headed back to Roxy.

When Tandy pushed through the swing door to the kitchen, Roxy was quickly finishing up a call on her cell phone. Tandy went to the stove, grabbed the teakettle, and filled it with more water to refresh their cups. She had managed to collect herself after her earlier outburst. Roxy was used to her tantrums. When Phil began his rise at the firm, Tandy began her rise in society. She and Roxy had met at a party for one of Phil's colleagues and had become fast friends. Tandy had made sure to nurture the friendship when she learned of Roxy's caliber of clientele. To Tandy, having a friend in the publicity business would prove priceless. She began by getting suggestions from Roxy on which events received big press. As they got to know each other, Roxy recommended parties and events to boost Tandy's visibility; she also steered Tandy in the direction of fashion, inviting her to shows and getting her in with the designers. From time to time Tandy would give her gifts or lunches or special-events tickets that Roxy could not get herself, and she would pay Roxy a fee for acting like an agent by getting her coverage in magazines, newspapers, and the occasional television interview. While Tandy might throw an occasional outburst, she made sure Roxy knew not to take it personally.

"Rox, between you and me, I need to re-create my image. It's been a year, and frankly, I need to find an income stream for myself. I'm not panicked or anything, but I would like to be out there working, taking care of me for a change. And extra cash wouldn't hurt." Tandy tried to get across the urgency without sounding destitute. Her hope was that Roxy would help her figure a way into some kind of salaried position that would keep her dignity intact. "I haven't worked for money in decades, but I've done charity work for children and women, and I've been a beacon for fashion, if I say so myself." Tandy chuckled, hoping to keep the mood light.

"The first thing that comes to mind is a foundation on stroke awareness, set up in Phil's name. We've talked about this before. It's only been a year since his death. You could still come up with something that would raise a lot of money for a good cause and give you a salary. Lots of widows do that, especially when they need money," Roxy said sincerely.

Tandy wrinkled up her nose as if she smelled something bad. "That widow thing is dead. Pardon the pun." Tandy smiled. "Seriously, though, as much as I respected Phil and know that his death could have been prevented if he had taken better care of himself, I don't want to associate myself with death. I'd rather do something new, fresh. I know we can come up with something."

As Tandy finished her sentence, the swing door of the kitchen blew forward, and the portly consignment man sauntered in. "There you are, Tandy. I wanted to go over the items that I've reviewed. First in the living room, you have a couple of respectable pieces that I could probably fetch a decent dollar for, but as far as the sofa and chairs go, my clientele don't generally—"

Tandy stood in astonishment as this lowly white man addressed her in her kitchen by her first name as if she were the help. "You know what? Let's go into the foyer and finish this conversation." She excused herself from Roxy and walked him toward the elevator. As they moved to her front door,

Tandy couldn't help but think that this sorry-ass man would not have come into her kitchen, called her by her first name, dismissed her furniture in front of her guest had she not been black.

"I can have those end tables and lamps picked up by the end of the week, if you like," he offered as Tandy pressed the elevator button in an effort to get this rude man out of her home as quickly as possible.

"That won't be necessary. I've decided not to sell them after all." As if on cue, the elevator doors opened, and Tandy bade him farewell.

He tried to salvage his sale. "I don't understand . . . I thought you—"

"You don't have to understand. Bye-bye." And the elevator doors closed.

Tandy put on her best face in an attempt to mask her humiliation before heading back to the kitchen. She asked Roxy to join her in the living room. Tandy needed a change of scenery to think about her publicity plan. Once seated, Tandy started in again, anxious to change the mood. "I'm meeting with Dana Trip next week. She's divorcing her husband. Do you think there is anything she and I could do together?"

"I think you should focus on yourself and not align yourself with anyone right now."

"Okay, then how can we get a fluff piece about me in one of these damn magazines within the next few months?" Tandy asked forcefully.

Much to Tandy's disappointment, Roxy looked at her watch and stood up. "I promise, I'm already thinking about your magazine piece. I didn't realize how late it had gotten. I've got to run. And Tandy, why didn't you tell me you were selling your things? I know some really good people who can get you excellent prices."

"Oh, I'm not actually going to go through with it. Since Phil died, I've been toying with getting rid of all of this stuff, because it reminds me of him. You know, we picked everything out together. But thank you. If I do decide to part with anything, you'll be the first to know."

After Roxy left, Tandy returned to the living room and sat back down, massaging her temples to ease the headache she felt coming on. How had she let Roxy run into that fucking consignment prick? *I never should have let his sweaty ass up here when he showed up so early,* she thought. But that encounter was not all that was bothering her. Roxy had not helped her come up with a plan to relieve her current situation. She vowed to have something in mind by the time she and Dana had lunch. As things stood now, Dana was looking like her only hope.

"ᴀɴᴅ what did you get this one for?" Ed asked Lauren, with his chin nestled in the crook of her neck. He was looking at the blue ribbon pinned to her cracked corkboard, along with her many other high school honors. The array of awards, certificates, and trophies was immortalized in her childhood room.

"Westchester regionals riding. I think that was for jumping," Lauren answered, feeling a mixture of comfort and awkwardness with him in the bedroom where she used to adjust the rubber bands on her braces.

"You took second place. Impressive," Ed said proudly, and began nuzzling Lauren's ears.

"But it was only regionals. I missed nationals that year with a broken foot." She neglected to mention that she had lost interest in riding and lacrosse and tennis her junior year, around the same time she started hanging out and partying with Margy. Ed seemed so impressed with the image of her as this all-American privileged suburban girl that she did not want to disappoint him with the truth.

"You got about twenty-five more awards than I did in high school."

"Yeah, but who has more now?" Lauren asked, turning to look at him directly. He tightened his grip around her waist, and her insides jumped in fear and anticipation. They were supposed to be getting dressed for the engagement reception Lauren's parents were hosting in two hours. Instead, Ed had taken a detour from his bedroom, in the guest wing of the colonial mansion. He had demanded that Lauren give him a tour of the bedroom she grew up in. Noticing the look of genuine interest on Ed's face as he learned everything about her, Lauren quickly got over her embarrassment. She was thankful her mother had long ago removed the Prince posters, but Grace had kept everything else in its place—the elementary, middle, and high school diplomas, the stuffed bunnies and lambs left over from many an Easter basket, the Mardi Gras beads from a family vacation draped across the vanity mirror. The Tiffany silver teddy-bear bank, polished to a high sheen, still sat on the chest of drawers beside the aging white leather jewelry box, complete with spinning white ballerina inside. The room could have been a shrine to Lauren the woman-child. Grace had left the room as she wanted to remember it—or, more accurately, as she wanted to remember Lauren the former overachiever.

Still holding tight to Lauren's midsection, Ed steered her to the French-paned double windows overlooking rolling green lawns checkered with pine trees. "How many poor boys climbed up that window trying to get into your pants?" he asked suggestively as he ran his hands up and down Lauren's bare arms, making his way to the tips of her fingers. He stopped at her hips and secured her in place.

"All the boys in this neighborhood were afraid of my father."

"I wouldn't have been," Ed told her as he moved his hands toward her jeans zipper, seeming to interpret her statement about her father as a dare.

Lauren ignored the challenging tone in his voice. He was a man's man, even when it came to her father. Of course, Ed was always very respectful, overly so at times. He would have been a prize to most future in-laws, but Lauren's parents were not most in-laws, and Lauren was their only child. They had raised her to be a future leader, and they had made sure she was financially comfortable, so she would never have to depend on a man for anything. Lauren also knew her parents were looking forward to having grandchildren. Whenever that topic was broached, Lauren changed the subject. There were still too many other hurdles to surmount before that sore spot became an issue as well. There was the matter of the first Mrs. Thomas, a social acquaintance of her parents—their contemporary. But with his consummate charm, Ed had managed to convince the Martins of his sincere love for Lauren. He assured them that his intentions were good, that he wanted to be a fine husband to her. He had secured their blessing, if not their total approval.

Lauren momentarily forgot about her parents as Ed began to press against her from behind. She involuntarily swayed her hips against his crotch in response. He had unzipped her jeans and slid his hands inside her panties before she fully realized what was happening. Then his fingers made their way inside of her, gently stroking and maneuvering the swollen lips aside in search of her most coveted spot. His movements froze her in place, his touch so pleasurable she did not want to interfere. Her head fell forward, and her eyes slitted—half seeing her childhood playground, half realizing she was in the same room where she had lost her virginity with Derek Miles at the age of sixteen. But on that night her mother and father had been attending a black-tie affair in Manhattan. This evening Daddy Earl was at the barbershop, ten minutes away from their New Rochelle house, and Grace was finalizing the placement of the flowers around the fiberglass-covered pool area.

There was excitement and danger to what they were doing, with so many people milling around below in preparation for their engagement party. Lauren felt naughty and enticing all at once. When she could take his fondling no more, she almost begged him to enter her, but he wouldn't give in so easily.

"Are you sure? Your mother's downstairs."

Lauren moaned, "Yes," as she felt his hardness press against her now-bare ass. She wanted Ed inside of her more than ever. There was an urgency to what they were about to do. It was their right. They were in love. They were to be married. And when Ed did enter her, he forcefully yet skillfully moved in and out. Never before had she felt so strongly as if they belonged together, to each other. Lauren's breath came faster and faster until the window she was leaning against fogged over, obscuring the yard, erasing all that had come before Ed Thomas. His smile, his eyes, the lemon-shaped birthmark at the small of his back, the curly hairs on his chest all flashed before her. She adored every part of him; all that they shared was sacred to her. Lauren's body began to convulse. Her wet mouth pressed against the slippery pane, begging for more, begging for a reprieve.

There had always been an intensity to their lovemaking, but today it was different—primal and possessive. It was early fall, Lauren's favorite time of year, especially at her childhood home. It signified the end of a satisfyingly packed summer at Martha's Vineyard, Antibes, and her grandfather's farm in Savannah. Yet the onset of fall always promised even more discovery, bringing the varied hues of the leaves, ranging from crimson to burgundy to fiery orange to burnt sienna. Hot colors for the onset of cool.

With Ed panting in satisfaction behind her, and her body and mind feeling released of any stress or worries, Lauren felt high. Ed was all she wanted or needed. As she slowly pulled up her panties and jeans, she turned around to gaze at Ed and saw the same look in his eyes. At that moment Lauren knew they needed only each other.

Then the door blew open. Lauren wasn't sure if Ed had zipped his pants up. She didn't know if she had pulled down the T-shirt that had risen above her breasts. What she saw was her mother's full figure standing in the doorway of her bedroom. Immediately, Lauren felt as though she were still in high school and had stayed on the phone too long or too late—except this was worse, much worse. By the time Ed turned around and saw Grace as well, they were all looking sufficiently uncomfortable. Grace was already dressed for the evening, in a chic charcoal-gray calf-length dress and a triple strand of double-knotted pearls. She seemed to look beyond their shoulders, out toward the grounds, not directly at them. Her jaw was tight, but Lauren could see that her mother was clinging to whatever manners she could muster under the circumstances. It was apparent from the closeness of the air and the sweat on Ed's brow that some kind of conjugal activity had taken place.

Ed was the first to speak. "Have any of the guests arrived?"

Grace refused to humor his attempt at normalcy and curtly stated, "The reception does not begin for another hour and a half. I won't be expecting anyone until then. But I would appreciate the two of you joining the photographer for your announcement photos."

"I'm about to get dressed now, Mother," Lauren interjected as Ed began heading toward the door.

"Okay, Grace, I'll go get ready," he said, stepping past her. Even he did not want to have an exchange with Grace.

Lauren was transfixed. Her high plummeted. Grace had busted them fucking in a curtainless window at four o'clock in the afternoon. Lauren had never even had the sex talk with her mother, and now this had happened.

Once Ed was out of earshot, her mother simply rolled her eyes, looked Lauren over from head to toe, and stepped fully inside the room. She firmly shut the door behind her. Lauren could feel herself squirm in anticipation of a confrontation.

"What's up, Mom? I'm going to take a quick shower and get dressed," she said in an attempt to rush her mother out of the room. She was not in the mood to have a discussion right now. But Grace advanced on Lauren, joining her in front of the slightly foggy window. Lauren noticed her lip prints on the pane. Her mother was undaunted.

"Lauren, your father and I have supported you in pretty much all of your endeavors your whole life. And we support you now."

Lauren wished her mother would get to the point.

"And I am very proud of you for all of your accomplishments, for always working hard," Grace said, then hesitated. "Always being a lady. That's what brings us joy."

"Thank you, Mother, I appreciate that. Now I'm going to take a shower."

"Hear me out, Lauren. Just hear me out."

"Hear you out about what?"

"As you step into your marriage, I hope *you* know your own worth."

"Yes, Mother. You and Daddy have instilled that in me." It was the answer Lauren knew her mother wanted to hear. The one that would make her feel she had done her job as a parent.

"I realize you think I don't ever know what I'm talking about, that I'm always meddling, but I want you to understand how high your stock is on your own merits. Ed Thomas should consider himself a lucky man to call you his wife."

Lauren had an idea what her mother was getting at, but she had no desire to go there. "Yes, well, I consider myself rather fortunate to have him as my fiancé as well."

"Lauren, I just want you to remember who *you* are. Don't lose that."

Lauren threw her hands up. "Don't lose that? If anything, I'm going to find myself even more, being married to Ed. He supports me and I support him. I'm not going to lose anything. Hopefully, I'm going to grow as a woman, as a wife, and with a man who has my back growing alongside me. Why do you have to be such a killjoy?"

Grace shook her head and sighed. "You misunderstand me, Lauren. All I want for you is your happiness. It's just that I've been around, I've seen a lot, and I want you to avoid the pitfalls of, of . . ."

"Of Ed and Claudia?"

"I didn't say that."

"But I'm sure that's what you meant. Listen, I know you may be trying to help, but Ed has already come clean with me about everything in his past. Everything. And that was a long time ago. Ed and I truly love and appreciate each other. And we are going to last. And maybe, Mother, maybe one day you'll realize that, and I'll be the better for it. Can't you just be happy for me? For us?"

. . .

Lauren's reminiscence was broken by the sound of her mother's voice coming over the intercom system, but she continued to stare out the window of her innocence. It was the fifth fall since that conversation between mother and daughter. Lauren wondered if she was better off now.

"Lauren. Lauren!" Grace's voice boomed through the speaker.

"Yes, Mother," Lauren called back, not removing her eyes from the falling leaves.

"Pick up the phone, I can't hear you very well."

Lauren backed away from the window. She could almost see her lip prints on the pane from five years before. She picked up the newly installed intercom phone and said, "Yes?"

"Did you want to come down for a mimosa before Ed arrives?"

Lauren did not respond. She was thinking about the last couple of months she'd spent at the Vineyard. Were it not for Manny and Tandy, she would not have had very much company, what with all of Ed's traveling.

"Lauren?"

Lauren swallowed hard before answering. She had come up from the city to New Rochelle the night before, with Ed's promise that he would join her today. Much to her disappointment, Ed had called to say he would have to cancel. She dreaded telling her mother. "He's not going to be able to make it today," she said into the phone. Grace's tense silence begged an explanation. "He had an unexpected meeting."

"On a Sunday afternoon?"

"Yes, Mother. But it's about to be Monday in Hong Kong, and he's doing business there."

Lauren heard the "hmmph" in her mother's breath before she spoke. "I remember a time when Ed wouldn't dare turn down an invitation to this house—when he considered it a privilege."

Lauren remembered that time, too. She wished she could rewind her life to that place and figure out what went wrong.

Rasheema Lawrence's burgundy-tinted arched eyebrows raised again as she read over the deed to the condominium she and her husband were closing on today.

"And the lien search was clear?" she demanded through shiny full lips outlined in dark brown pencil.

The wiry man with the blond curly-top from the title-search company, Oscar Kratt, nodded and said, "Yes ma'am," eager to prove that he had done his job. As Manny was discovering, nobody wanted to suffer the wrath of Rasheema.

Everyone sitting around the blond wood oblong table in Manny's brightly lit conference room nodded. Though it cost him way too much rent, Manny had office space at Sixty-fifth Street and Columbus Avenue. He used a per diem receptionist, calling a temp agency when clients showed up. His goofy-looking personal assistant cost him forty thousand a year plus a bonus every time the young man brought in a listing or referral. But the expenses were worth it. The office made the agency look sound, a stable, growing business.

Rasheema fit every physical stereotype of a young NBA millionaire's wife. Manny imagined that the twenty-seven-year-old was attractive beneath the layers of blond hair dye, weave, and green contacts. She wore designer monograms from her pink-tinted chrome Chanel glasses to her Louis Vuitton leather jacket, from her Dolce & Gabbana skintight T-shirt to her Gucci belt, down to her Prada shoes. She was a designer billboard, only she hadn't bothered to conceal the labels on the inside of her clothes. Her ensemble screamed to the world, "Look at me, I'm wearing expensive designer clothing!" She and her Afro-wearing, overgrown child of a husband were newer than nouveau riche and were not even ghetto fabulous. At first they just seemed to be plain ghetto, with the distinguishing characteristic of a hundred-million-dollar NBA contract. Despite appearances, Manny had come to realize, Rasheema had them all fooled. He watched her meticulously reading over the closing documents.

Manny was certain that the seller's broker, Gerald Locke, an uptight WASP recently out of the closet, hadn't expected the closing to be so protracted. Gerald was such a snob he probably assumed that the Lawrences would blindly sign all of the closing documents without reading them, especially since there was no bank involved. The Lawrences were paying cash for the five-million-dollar penthouse condominium at Riverside Drive and Ninety-fifth Street. Unlike most New York Knicks, Faheed Lawrence had decided to live in the city instead of Purchase, New York, or Englewood, New Jersey, or Stamford, Connecticut—or perhaps it would be more accurate to say that his wife had made the decision for them. She thought the city would be a better place to jump-start her modeling career. The woman was delusional, Manny thought. Rasheema had proudly informed Manny when he started showing them property that her credits included the side of a hair-relaxer box; a billboard for alligator stilettos, displayed only in Detroit and Chicago; and, as Manny embarrassingly discovered, she was a "booty" girl in several rap videos. So many, in fact, that a teenage boy in an apartment Manny had shown the Lawrences on West End Avenue had asked her to autograph the poster of her well-oiled booty prominently displayed on his wall.

When the couple contacted Manny after seeing several of his ads in magazines two months ago, he agreed to take them on as clients, figuring they would buy quickly. Tacky as they seemed, a five-million-dollar cash deal was worth any shame he might endure, especially considering how flat the market was. Entertainment money, Manny had learned, was usually recession-proof.

In spite of her appearance and misplaced aspirations, Manny kind of liked Rasheema. She knew how to handle Faheed, and much to the surprise of the white folks congregated around the table—all waiting to get a piece of the Lawrences' basketball money—she knew how to manage their affairs. It was also refreshing to deal with someone who was so real, even if he did occasionally feel like he was baby-sitting.

"If you would like, Mrs. Lawrence, you can also pay your property taxes for the remainder of the quarter to my title company," Oscar said, obviously feeling it was necessary to address Rasheema only now. Not that Manny could blame Oscar. Faheed was sitting in his chair with his head bopping and six-inch Afro flipping back and forth. His eyes darted everywhere in the room other than at the participants. He glanced at the colorful Michael Ray Charles posters on the wall, at the white KRUPS coffeemaker on the marble corner table, out the twelfth-floor window overlooking Columbus Avenue. He barely looked up long enough to sign the closing documents. Manny wondered what Faheed might be thinking; he had definitely checked out of the closing. He reminded Manny of a street person living an alternative life in his head, as if he were playing a pickup game of one-on-one in his own mind.

Meanwhile, Rasheema stared at Oscar quizzically and said, "When are the taxes due?"

"At the end of the next quarter."

"Which would be?"

"Mid-January."

Setting down the document, Rasheema stared at Oscar as if he were crazy. "It's October now. Why would I give your company my money to earn interest on until then?"

"Well, it's common practice," Oscar began, before Rasheema abruptly cut him off.

"No, thank you, I'll keep my own money until the taxes are due, and I'll keep my own canceled check as a record that we paid our taxes," she said before turning to her white male attorney, who looked like he would rather be playing a round of golf than sitting here with them. "What's next?" she asked.

In response, the pasty-skinned seller's lawyer, acting on behalf of his absentee clients, took the lead and informed Rasheema that the remaining taxes for the quarter were due, as well as the prorated maintenance fee for the remainder of the month. He then handed Rasheema the supporting documentation, and home girl promptly pulled out her two-way pager and began using it as a calculator, cross-checking the tax and maintenance-fee figures. Her expression resembled that of an overly aggressive cross-examiner waiting to find an inconsistency in the witness's testimony. After completing her calculations, she carefully wrote out the two additional checks. She asked, "Who gets these?"

Tentatively, Oscar raised his hand and told Rasheema, "I'll take the one for the remaining taxes, and I believe the seller's attorney will take the maintenance-fee check."

"So, I presume I don't have to write any more checks today," she announced.

Manny told her that was correct, especially since he had his hundred-and-twenty-five-thousand-dollar check in his coat pocket and was anxious to get on with the day. He and Trenton were going to a straight party with Lauren later on, and then to the Dive in the Village. Trenton was always more available on the days Manny was collecting commission checks. Also, Manny was trying to make Trenton feel more comfortable around his friends.

"Doesn't the settlement sheet need to be signed?" the pasty lawyer asked, looking at Gerald Locke and then at Manny. He was referring to the sheet that listed all of the payout information: who received what money in the closing.

"Oh, yes it does," Locke began, then said what Manny was thinking. "But it hasn't been filled out yet. We can just all sign it, and we'll fill in the numbers later."

Even though it was common practice, Manny could see by the look on Rasheema's face that she wasn't going to put her name on anything without knowing exactly what she was signing. As their broker, Manny felt obligated to suggest filling out the settlement sheet appropriately and then sending it to the Lawrences. The absence of the payout information would not stop the closing from going through, but Rasheema's attitude about signing an incomplete form would prolong the already endless meeting.

Rasheema immediately accepted Manny's suggestion and gathered up her belongings before telling her lawyer, "I'll bind my own closing documents." Then she stood up, glanced down at the still-seated Faheed, and said, "Come on, Boo." Obligingly, he bopped up, all six feet ten inches of him, and followed his wife, who looked more like his older fly sister than his spouse.

After Manny ushered everyone out of the conference room, he sighed in relief. He then headed to his office to check his voice mail. As he was reaching for his high-back leather swivel chair, it spun around to a grinning shirtless Trenton.

"Surprise," he said, grabbing Manny to him. Falling into Trenton's lap, Manny knew in the back of his mind that it was no "surprise" that Trenton had shown up at his office on the day of a closing. Trenton could sniff out money better than a hound tracking the scent of a missing child. But as Trenton began rubbing Manny's legs and then his groin, Manny didn't care why his lover had shown up; he was too lost in the moment.

FOURTEEN

TANDY had been waiting at JoJo's by the narrow bar for ten minutes, being shoved from side to side as busy waitresses whisked past carrying trays filled with drinks. She hated to wait. And while JoJo's was one of her favorite restaurants for lunch, today the green and purple decor, along with the darkness of the room, was exacerbating her already foul mood. If she didn't need Dana so much, she would have left by now. This lunch was important. She had to get it together. Dana, flighty as ever, would arrive eventually.

Finally, Tandy, looking out of the iron-barred windows of the English basement of the brownstone-turned-restaurant, could see Dana walking down Sixty-fourth Street, talking on her hands-free cell phone with a dangling mouthpiece that jumped as she gesticulated wildly. Stepping down into the restaurant, she continued to speak loudly enough for people in the back to hear her. She motioned to Tandy with a nod and a wave, holding up an index finger to say she would be there in a moment. Tandy turned her nose up, annoyed at the dismissive gesture, but quickly checked herself as she told the hostess, "We're all here," thankful that Dana was a white woman, acting rude and classless. At last Dana snapped her tiny Motorola shut and turned her attention properly to Tandy.

Once seated, Dana could not wait to share her new spiritual experience. She raved about her new guru. "Shuram studied with a Bartuzi chief in India. They believe that all life evolves from one place. Such that we are as much an ant as we are a leaf on that plant over there. To be centered, we must be in harmony mentally, physically, and spiritually . . ." Dana went on and on, excited about the harmony she'd found through the Stonemark Forum. "The first step was standing up in a room with about one hundred people and shedding your skin, the way a snake sheds its skin. The process is amazing. It's metaphoric for all of the layers we place between our inner selves and the outer world."

Tandy could barely contain herself. As she sat across from Dana, pushing the salad on her plate around with a fork, she smiled and nodded and added the occasional "uh-huh," feeling completely annoyed and bored. To amuse herself, she began to watch Dana's collagen-enhanced lips flop up and down as she spoke. Her mouth looked like pinched sausages, but Tandy had to admit the lipstick and liner stayed put throughout the first cocktail (juice for Dana, chardonnay for Tandy), a couple bites of salad, and rapid chatter. Tandy had to respect a woman who knew how to apply makeup well and makeup that lasted.

"Charlie, of course, thinks I'm completely crazy, which is why I'm divorcing him. Plus, I discovered that he is incapable of shedding his skin. But with the help of Shuram, I'm divorcing him the smart way. Shuram has already counseled me on seizing my destiny and not allowing Charlie to take advantage of me, like he did his first and second wives. Shuram's been a great adviser."

As the salads were replaced by the entrées—monkfish for Tandy, since protein was always good for the muscles; ginger carrot soup for Dana, because she was a brand-new vegetarian—Dana's phone chirped loudly enough to make the other patrons turn their heads with loathing. Dana didn't seem to notice as she blared into her phone.

Hanging up, she sported a big grin that spread those lips wide across her face. "That was my attorney. He's one of Shuram's advisers as well. He is brilliant. Anyway, he's helping me organize my assets before I tell Charlie I'm divorcing him."

Tandy loved the fact that Dana was the type of person who was interested only in her own life. Throughout the entire lunch, Dana had barely asked Tandy how she was doing. To Tandy, that was just as well, since she intended to indulge Dana for as long as necessary. When an opening presented itself, Tandy planned to insinuate herself deeply into Dana's life.

"Really? Is he marking certain assets that you'll get in the divorce?" inquired Tandy.

"No. Even better. Charlie, being the greedy bugger that he is, put a few buildings that he owned into my name so his last ex-wife couldn't get them as they were finalizing their divorce. We're going to sell them before Charlie has a clue."

"Wow. But isn't he suspicious already? I mean, it's clear that you really are done with him."

Waving her hands as if she had it all figured out, and tossing her straw-blond, overly processed hair, Dana replied with the utmost confidence. "As long as I fuck him and suck his dick the way he likes it every Friday night, Charlie thinks we are in marital bliss. And believe me, Shuram gave me some good tips on keeping Charlie happy, not that I needed them." Dana cracked up, and Tandy laughed right along, grossed out by the image of surgically enhanced, nipped-and-tucked Dana—who probably had more scars than a war vet under her clothes—performing fellatio on the round, balding Charlie.

Anxious to keep her thoughts clear, if not pure, Tandy pressed on about the buildings. She could feel a good idea coming, even if it hadn't jelled yet. "What buildings? Where?" She tried not to sound overly anxious, but she was getting excited.

Tandy's excitement turned to elation as Dana described one of the three buildings. It was located in Harlem, about thirty-five thousand square feet, and worth, according to Dana, about twenty-five million dollars.

"If I can get thirty million for it, I would be thrilled. I want to unload the thing as soon as possible. I mean, what do I need a building up in Harlem for?"

"You are so right. Thirty million, and it's on One-twenty-fifth near the West Side Highway? Hmmm?"

"What? You want to buy it?"

With a chuckle Tandy responded, "No, no, no. But let me think about it some more. Maybe I can help you out. I know people in that neighborhood who may be interested."

Looking confused, Dana replied, "In that neighborhood? But Tandy, can someone from that neighborhood afford that much? I am totally not negotiable. I will accept nothing less, not one nickel less, than thirty million dollars. I'm not trying to be greedy, but as Shuram has counseled me, I want to get what I believe I'm worth."

"Oh, I completely understand. If I can be of help, I'll let you know." Tandy smiled, her mood high. Dana's new guru was not as crazy as Tandy had first thought. That property was the Sugar Hill Building, a very important and grand landmark in Harlem. The space would command a lot more than thirty million; it was simply a matter of finding the right buyers.

FIFTEEN

LAUREN was thrilled when Tandy called and suggested they get together for a round of golf at the Westchester, especially since they were having such mild weather for October. They might as well take advantage. Tandy was not a member of the club, though she was fully aware of the Thomases' membership. As a passionate golfer, Ed belonged to many country clubs around the world. He had joined the Westchester Country Club twenty years earlier, when the membership was cheap. Tandy promised Lauren that they would have a fun girls' day playing golf, having lunch, and maybe even fitting in a massage before they headed back to the city.

Lauren had enjoyed playing golf since the summer she had turned thirteen. Her father had been an avid player and was anxious to cultivate an activity that he could do with his daughter. He was tenacious when it came to making sure Lauren went to her lessons. The instruction paid off. She learned the game well. She also came to love going out onto the beautiful open course. Her only regret was that she could not make more time to play.

Tandy and Lauren traveled from the city in Lauren's chauffeured Suburban. Watching Tandy as she talked into her cell phone, Lauren thought to herself that her friend looked flawless, as usual. She was wearing the perfect golfing outfit: cotton khaki slacks, a polo shirt, brown saddle golf shoes, and a visor placed over her perfectly blown-out hair. Somehow, no matter how good she looked, Lauren couldn't help but feel she had not quite pulled herself together when sitting next to Tandy. However, her perspective had nothing to do with how Tandy treated her. On the contrary, Tandy had always handled Lauren as if she were one of the girls, which was another reason Lauren enjoyed Tandy's company so much. Unlike her mother's other friends, Tandy had seemed to recognize the woman inside Lauren from the time she was a mere teenager.

At last Tandy shut her tiny cell phone and turned her attention to Lauren. "Sorry, that was Denise Mitchell from the Museum of Harlem. We've been talking about this children's wing for some time now. We may actually get it going this year. Has Ed talked to you about it? I know your name keeps coming up for the project."

Ed had not specifically mentioned the children's wing, but Lauren was beginning to feel she would not be able to escape the museum as one of her official marital obligations. "No. He's talked with me about the museum generally, but I'm not sure I have the time or energy to sit on a stuffy board. I hate long meetings." Lauren had learned to be direct about her feelings on philanthropic requests. She wanted Tandy to know right from the start that she did not intend to become a member of the board of trustees.

Understanding of Lauren, as usual, Tandy softened her tone. "I know what you mean. I hate them, too." Before Tandy could continue, the SUV rolled to a stop. They had arrived at the course. A caddie ran out to the car to greet Lauren and to take their bags to the clubhouse.

Stepping out of the truck, Lauren happened to get a peek into Tandy's purse. "Tandy! You're not still smoking?"

"With all of the stress I've been under lately, I started again. I know it's shameful. Don't tell anyone. I only do it when I'm alone."

"You always did like to sneak around for a smoke," Lauren joked.

"And if my memory serves me well, you did, too." They chuckled at the mention of a shared moment many years ago. Since that time Lauren had thought of that night fondly, not only as a reminder of her bond with Tandy but as a marker for Ed's entrance into her life.

Every summer Lauren's family went to Martha's Vineyard and stayed from June until September. Friends and family would congregate on the island at various times during those months, especially in August. Lauren's parents would throw a huge barbecue, inviting all of the black folks who came to the beach from New York, Boston, Atlanta, Chicago, Milwaukee, D.C., and Detroit. The party was for adults alone, and Lauren inevitably ended up being the only child there, unless she hooked up with the other kids elsewhere. When she was old enough, Lauren would assist her parents with preparations for a small allowance.

The summer Lauren was fifteen, she had helped her parents get things organized for the guests. Once people began arriving, Lauren excused herself, figuring she would eat after the company. An hour or so into the party, Lauren ventured out from her room, which was located on a wing in the back of the Cape Cod–shingled house, giving her privacy. She went directly to the kitchen, to grab a plate of chicken and potato salad, passing through a fairly empty living room, since most of the guests were outside. The caterer insisted that she also take a piece of strawberry-peach pie before the guests ate it all up. As she gathered the food to head back to her room, a tall, good-looking cinnamon-colored man walked in, and asked for club soda. He had spilled red wine on his pants. "You must be Grace's daughter. You're even more beautiful than your mother," the handsome man said to a blushing Lauren.

"I'm Lauren" was about all she could say.

"Well, Lauren, I'm Ed Thomas. And I've made a mess. Do you know where I can get something to clean it up?" Lauren was happy to help this new stranger who caused her heart to skip a beat with his intense stare and devastating smile. He asked her about her vacation on the island and told her about his summers spent working, which were vastly different from the way his children spent their vacations.

As he finished cleaning himself up, a dowdy, pale woman who looked like she could have been white, with wiry hair that seemed to have been washed in the kitchen sink with Palmolive dish detergent, waddled into the kitchen. "There you are! Did you get the stain out?" she asked him.

"Yes, Claudia, I did. Thanks to this lovely young lady, I think my pants will be good as new." He smiled in Lauren's direction. His wife's eyes followed, though her face never registered a smile or anything at all friendly.

"Well, isn't that lucky," the woman said, staring at Lauren's young body from top to bottom.

"Nice meeting you, Lauren," Ed said as he and his wife left the room.

"Brrrr." Lauren shivered at the cold reception Claudia Thomas had given her. As she walked back through the house toward her room, she bumped into Tandy coming out of the bathroom. "Where are you headed with all of that good loot?" Tandy asked.

"Back to my room." Lauren smiled. Mrs. Brooks—or Tandy, as she'd insisted Lauren call her since she turned thirteen—was not a very close friend of her parents. They saw her at the required social events and at the occasional summer party. Yet she was the only one who talked to Lauren like a grown-up, instead of making the perfunctory greetings and how-is-school conversation she was subjected to from all the other adults.

"I don't blame you. I wouldn't want to hang out with all of these old fogies, either. Mind some company?" Lauren shook her head, and Tandy took her arm and headed them back to Lauren's room.

"Why don't we sit out on the deck? It's such a lovely night," Tandy said in her smooth yet husky voice. She then stepped out onto the terrace of Lauren's room. Lauren joined her, and sat with her plate in her hands. The two of them stayed in comfortable silence while Lauren picked at her food. Lauren glanced sideways at Tandy, who seemed deep in thought. Lauren dared not disturb her reverie. She felt privileged to have Tandy all to herself. She had often watched Tandy with her daughter, Deja. The two of them were so coordinated, with their matching straw sun hats, taking morning walks together along Martha's Vineyard's renowned beach for the African-American elite, the Inkwell. Even though Deja was just a young girl, she and Tandy seemed to share a closeness Lauren had never experienced with her own mother.

Lauren finished eating, and Tandy reached into her purse to pull out a cigarette. "Mind if I smoke?"

"No, not at all." As Tandy lit up the cigarette, Lauren followed it to Tandy's confident lips and watched the smoke emanate, making curlicues appear in the air from Tandy's lungs. Lauren's parents had no idea that their daughter smoked. After all, she did it only occasionally.

Tandy, emerging from her contemplative mood, took note of the longing on Lauren's face and asked if she wanted one. "Don't worry, no one will see you back here. I promise I won't tell your mother, as long as you promise not to tell Phil."

"It's a deal," Lauren said, taking the cigarette from Tandy and lighting it, suddenly feeling so cool. She wondered why Tandy was content to be with her for such a long time instead of being with the rest of the adults, but she feared that Tandy would take the question as an excuse to leave. They continued to sit on the slightly damp wooden planks, smoking and looking at the stars. Just when Lauren felt she could no longer ignore the splinter working its way into her cool bare thigh, Tandy began to give Lauren background information on everyone in attendance at the party: who they were, what they did for a living, and where they lived. Lauren remained riveted as Tandy told bold gossip about the adults, something Grace would certainly not do, believing that such talk was not appropriate for children. Tandy spoke to Lauren as if they were on the same level. She finally got around to Ed and Claudia Thomas.

"They live in St. Louis. He has a bottling company."

Tandy knew everything about everyone, Lauren thought, including the gorgeous man she'd met in the kitchen. "I met him a little while ago," she said. "He was really nice." For the first time in their discussion, Lauren was deeply interested. "He actually spoke to me like I was a person. Not like his wife. She seemed so mean."

"You mean she was a bitch. I know Claudia, and she is a miserable person." Tandy leaned in to Lauren conspiratorially, apparently eager to share her gossip.

"Yeah, well, she doesn't have to take it out on the rest of the world," Lauren responded.

"You're right, Lauren. But Claudia sees what her husband is. And he is one sexy man. Don't you agree? Tell the truth."

"He is handsome," Lauren answered, blushing again as she thought about the conversation with Ed. She felt as if she and Tandy were girlfriends plotting to gain the affections of the new boy in the neighborhood. Tandy leaned back and rested one of her elbows on the deck. Her smooth, tanned shoulders glistened in the moonlight. Taking a long drag on her cigarette, she blew out the smoke in a mystical haze before saying, "Boy oh boy, he is fine, charming, and powerful. He's going to be one of those people we watch in awe, Lauren. He is on a fast track and has the full package to make it happen. Claudia, on the other hand, will get left behind, and she sees it coming." Tandy paused and seemed to gather her thoughts. "She knows that other women, young and old, look at Ed, and that Ed may look back from time to time. It will take more than a woman like Claudia to keep him in check. He needs a worldly woman. A woman with a vision for herself. Someone who can run with him on that track, not someone who will hold him back. Love alone is not enough."

Tandy had been talking almost to herself but now turned her attention back to Lauren. "If there is one thing I can teach you, dear, it's that love is not what keeps a marriage together. A strong woman who is clear about what she wants out of life and out of her man keeps a marriage afloat. The wife must be at least as ambitious as her husband, if he is an ambitious man. And why would anyone marry a man with no ambition? Men are hard enough to deal with. When you are married to them, they'd better at least work hard." Tandy laughed.

After what seemed to Lauren like hours of talking, Tandy stood and meticulously readjusted her chic sarong skirt and slipped back into her turquoise sandals. Her rich skin, along with her silky black hair, made her look like she should be on some far-off beach in Morocco instead of here at this party with Lauren's parents' stuffy friends.

"I better go and show my face, even though I'd much rather hang out here with you all night."

Lauren beamed. She, too, could have stayed outside with Tandy for the rest of the evening, especially if it meant yummy girl talk about that charming man. Tandy had given Lauren a peek into the grown-up world. From that day on, Lauren felt like she was a special aunt. If she ever needed advice or guidance, she went to Tandy for an honest opinion.

Remembering that special evening made Lauren feel happy that she and Tandy had grown together as friends when Lauren grew into womanhood. Lauren had also thought it prophetic that Tandy was there the night she met Ed, and had almost predicted that Ed's first marriage would not last. Not that Lauren had anticipated being a second wife, but fate had planned for her and Ed to be together. Tandy had been around, almost as if to bless their meeting. So when she brought up Lauren's involvement with the Museum of Harlem for the second time that day, Lauren listened.

Riding in the cart, with Lauren driving, Tandy began again. "Lauren, I'd hate for you to feel like I'm pestering you, but I believe that you could spearhead the move for the children's arm at the museum. You are the perfect choice. And trust me, once you have set up a big pet project, people will understand that you don't have time for other ventures and will leave you alone."

"What kind of time commitment will I be in for? You know I'm trying to focus on my work."

"I understand, and your work is very important. You should be focusing on that. The first big push won't require so much of your time . . . What I'm about to tell you is privileged museum business. Obviously, you can discuss it with Ed, since he already knows about it." Lauren waited, dreading news that might draw her in, but realizing her duty to her marriage and love for Ed required that she be open to what Tandy was about to say. "The museum's lease is up at the end of the year, at which time we will be either paying higher rent or moving into a new space. If we stay where we are, we will being paying more rent and won't be able to launch the children's wing, because there is not enough room." Lauren continued listening as she climbed out of the cart to grab her wood for the fifteenth hole. Tandy stood as well, talking measuredly. "But I know of a building for sale in a great location in Harlem that would be perfect for the museum's expansion."

Lauren was beginning to see where Tandy was going. Lauren pulled out her Big Bertha driver and readied herself at the tee box. She placed her ball on the tee and took her stance, legs wide apart, knees slightly bent, head down, eyes on the ball. Tandy had stopped talking, respecting Lauren's shot. With a loud ping, the Pinnacle 2 soared into the air, flying like a missile to a direct target. "Nice shot," Tandy said in earnest.

"Thank you."

Tandy took her turn, hitting the ball with a decent shot, but not into the middle of the fairway like Lauren's.

As they climbed back into the cart, Tandy continued, "I'm going to be direct with you, Lauren. If you and Ed purchase this building and then lease the space to the museum, your contribution to Harlem would forever stand tall as the Thomas Museum of Harlem."

"I don't need my name on the building. That seems kind of obnoxious."

"Lauren, please. Look at the hospitals, colleges, mainstream museums, or any kind of building or organization that has received financial support from a major donor. That is a legacy. I know you're young, but you should be thinking that way. If not for your own children, for other black children. One day you'll understand what I'm talking about. They need to know about you, and they need to know that African-Americans have buildings named after them. They need to know about your contributions to society."

"What would the building cost?" Lauren asked with an expression that told Tandy she knew the building would be quite expensive.

"Thirty-five to forty million. But definitely not more than that," Tandy responded as if she were talking about a bargain.

"Forty million dollars? I don't know, Tandy. That's a lot of money." Lauren had learned that people thought being a billionaire meant you had endless money to lend, donate, spend, invest, or throw away.

"I know, but your accountants can figure out ways for you to write off a large piece of it. Maybe you don't buy it all outright. Listen, why don't you think about it. Talk with Ed and your accountants. It would be such a good move for you, Lauren. I want to see you take your place where you belong. The museum would be a natural."

"I'll think about it," Lauren promised. "But for the rest of the day, I don't want to talk about the Museum of Harlem or anything else that has to do with me giving money away to anybody. Deal?"

"I won't say another word." Tandy was now putting in on the fifteenth hole. Lauren had already beaten her on the hole with a one under par. Watching Tandy getting ready to putt, Lauren thought what a conscientious mentor her friend had been over the years. Tandy had been around for a long time, had seen many things and many folks come and go. *Maybe I should listen.* If nothing else, Tandy was right about one thing: With a huge commitment to the museum, Lauren could thwart all the other annoying requests, citing the museum as her time-consuming pet project. She also knew that Ed would appreciate her involvement and certainly would have more respect for that activity than for her freelance producing gigs. The idea of working with children did appeal to her. This was a calling that Lauren was beginning to think she might have to answer.

THE next day, seated in the back of the chauffeured Lincoln Town Car, Tandy reviewed her conversation with Lauren, trying to contain her anxiety that Lauren might deflect the suggestion and not even discuss it with Ed. Tandy had learned that making things happen in New York City as a middle-aged woman without a partner was not easy. Occasionally—just once in a while—she wished Phil were still around.

Tandy swiveled around in her vanity chair and yelled out once more. "Phil? Phil, are you all right?" After getting no answer, she slowly rose to check on him. "What on earth are you doing in there? Why don't you answer me?" she muttered under her breath, annoyed at his clumsiness and frustrated by his lack of response.

As she stood to walk toward the bathroom, Tandy noticed that her gown from the evening's festivities had fallen off the hanger. She was momentarily mortified about a possible tear in the delicate fabric. She leaned down and picked up the dress, cradling it as if it were a baby. She carefully replaced the precious dress on the wooden hanger, this time making certain it was secure. Then she turned her attention back to determining what her oaf of a husband had done this time.

Slowly and carefully peeking into the bathroom, Tandy stopped short as she caught sight of Phil's naked body lying on the floor. He resembled a beached whale, yet far less imposing. The water from the showerhead cascaded over him like a waterfall, but nothing about the scene was romantic. Blood on his forehead oozed onto the gray marble floor, mixing with the water. Shards of tiny glass from a broken piece of the shower door glistened like diamonds. Phil's eyes begged Tandy for help, even though his voice was barely a whisper. The image of her naked, vulnerable husband lying sprawled like a helpless animal told her to move into action. But she was frozen. Stricken by fear and maybe a little hope, she remained at a standstill and began to count to herself. She counted the money she would no longer have to share with Phil. She counted the life-insurance policy she would cash in on. She counted the number of times she would no longer have to fuck him. She counted the extra feet of closet space she would have. She counted the miserable years he had bored her with his dullness and his stupid jokes. She counted the number of pounds he had gained since they had gotten married—fifty. But more than anything, she counted her freedom from him without the trouble of a messy divorce, and that was priceless.

At the sound of a loud gurgle that finally escaped Phil's throat, Tandy was propelled into action. She quickly dialed 911. But by the time the paramedics arrived, Phil was gone. She would forever wonder if she could have saved him.

The portly Dominican driver interrupted her thoughts: "Mrs. Brooks? Mrs. Brooks? What is that address again?"

"Oh. One-eighteen Striver's Row." Tandy often thought of that evening, more and more as of late, with all of the financial woes she was experiencing. While her parents had not been rich, she had never wanted for anything. In adulthood, living in New York had been fun, exciting, and glamorous. But with all of the thrills came a huge price tag. Tandy often joked with her friends and colleagues that to live in New York, one had to have very deep pockets. Wealth was a relative concept, but Tandy knew too well that to survive, she would need more money than she had ever earned personally in her entire life. God had sent her a gift in Dana Trip. She planned to use it.

As the driver helped her from the car, she instructed him to wait exactly where he was. She climbed the stairs of the beautiful brownstone that dated back to the turn of the century. While she believed that Manny was a hanger-on of sorts, she had to admit that he had taste and style. He didn't disappoint when he answered the door dressed in tailored gray tweed pants and a white linen shirt with driving moccasins. He greeted her with a *baisé*, air-kissing her on each cheek. He was a great charmer, Tandy thought, and an even greater bullshitter.

Today Tandy would trade on all of those qualities. She knew Manny wanted to be considered an insider in the black bourgeois scene of New York, but as a simple broker, he would never have the clout to get very far. Tandy also knew that Manny needed money. He had confided in her the rising costs of refurbishing this brownstone, and by the looks of the kitchen and a few holes in the wall, he could benefit from some fast cash. She also knew he had become a sugar daddy to a greedy boy toy. Those were very expensive accoutrements in New York City.

After Manny brought her a Jensen glass filled with vodka and cranberry juice on ice, Tandy began her pitch. She would not leave his house until he agreed to the terms. "I have a deal for you that will give you the money and the clout you want," she began, having decided to be direct.

Manny heard the words and was all ears. Tandy was a reliable source of clientele. Even though her most recent referrals, the Joneses, were annoying him, they would still prove to be money in his pocket. And at least they were the sort of low-key, well-educated, cash-rich blacks who could get approved by many Upper East Side co-op boards, albeit probably not in the most restrictive of buildings. Throughout his long career, Manny had dealt with all types of apartment sales in which no financing was allowed and people were required to show that they were liquid five times the amount of the apartment they hoped to purchase. However, he had never made it into the very rigid co-ops—the buildings that would not accept anyone who was black or Jewish; essentially anyone non-WASP. No problem for Manny; he simply ignored those co-ops' existence. With Tandy making a trip to Harlem to approach him directly about making money, she had to be for real. But, not wanting to sound desperate, Manny said, "Money isn't everything."

"Maybe not, but money is very very important in the world we live in."

"True that is," Manny mockingly agreed.

"And don't forget the clout," Tandy went on. "A friend of mine, Dana Trip, is selling the Sugar Hill Building. At one time it was residential, but now I believe it's a mixture of residential and commercial space. The building is a perfect location for the Museum of Harlem."

"I know where you mean. The building *is* in a great location. They were going to try to put a Barneys or Jeffrey's there, but they never got off the ground." Manny prided himself on knowing a little bit of something on most significant New York properties. He also knew it was a massive landmark building and would command more than any commercial building ever had in Harlem.

"I don't know anything about that, but what I do know is that Dana wants thirty million for the building, and she would sell yesterday."

Manny listened and thought. "Thirty million? That seems low for the Sugar Hill Building. The Dwight office building sold for twenty million last year, and it's half the size and doesn't have the historical significance, and the location was not nearly as good. I'll double-check the commercial market, but I have a feeling it's worth more than thirty million."

"Dana doesn't know about Harlem or its market. As far as she is concerned, anything above Ninety-fifth Street is a black hole, pardon the pun."

They both chuckled. Manny was well aware of certain white folks' perceptions of Harlem; for that matter, some black folks shared it, too.

Tandy continued, "Anyway, I was thinking you could be her broker."

"Usually, I refer commercial property to a colleague of mine. It's not my specialty," Manny admitted.

"You can do this deal. And I'm guessing that you don't even need to find a buyer. You could be the exclusive broker. If I've read my people right, Lauren and Ed are apt to buy the building through their foundation for the Museum of Harlem. Lauren thinks the building will cost forty million and is prepared to pay as much. So basically, all you would need to do is draw up the papers."

Manny was astonished. He was already doing the math on 6 percent of forty million. Tandy was great. "I appreciate you pulling everyone together. Of course, being an attorney, you will receive your normal referral fee." In New York, lawyers who referred clients to brokers got 10 to 20 percent of the broker's cut as a referral fee. Tandy, of course, had brought that fact to Manny's attention, so he had often given her referral fees for the people she sent his way. Today, however, Manny could tell by her tight-lipped expression that she had another idea altogether.

"I mentioned you to Dana, and I told her you were a specialist on Harlem. I'm pretty sure she will use you as her broker. She just wants to be assured of getting thirty million for the building."

Manny was confident. "Oh, she could get at least that much. If what you say is true about Ed and Lauren's foundation being willing to pay forty million, we already have the deal. This should be a no-brainer."

Tandy appeared hesitant. She crossed and recrossed her legs in the narrow black pencil skirt. She opened and shut her purse without removing anything. "Listen, Manny, this is a delicate situation. What I'm saying to you is that Dana only wants thirty million. Quite frankly, she's not even expecting that, but if she gets it, she'll be more than satisfied."

Manny was watching Tandy. She seemed a little uncomfortable getting all of her thoughts to escape her mouth, as if she had a hairball caught in her throat. "So, you told her about me, I'll arrange a pitch meeting to convince her to use me, and then we'll do the deal. Should I call her, or would she feel more—"

Tandy cut him off. "It won't be a problem meeting her, but I want you to sign a net-exclusive broker's deal with her."

"Excuse me?" Manny was not sure he understood.

"Have her sign a net-exclusive deal."

Manny's eyes widened at the suggestion. Tandy was an attorney. She had to know that the law did not allow real estate brokers to receive a commission higher than 6 percent. With net-exclusive agreements, there was potentially no cap on a broker's commission. Essentially, a seller would set the price he wanted for his property, and a broker would get all monies above that amount as his commission. These types of deals had been outlawed because of the abuse they invited by unscrupulous brokers.

"Phil and I signed a broker to a net-exclusive when we sold our apartment in the Village."

"That must have been a while ago, because net-exclusives have been illegal for the past five years. I'm sorry, but I can still give you a great referral fee, and with Lauren and Ed involved, there is a commission to share. We still come out well at one point eight million." Manny had learned how to calculate 6 percent quickly and easily. At almost two million dollars, it would be his largest commission.

"True, Manny, but if you sell the building for forty million and sign a net-exclusive deal with Dana, guaranteeing her thirty million, that's a ten-million-dollar commission. And since I'm willing to go halfsies with you, that's five million for each of us."

Perhaps Tandy was not hearing him. Manny tried again. "But net-exclusives are illegal now."

"Says who?"

"The REBNY. I could lose my license, my business."

"Not if it's a private agreement."

Manny did not know why he was even entertaining this conversation, but he asked, "A private agreement?"

"Yes, Manny. It would be between you and Dana only. Hell, the ten million we get might as well be considered a gift, and there's no crime in that. It would not be a publicly filed document. The agreement would be a formality, making her aware that you will get her the thirty million she wants for her building and that anything over, you keep. Believe me, Manny, she's thinking it would be a small miracle for anyone to pay that much for real estate in Harlem. And to simplify the matter even more, the entire purchase amount could be made directly out to Marks Realty and put into an escrow account. Then you could cut the thirty-million-dollar check to Dana directly."

Manny had the urge to stand up. He wanted to clear his head. Tandy certainly seemed to have the whole scheme figured out, but it was at the very least unethical.

"Won't Dana's attorneys tell her the net-exclusive isn't—"

She interrupted again. She obviously was not open to what he had to say. "Manny, there is no reason we can't pull this off. Dana wants to sell. Her lawyer is some fruit involved with this cult she's in, Stonemark. Besides, as I said, the agreement between you and Dana is between you and Dana. The kooky lawyer won't have anything to do with your arrangement. Everything will be above-board." Tandy was talking fast now, her words running together like she had it all figured out.

"Oh, she's doing Stonemark. I've heard great things about them," Manny commented from his haze. He had not given much thought to the extra ten million coming out of Lauren and Ed's pocket.

"Whatever. Lauren wants to do something for the community. Dana wants her thirty million. It's win-win for everybody." Tandy's eyes looked a little wild.

Manny realized that although he had stood up moments before, he was frozen in the middle of his rug. He studied Tandy closer. Her request revealed something in her that he had not seen before. He figured that since Phil's death her money might have been tight, but he didn't fully under-stand her need to go to such extremes. Then again, five million dollars in cash was a strong incentive for anyone.

As Tandy sensed Manny pondering her proposal, she began a full-court press to push him over the edge. "Manny," she began earnestly, "you are probably wondering why I would go to such great lengths for money." She looked down, searching for the words, seemingly embarrassed but determined. "When Phil died, he left me in mounds of debt. I can't sell the apartment because it's completely leveraged. Believe me, I've tried, and I continue to try to cover my debts in other ways. Deja has all of the cash that's available. I can't touch it. If I don't get some money soon from somewhere, the banks are going to foreclose on me, and then what would I do?"

Manny had always thought of Tandy as a strong woman, but today she sat in his Ralph Lauren slipper chair looking crumpled and defeated. A single tear slowly trickled down her cheek.

Passing a couple of tissues to her, Manny realized that, ethical or not, it might be his turn to help Tandy. She had been so good to him for many years. She needed him. He wouldn't disappoint her. After all, she didn't just bring this deal to benefit her; Manny would also get five million. He would help her out—as Tandy said, if he handled everything correctly and carefully, no one would ever find out.

Overshadowing his fear of getting caught was his excitement at being hand-delivered not only the financial opportunity of his life but the deal that would finally signify he was a major player in Manhattan real estate. Not bad for a country boy.

SEVENTEEN

TANDY did not waste any time. True to her word, she arranged a meeting between Manny and Dana Trip for the next afternoon. Dana chose a teahouse on the corner of Lexington and Eighty-second Street. When Manny walked through the green wooden door, the sweet music of wind chimes echoed through the air, the peaceful sound marking the restaurant as one of New York City's many false havens. The space was long and cavernous, with many different-sized Buddhas and elephants decorating the shelves that lined the bamboo walls. There were ten or so low square wooden tables with fancy silk pillows surrounding them. Manny immediately recognized Dana by the description Tandy had given him. With her shiny pink microdermabrasioned skin, unnaturally full lips, perfectly coiffed bright blond hair, and finely made clothing, no one ever would have imagined that she hailed from any place other than Park Avenue. Surely, no one would have suspected that she originated from Omaha, Nebraska. However, Manny could immediately understand how she managed to marry well. Women like her got plucked up quickly as the replacement wife: young, pleasant to look at, eager to please, not bitter. Until they became bored with their old man of a husband and fell prey to the brainwashing of the guru of the month.

She waved at Manny as soon as he entered. Apparently, Tandy had described him well. He walked toward Dana, confident, certain he looked every bit as rich as she did. As he reached her, he leaned down, and gave her a large white smile that exclaimed, "You can trust me. I'm a likable guy."

"Tandy was right. You are so cute, so cute. I could just eat you up right here, right now." Dana beamed.

Manny continued to smile, disgusted by the thought of her bloated lips eating him. "Nice to meet you, too." He made sure he sounded sufficiently open, informal, in a tone he gathered she could appreciate, being spiritually astute.

"Tandy told me all about you," she said, looking him up and down before gesturing him to sit in the chair closest to hers. Immediately, she placed her manicured hand on the arm of his cashmere sport jacket.

"Hopefully not *all* about me!" Manny joked, maintaining the casual tone. He always took his cues from potential clients.

"You are such a charmer, just as Tandy said!" Dana laughed, and her eyes continued to appraise him.

She took the liberty of ordering him some lavender tea before grilling him. She probably assumed she was saving him the embarrassment of asking for Lipton with extra sugar.

"So, you're the Harlem guy, huh?" she said.

"Well, I broker real estate in Harlem and all over Manhattan: Tribeca, SoHo, the Village, Upper East Side, Upper West," he explained, adding, "and I am also a Harlem resident."

"I don't mean to be rude, but you look like you stepped right off of Madison Avenue. I did not know that people from Harlem were so stylish."

She was more ignorant than he'd been expecting, but he reminded himself of the ten-million-dollar commission. Playing light and sweet, he said, "Oh, we come in all shapes and sizes up in Harlem."

Dana looked at him with a blank expression, as if she hadn't heard or understood, before bluntly asking, "So you really think you could get me thirty million for my building up there?"

With the utmost confidence, Manny replied, "I'm certain of it. I've had over fifteen years of experience in the business, and several of my clients have purchased property in Harlem. People find it very desirable for their personal residences as well as for their businesses. Some people also like to buy in Harlem for investment reasons."

Apparently focused only on her agenda, Dana continued, "Tandy said you could guarantee me thirty million."

Tandy had done her part; now Manny would take his turn at managing one of the most delicate moments in this nascent transaction. "I am extremely optimistic that I will be able to secure that amount for you."

She regarded him skeptically for the first time and began fiddling with the diamond ring on her finger. It was at least ten carats. "Extremely optimistic?"

"Yes."

"Fine, then. What about this agreement Tandy mentioned to me?"

Manny's heart began to beat a little faster as he prepared to explain to this unsuspecting woman about the document that could make him and Tandy millionaires. But before he had the chance to speak, a black clay teapot was placed in front of him along with a matching cup. Nervously, he took the opportunity to pour himself some of the hot brew before working up the nerve to pitch her the idea of signing a net-exclusive agreement.

He cleared his throat. "Yes, well, it's called a net-exclusive agreement. Simply put, the contract would state the price for which you want to sell your building, which is thirty million; and the contract would also spell out that my firm would retain any amount received on the sale of your building above your stipulated price as a commission fee."

"But you'll get me my thirty million?"

"That's the plan."

"I don't care what you keep as long as I get my thirty million." The woman was fixated.

"Then you understand the net-exclusive agreement."

"What you explained to me is *all* Tandy was talking about?"

"Yes, I guess it was," Manny said, now understanding what Tandy had meant about her college friend simply wanting her thirty million.

"Well, that's not so complicated."

"The only other part is that my firm would receive the check for the sale amount in its escrow account, and we would cut you the check for thirty million immediately after the closing."

"That's fine," Dana began, looking around the long tearoom as if the other patrons might be eavesdropping, "but I'm trying to keep this whole thing kind of quiet, you know."

"Well, you realize that upon closing, your sale of the building will be a matter of public record. So I don't know how quiet you're going to be able to keep it."

"But that won't be until after I get my money, right?"

"Right, nothing will be publicly filed until after the closing."

"That's fine, but this net-agreement thing. What about that? That won't tip anyone off, will it?"

"That's a private agreement between my firm and you. No one needs to know about that but us, dear." Manny was assuaging her fears and his own. She did not want her husband to get wind of what she was up to. And Manny didn't want anyone to know about this illegal contract they were entering into. Discretion was best for them both. He judged by the expression on her face that she was ready to immediately move forward, but he dared not be presumptuous.

"When can you have all of the papers drawn up? Are there a lot?" she asked.

"No, just the net-exclusive and a power-of-attorney agreement to authorize my firm to receive the sale price in an escrow account. I could have them done tomorrow."

"That's a little soon. You have to meet Shuram Alita first. He'll want you to do a cleansing before I sign anything."

"A cleansing?"

"Yes, a shedding process, a purification. You don't mind, do you? I no longer do business with anyone unless they have gone through a cleansing with me and Shuram Alita has met them."

"Of course not. I could always use a good cleansing."

"Me, too. Tandy will also have to be cleansed, since she introduced me to you. We'll all do it together," Dana said, licking her peach-colored lips. "So, I'll be in touch, but I like you. I'm sure Shuram will like you, too—you have an inner light and nice taste in clothes."

Only in Manhattan would the spiritually enlightened person equate one's inner light with his outer attire. Everything appeared to be skin-deep these days in Manny's world.

EIGHTEEN

A FTER all these years, Lauren still felt awkward walking through the imposing chrome doors of the Thomas Building on the corner of Lexington and Fifty-seventh Street. When she had been merely an employee of Ed's company, coming and going like all of the other drones who blindly traveled to and from work, head down, coffee in hand, minds on the end of the day even at seven in the morning, she had just been doing a job. There had not been much at stake for Lauren six years ago, when she was fresh out of business school, beginning a career that offered great health benefits but no real allure for her, though her competitive nature made her aggressive in it. But she had been doing what made her parents proud after they'd paid for twelve years of private school and six years of college.

"Good afternoon, Mrs. Thomas. Right this way," Joe, one of the few long-standing security guards, said to her. She had joined the visitors' line to show her ID like all of the other nonemployees of the Thomas Building. She didn't feel right stepping in front of anyone because her husband owned the building and occupied twenty of the forty floors.

Lauren self-consciously waved Joe off, still not moving from her place behind half a dozen other people.

"Please, Mrs. Thomas, please. Your husband would fire me if he saw you waiting like this. Please allow me to escort you upstairs."

Lauren gave in and rather reluctantly stepped in front of the other visitors, who were staring at her curiously with looks that said, "Who are you to bypass the security checkpoint?"

Lauren followed behind Joe down the long steel, glass, and onyx corridor to elevator bank three, which serviced the thirtieth through the fortieth floors. The security guard ceremoniously waved his hands this way and that, like a police escort clearing the way for a dignitary. Lauren was tempted to tell him to knock it off and let her go on upstairs by herself, but he was taking his job so seriously, she was hesitant to interrupt his routine.

He radioed up to inform someone that she was coming. "I've got Mrs. Thomas coming up on number eight. Yes, yes, I'm going to escort her. You can meet us at the top. I'm going to put the elevator on express."

Stepping into the elevator, Lauren hardly felt or looked the part of Ed Thomas's wife in her vintage Levi's, white tank top, black cashmere sweater casually tied around her shoulders, black loafers, and hair tousled carelessly. Since she still had a hint of her tan from the end of those long summer days on the Inkwell, she barely wore makeup. Not that the occasion was informal. She had business to discuss with Ed.

As she reached the fortieth floor, another plain-clothed security guard met her. Lauren imagined how Tandy would scold her if she saw her now: "You young girls will wear just any old thing out on the street, coming out of the house with your hair all over your head. And to see your husband, no less. Put yourself on a nice Valentino or Armani suit, step out in style." Lauren chuckled at the thought. Even though Tandy was the hippest of all of Lauren's mother's friends and had become one of her closest confidantes, she could occasionally be a bit long in the tooth when it came to keeping up appearances. But Lauren knew that Tandy's physical beauty was a part of her legend: Evidently looking the part worked for her. She was an amazing woman in Lauren's eyes; she had always looked out for Lauren when all of Ed's other contemporaries treated her with apparent disdain. Tandy, Lauren warmly thought, had truly befriended her.

When Lauren reached the first set of double doors, she was met with mammoth, intricate steel and mahogany sculptures, museum-quality reproductions of ancient Mayan ruins that Ed had commissioned. She was greeted by Ed's personal secretary, Margaret.

"Mrs. Thomas." Margaret looked at her over the same green-tinted spectacles she had been wearing since Lauren met her. "What a pleasant surprise." She had been Ed's secretary for over a decade and had always treated Lauren with kindness and respect.

"Nice to see you, Margaret. How've you been?"

"Well, thank you, very well," she said with a strained smile. Lauren remembered that the older woman had diabetes and her eyesight was failing. The spectacles enlarged fathomless black eyes that expressed the difficulties the middle-aged African-American woman had experienced. Despite her close-cut red hair and handsome, stylish charcoal-gray Brooks Brothers suit, Margaret looked tired and worn.

God bless Margaret, Lauren thought. She never complained about the eight-year-old autistic grandson she had cared for since her daughter overdosed on drugs when he was only seven weeks old. She quietly and diligently went about her work in a professional manner. Ed was lucky to have her.

Lauren smiled back at Margaret as Sophie appeared from behind the second set of ceremonial doors. As classy and understated as Margaret was, Ed's personal assistant was her antithesis. Where Margaret was soft, round, and welcoming, everything about Sophie was razor-sharp, from her jawline to her teeth to her bony body to her angular clothes to her tongue. She couched all of her statements as backhanded compliments.

"Lauren! How ahh you, dear? Did Ed know you were coming?" she asked with a broad fake smile before sidling up next to Lauren and attempting to give her a familiar hug, as if they were long-lost buddies.

"No, I was in the neighborhood and thought I'd stop by," Lauren found herself answering, even though she hated explaining to this woman why she was coming to visit her husband. She felt such powerlessness over her relationship.

"Of course, of course. I'm sure Ed will be delighted to see you," Sophie said with salt in her eyes, as if she had given Lauren the okay to see her man.

Lauren managed her own fake smile. She felt like she was shrinking as Sophie looked her over, taking inventory of Lauren's very being.

"Listen, why don't I take you to Ed's sitting room while he finishes up his conference call. I'm sure he'll only be a moment," Sophie told Lauren without giving her an opportunity to object.

Obediently, Lauren followed Sophie down the paneled hallway, covered with 1950s black-and-white Gordon Parks photos of people on the streets of Harlem. As Sophie ushered her into Ed's private quarters, a room she had become quite familiar with while still working for Thomas Industries, Lauren became nostalgic. In the early days of their relationship, when Ed was still courting her, they'd had a number of trysts on the weathered leather sofa.

"Have a seat, dear. May I bring you something?" Sophie asked.

Lauren said no thank you to both. She didn't need Sophie instructing her to sit down. That was the last thing Lauren wanted to do. For some reason, she began to feel antsy inside Ed's cavernous personal quarters. The room was filled with the accolades of a lifetime, ranging from honorary degrees from universities around the world, to golf trophies, to three separate photographs alongside three presidents of the United States, to personal photos of Ed's two adult sons, who were only a few years younger than Lauren. They had graduated from Yale. Lauren looked around the dimly lit room for photos of herself. She couldn't find any on the walls. She walked over to Ed's desk and noticed a small silver frame behind a leather cup of pens, pencils, rubber bands, and whatnots. The three-by-five photo of Lauren and Ed from their wedding day easily could have blended in with the rest of the clutter on the overcrowded desk. But Lauren was keenly aware of its existence. She picked it up. A pang of sadness touched her to see the small representation of such a large day in her life. To Ed, she was a five-inch framed memory amid the mountain of his career.

By the time Ed finally joined Lauren, she was feeling almost like an interloper in his world. When he walked toward her, she searched his face for any sign that he was still as madly in love with her as she was with him.

"Hello, Mrs. Thomas," he said, and her heart raced a little as she looked at him in his crisp white shirt, sleeves rolled up to the elbows, exposing powerful forearms. For a moment she couldn't look him in the face and instead watched the veins pulsating in his arms. Simultaneously, she was attracted to him and intimidated.

"What brings you to my neck of the woods?" he asked as he stood over his desk shuffling a few papers. Lauren wondered where her kiss was. A part of her wished he would just grab her and throw her down on the old familiar couch and fuck the hell out of her, like old times.

"Working in midtown and decided to stop by. I wanted to talk to you about something in particular."

For the first time, he glanced up and seemed to take notice of Lauren. He appeared concerned. A wave of relief swept over her at even this minimal show of affection. She couldn't put her finger on why, but she was feeling vulnerable and out of sorts.

"Is everything all right?"

"Yes, yes," Lauren assured him as she moved nearer. She wanted to feel his arms around her, but she dared not initiate anything. This was his territory. He did not like her to be too forward; nor did he like her to be a bad girl, unless it was on his terms. She obliged. Still, she moved closer and tried her best not to have a lame "Notice me, please!" expression on her face. Why was she getting so clammy?

"Well? Spit it out. What's on your mind?" he said, reaching out and grabbing her by the waist, pulling her to him. Lauren was thrilled by his touch and felt instantly at ease.

"Well," she began, wanting to make the best presentation, "you know how you've been telling me I need to be more civic-minded and get more involved in the community? I've thought of something I would like to do . . . us to do . . . or our foundation."

Ed raised his eyebrows in curiosity. Lauren felt like she was making a pitch to her father to buy her a car for her sixteenth birthday.

"And what do you have up your sleeve, young lady?" If Lauren was not mistaken, he sounded pleased. His tone gave her confidence.

"You're committed to the Museum of Harlem, and you've been encouraging me to join the board for years—or any board, for that matter." She stopped to see if he appreciated her self-deprecating humor, especially since he had been riding her to accept at least a few of the invitations to join some boards.

"Does this mean you've reconsidered?" Ed began hopefully.

"No, not about joining the museum's board, but I would like to become involved in another way." Lauren took a deep breath. She knew her husband was a very wealthy man, but even still, thirty-five to forty million for a building was a lot of money, no matter how much he had.

"Tandy informed me that the lease on the current space for the museum will be expiring soon. I think we should buy the Sugar Hill Building in Harlem for the museum," Lauren quickly said before losing the nerve. Ed was staring at her, and she couldn't blame him. The idea had come out of left field.

"Buy the Sugar Hill Building?"

Taking a seat in his large leather wingback chair, he pulled her down on his lap and encouraged her to continue with her "bright idea." Lauren eagerly nodded as Ed began playing with her earlobes.

"Yes, I think the foundation should buy the building and lease the space to the museum. The Sugar Hill Building is large enough to do a whole children's wing. I really think the museum needs to be accessible to the youth. The interest in art should start at a young age, or at least the exposure. Why should the children in Manhattan have their own museum and not our kids in Harlem?"

Now Ed was kissing Lauren's neck as he whispered, "You sound so passionate about this."

"I am," Lauren said under her breath, feeling her body respond to Ed's butterfly kisses working their way down her spine.

"And how much would this Sugar Hill Building set us back?"

"Thirty-five, forty million." Lauren gasped as Ed bit her shoulder and flung her sweater to the carpeted floor.

"You don't make cheap requests, do you?"

"What kind of girl do you think I am?"

"A ... very ... expensive one," he said, pulling her firm breasts out of her bra and placing her nipples in his mouth.

Lauren groaned at his touch, and her entire body filled with goose bumps. Her mind was no longer on business as Ed said, "You're a very clever girl. For that amount of money in Harlem, the museum will be getting a new name, Mrs. Thomas." Ed began working his tongue over her taut tummy, moving south down her belly to her lace underwear. He was now unzipping her jeans.

"I don't know about you, but I'd like some lunch," Ed said before practically ripping off her jeans. Lauren's head rolled back, and ecstasy overcame her. The rest of the world's desires for her would have to wait. She was concentrating on her own rapture as Ed's mouth and tongue explored her most secret places.

NINETEEN

FIVE-FORTY-FIVE A.M., and Manny was right on time. With such an early call, Manny was thankful the uptown barbershop was in his neighborhood. Moneybags Ed Thomas had called and told him he wanted to discuss something important. Whatever the request, Manny figured he would do his damnedest to see it through. Pleasing Ed Thomas could be his ticket to true playerdom.

The barbershop sat in the middle of a decrepit block, dispelling the image that a billionaire might drop by at any time. As Manny approached the storefront, he saw the Rolls-Royce, with the driver in the front seat reading the paper. How anyone could actually read at this early hour was beyond Manny.

Peering inside the store, Manny rapped on the shaded glass door, hoping someone would hear him. Ed emerged from a back room, cell phone to his ear—never too far away from the making of a business deal. He let Manny inside and indicated a chair. Manny sat where he was told and waited for Ed to finish his call. The room reminded Manny of the shop where his father had taken him to get his hair cut when he was a boy, a place where black men came together to exchange stories, counsel one another, play the numbers, and make deals.

Ed hung up and joked, "Hey, Manny. How are you feeling? This too early for you?," seeming as though he had been awake for hours. To date, this was the longest exchange they had shared.

"You know, this is not my favorite time of the day," Manny said with a smile, bowing his head in deference.

"When we're done, you can go back to bed. I wanted to meet when we could speak privately. The owner, Will, will be here at six. We have a few moments before he arrives," explained Ed.

"Is this your barbershop? I mean, since you have a key and all." Manny had not heard that Ed owned a barbershop, but anything was possible.

"No. I helped Will out a few years back, when he was trying to branch out on his own." Ed spoke with a smile in his eye that reflected his apparent pride. "He needed some financial assistance and business guidance, initially. I bought this place for him, and I keep a key—you know, so I can come on in for a haircut and shave and be ready for him when he gets here."

Manny nodded, acknowledging Ed's empathy, and Ed continued, "I like to help people, Manny. When I see someone who works hard but can't seem to get a break, if I can help them out, I enjoy doing it. That's the beauty of having money and resources." Again Manny nodded, anxious for Ed to get to the reason he'd called. "Like you, Manny. I would love to help you out. You know Lauren and I send referrals your way whenever we meet someone interested in buying a place. I called you here because I wanted to ask you to help me find a building that our foundation can buy for the Museum of Harlem. The building should be thirty to thirty-five thousand square feet, in Harlem, and should cost no more than fifty million, but I would prefer if the price came in closer to thirty."

"Of course I'll find a place for you, Ed. Whatever you want." *Tandy knew the game* was all Manny could think. Tandy was ahead of the curve on this scheme; she had the building and the buyer pegged. Manny just hoped that Dana's attorney was as flaky as Tandy had led him to believe. But judging by the way Tandy had handled things so far, Manny believed he could trust her. Not only was she right, but Ed had said he would go up to fifty million. He would talk to Tandy; maybe they should increase their take from five million apiece to ten.

"I appreciate that, Manny. I knew I could count on you. I want you to know, though, that after today this is completely Lauren's project. She will contact you about the building, and she will manage the entire purchase." The circumstances were getting better and better for Manny. No Ed in the deal would make the transaction that much easier. Ed was a shark, Lauren a lamb. This meeting had definitely been worth getting up for.

Neither man mentioned Sugar Hill. Manny didn't want his job to look too easy. He hoped to make the impression that he had to do some research and footwork to come up with the perfect building for Ed's requirements. He did not know how much Ed knew; anything was possible. Thomas was an *utter* businessman and would hold all of his cards to his chest. He might know the building was for sale and want Manny to be the first to name a price.

But Ed was not finished with him yet. "I have another small matter for you as well."

Manny was feeling so good that if Ed had asked him to get naked and ride on top of the car, he would have.

"I have a friend who needs an apartment of her own. In fact, you've met her." He paused, giving Manny time to understand what was about to go down. "She is a great girl. Very talented. She came from nothing, the ghetto of Compton. She had no formal dance training and practically walked into the ballet world and made them take notice and embrace her. But you know, despite her talent, the life of a dancer is tough. She makes no money and really needs some help. As a gift to her, I'm buying her an apartment. She will own it outright and can do with it as she pleases, if and when she decides to move on." Ed spoke very fast, but Manny followed every word. "She's a good kid. She deserves a leg up for a change."

"And you have to be that leg?" Manny was no longer feeling on top of the world. "Does Lauren know that you are buying this dancer a home?" He didn't want to alienate Ed, but how could he ask Manny, one of Lauren's best friends, to be an accomplice in his affair?

Ed regarded Manny carefully, looking him deeply in the eyes. He gestured broadly and nodded as he spoke. "Manny, come on. You're a man." Ed tipped his head to the side, giving Manny the impression that he wanted to add, "Even though you are a homosexual." Ed continued, "You know how these things go. Lauren has nothing to do with this. I love her dearly. As far as I'm concerned, no other woman can touch her. But my friend Alyssia is alone in the world. She has no one to help her, and she deserves a little break. She works hard. When all is said and done, Lauren and I will grow old together, and Alyssia will have something that will at least get her through. My wife does not need to know anything about any of this. Knowledge of this situation would only be hurtful and complicate a situation that does not need confusion."

Ed sounded to Manny as though he had this affair under control. Clearly, he knew it would not be long-term. Lauren was his first priority. He was just spreading the wealth around. Charity work. Still, Manny was conflicted. He did not have a good feeling about what Ed was asking him to do. The request was a direct betrayal of Lauren, someone very special to him.

"How am I supposed to face Lauren after a day showing your girlfriend property?"

Ed gave Manny a sideways glance before taking a seat in the barber's chair. His previous congenial expression was gone. In its place was a face of stone—one Manny was certain several lesser adversaries had seen over the years before being gobbled up by Thomas Industries. Any patience he'd had with Manny had dissipated. "You're getting self-righteous with me?" he condescended.

"But Lauren's my best friend."

"Manny, come on. Who do you think you're kidding? You are your own best friend. I know you found Terrence Brown's girlfriend an apartment, just to mention one of many."

Meekly, Manny said, "Terrence's wife was not my friend. That was different."

"Your naive act is killing me, Manny. Look, Lauren knows what she signed up for when she married me. There's no need for you to be the morality police here."

"I think I would be more comfortable—"

Ed shut him down. "With me getting another broker. Someone who would talk, spread my business around town, embarrass my family?"

How was it that Ed had the ability to turn the situation around and make Manny feel like finding the mistress an apartment was his personal duty? Manny was now on the defense. He said, "That's not what I'm suggesting, Ed."

"Or are you suggesting that I find another person to broker the deal for the foundation?" Ed pointedly asked, knowing he was hitting Manny where it really hurt. Softening his tone, Ed added, "With you on board, it's a win-win. You can make sure no one gets hurt, and you can have a respectable payday."

He looked confident that Manny would consent. Obviously, he knew that for Manny, a commission check was much-needed money in the bank. And how could Manny possibly say no? Ed had just handed him a thirty-plus-million-dollar deal.

"So when Alyssia calls, be nice and find her something sweet, preferably in the West Village, a town house with a garage. Stay under three million." At that, Ed's phone chirped, and Manny was summarily dismissed, as if he were the hired help—which, in a way, he thought miserably, he was.

Walking down a slowly awakening 125th Street, Manny checked his watch. His meeting with Ed had taken exactly fifteen minutes. Stopping on the corner to wait for the light, Manny looked up and saw the Museum of Harlem. He felt awful about Lauren's predicament. But as Ed had said, Manny did know how these things went. Men like Ed were hard-pressed to be one-woman men. Manny had no doubt that Ed loved Lauren, but no one woman would be enough for a man of Ed's energy, wealth, looks, and opportunity.

Thinking more about the situation, Manny told himself that it was fortunate Ed had come to him. With Manny on the case, rumors of Ed and his mistress were less likely to leak. Manny could even possibly derail the affair as he got to know the girl. But thinking of his first meeting with Alyssia and her apparent aggression, he knew she would not be so easily put aside. She was the type who, once she had her claws in a man, would no sooner release her grip than a lion would stop tearing into a wildebeest for her weekly dinner. Manny decided he would tell Ed that he would not accept a commission off of this deal. He had to draw a line between right and wrong somewhere.

Continuing up Malcolm X Boulevard, past the Schomburg Center, Manny couldn't help but wonder if his moral barometer was broken. He was about to do some pretty sleazy things. But he had not created the game. Everyone around him was in the business of doing whatever was required to satisfy their desires, which they deemed needs. The more he thought, the more he began to understand that in the world of high finance and big players, corruption came with the territory. If he, Manny Marks, was ever going to get out from under the lifestyle of the basic salesman, he would have to step up his game.

Tandy had shown him the writing on the wall. If he wanted the life he had dreamed of since childhood, he would have to take some risks—even though his grandmother used to say to him, "Just because everyone is doing it doesn't mean you have to do it, too." Manny was beginning to believe that in this world, following the lead of a billionaire and a New York socialite who had raised millions of dollars would be the acceptable exception to the rule.

TWENTY

Mᴀɴɴʏ's head reeled as he read the vicious words beneath the photo of him and Lauren, taken as they were leaving Stephen L. Carter's book party. The black-and-white picture from *The New York Observer* depicted Manny carrying Lauren's books, coat, satchel, and his own briefcase, all the while trying to open the car door for her with a huge grin on his face. He had only been trying to be a gentleman. But New York's reigning town crier, "Gossip to Go Glo," had perverted the whole scene for her own purposes. In the subtitle, Glo referred to him as a "subterranean errand boy to Manhattan's upper crust. The only part of 'upper' he could ever aspire to be is the crust."

Manny knew the reason behind her venom. Several months back, he had refused to show the tabloid writer any more property than the dozen or so apartments she had seen with him; he had realized she was using him as a tour guide to view buildings that celebrities and socialites lived in. He knew she still held that slight against him, but he had never thought she would be so vindictive. He certainly did not deserve this treatment.

New York City's gossip queen was fucking with his reputation, and the timing could not be worse, considering he was in the midst of trying to pull together the biggest deal of his career. Manny had worked too damn hard—fifteen years of backbreaking labor and ass-kissing—to get to this point, and he had no intention of going backward. He could not. The fall would take him to a place he had no desire to visit again—a place where he was desperate for survival in New York City. He had been left alone, broke, and with limited options, a scary place to be.

Manny was devastated when Tommy died in the fall of 1984. No one in their family had even bothered to attend the small memorial Manny pulled together, as per the instructions Tommy left with one of his bartender buddies. Manny had not grasped how ill Tommy was. He had always put on a brave face in front of Manny and seemed to care only about partying and picking up boys during their brief time together. So the day Manny and a dozen of Tommy's friends sprinkled his ashes into the East River, Manny felt a void in the life he had come to love. There was also an economic reality: Manny had run out of cash, and with only two weeks remaining on Tommy's lease, he needed to find a way to make money, fast. Returning to Alabama was not an option. He would rather be cremated and tossed into the water with Tommy before heading back to Birmingham. When Tommy was alive, Manny had been too busy having fun to think about getting a real job. Their life together had been a carefree one. Now the harsh reality of his situation was hitting him. His cousin was no longer there to buffer him. As far as work was concerned, Manny certainly had not come to New York to get a mundane job. He needed something to suit his personality.

Manny began poking around, making inquiries of Tommy's friends and trying to formulate a plan. He was learning at a young age the importance of not only knowing people but being known. A job as a waiter or a salesperson in a clothing store wouldn't do. In fact, he had no idea what would be right for him, until Tojo showed up at the apartment. Tojo was a friend of Tommy's and had stopped over to sift through some old clothes. Manny would later think back to that day and replay it in his mind over and over again. He often wondered what would have happened if he had refused to meet Tojo's friend. Would that have stopped a chain of events that led him to the life he had come to know? Manny never dug too deep or reflected too much into his inner psyche. That sort of thinking gave him a headache. But it took very little thought to recognize that agreeing to meet Tojo's friend was one of the defining moments in his life.

"You know what you're going to do yet?" Tojo asked, pulling his shoulder-length thick blond hair into a green rubber band. He was an aging beautiful boy whose one remaining attribute was his shiny mane. His skin was deeply lined and damaged from too many sunny days spent in South Beach, and from too many drugs. Even his once electric blue eyes looked more like milky pool water than azure seas. He wore an expression on his face reminiscent of someone whose best days were behind him. But he always had plenty of stories to tell about the glory days. Manny wondered how much of Tojo's premature aging had to do with losing one too many friends to a mysterious deadly virus.

Manny told Tojo that he had not figured it out but was working on a plan.

Tojo stared at Manny hard as he continued to fiddle with his hair. "People like you up here. They think you're cute and charming. And we all love the southern drawl."

Manny didn't know who these people were, and he didn't know what that had to do with getting a job. "Yeah, but I still haven't found a job that lasts longer than a week at a time," he explained.

"You got to stop partying all night and show up on time. Tommy got you started on some bad habits."

Manny suddenly felt protective of Tommy; it hurt to have his cousin's name brought up in an unkind way. Besides, Manny hadn't even thought about partying since Tommy died. He had been spending most of his time feeling alone and overwhelmed.

"Yeah, well, I'm young. I'm free. I'm supposed to have some fun," Manny said with false bravado.

"You also want to stay alive. Where are you going to live? How are you going to support yourself?"

Though Tojo's words resonated, Manny defensively told him, "I'll figure it out."

"Look, I'm on your side here," Tojo said, softening his tone before moving toward Manny, his milky eyes becoming brighter. Manny wondered if Tojo was about to launch into one of his nostalgic stories from the 1970s about dancing on tables in Antibes and some French count wanting to buy him a chalet. Although Manny did enjoy Tojo's anecdotes, he was in no mood to hear one today.

Tojo didn't seem interested in going through Tommy's things. Instead, he was concentrating on Manny. "Hey, you're young and charming; not too bad-looking, either. I'd say you're very marketable."

"Marketable without a marketing degree, my grandparents would tell me. Maybe I should think about going to school, get some student loans, get my bachelor's of business or something," Manny pondered aloud.

"Maybe, maybe," Tojo said, sounding like he had other ideas. "You could do that. Or you could work someplace where you can make a hell of a lot more money than you would by getting your bachelor's degree. You can't get a job these days with just a bachelor's degree. Hell, you'll be in school ten years before you start making any money, and then you'll spend the rest of your life paying off your student loans. That's what happened to my brother. Now he's so beaten down, he can't even hold a steady job. College is only for the trust-fund kids."

To Manny it sounded like Tojo knew what he was talking about. Tojo came and sat next to him on the dingy sofa that had become his bed. Even after Tommy died, Manny couldn't bring himself to sleep in his cousin's bed. Tommy had been so proud of his indulgent king-size Serta, of all the pillows he had collected from thrift shops around the city. He used to tell Manny that each pillow told a different story and had a special purpose, and Tommy's mood would determine which pillow he slept on each night.

Tojo abruptly ran his hand over Manny's abdominal muscles. Manny was more taken aback than fearful. Tojo had never made a pass at him, and Manny felt uncomfortable seated so close to him.

"Don't get uptight, I'm not interested in you like that. You don't have an ounce of fat, and do you realize you don't look a day over sixteen," Tojo said, as if he were tabulating Manny's assets rather than flirting.

Manny didn't appreciate that comment, especially since he'd worked so hard to look older than his nineteen years and fit in with all of Tommy's friends. Still, he wondered what Tojo was getting at.

"Have you ever thought about modeling?"

"Well," Manny began. He had thought about modeling, but he didn't know how to get started.

"Or acting?" Tojo continued in earnest.

"I never thought about acting," Manny confessed.

Tojo sat forward, his mind obviously clicking. "I want you to meet a friend of mine, Alexander. He has a boutique talent/modeling agency. I think he could get you some work."

"Acting?"

"Maybe, or modeling. And he sometimes lets his clients stay at his place rent-free."

Manny raised his eyebrows. "Rent-free?" He hadn't heard of getting anything free in this town, even from his own cousin.

Tojo nodded. "It's common practice for young models to room with their agents."

This sounded too good to be true. "You think your friend will like me?"

"Definitely."

"And you think he could get me work?"

"Oh, he'll get you work. You really have a chance at a life in the city. And you're smart, too. I knew that about you the first time I met you. That, coupled with your looks, will take you to the next level."

Manny liked what Tojo was saying. He liked it a lot, maybe too much, he realized. He pushed his grandfather's words out of his mind: "The devil will come with flattery." Tojo saw something in him that no one else had seen, and he wanted to help. Why else would he be spending so much time with Manny, telling him how fabulous he was? Manny agreed to meet Tojo's friend.

Tojo had not lied; Alexander Bitcoff liked Manny very, very much. And Manny was infatuated with the lithe, fair-haired, silver-eyed trust-fund son of a media mogul. He was so worldly and so well read. Alexander had lived in the exotic places that Manny's mother had only hoped to visit; plus, he was educated, with degrees from several universities. He walked around quoting poetry and speaking Latin, impressing Manny with his knowledge of literature. Most thrilling to Manny was not that Alexander agreed to be his agent, but that he invited Manny to live in his luxurious Upper East Side home, along with two other young models from out west. Manny had only heard about such places in Manhattan; he certainly had not seen any during his yearlong stay in the city. The notion that such an expansive and extravagant retreat could exist behind a nondescript limestone facade intrigued Manny. Thus began his love affair with New York City real estate. It also marked the beginning of his not so loving relationship with Alexander.

"Oh no, she did not!" Trenton said, staring at Manny and Lauren's photo. Manny had not even heard him saunter into the kitchen. He had thought Trenton was still asleep after his late night on the town. "Oh no, Miss Glo did not dis you like that!"

Trenton was not making the situation any better. Why did he have to underscore how damaging the caption was?

Manny tried to play it off. "I'm not thinking about that woman."

"Hmmph, but she dogged your ass out," Trenton said.

Was Manny imagining it, or did his lover boy sound almost pleased by this public humiliation? Wherever Trenton was coming from, Manny was determined not to let him know he was under his skin.

Trenton would not let up. "But that's what your ass gets, hanging out with those uppity folks. Glo wouldn't have written that about you if Lauren and them treated you with more respect instead of like their—what did Glo say?—like their personal errand boy." Then he had the nerve to cackle.

"Trenton, you don't know what the fuck you're talking about," Manny snapped, having heard enough of Trenton's mouth. He couldn't help himself. A small part of him wondered if there was some truth to Trenton's words. Maybe if Lauren and Tandy treated him with more respect, others would view him in that light as well.

Trenton pulled open the refrigerator door with a self-satisfied smirk and unscrewed the cap of the half-empty Pepsi that Manny had bought last night. He began slurping it down directly from the bottle, then belched loudly. He tossed the empty bottle in the trash before turning back to Manny and saying, "Damn, niggah, you don't have to get so sensitive with me. I'm just trying to keep it real with you. You need to get your head out the clouds and figure out who your real friends are."

Manny was near his exploding point with Trenton. Not only had the man been out damn near all night partying, claiming to be cultivating new modeling contacts, but now he was riding him about those stupid comments. It was more than he could handle on an already rocky morning.

"Do me a favor, Trenton, just butt the fuck out. Why don't you go play one of your video games?"

"You think I like seeing my man played like a bitch in the newspaper?"

"Probably not, Trenton. It probably embarrasses you. That, or it gets you worried about whether or not it will affect my next commission check."

"Not really, none of my friends read this shit," Trenton said, before walking out to the living room.

Manny wanted to say, "That's 'cause none of your friends know how to read," but he stopped himself. Instead, he silently fumed. Trenton was already oohing and aahing in unison with Ricki Lake over the two obese sisters who had gotten pregnant by their cousin June Bug.

Something had to give. Manny hoped it wasn't him.

TWENTY-ONE

TANDY thrived on these board meetings. Sitting in the windowless room with beige walls and beige carpet where the only visible art was a painting of a pre–September 11 New York City skyline did not dampen the day's exhilaration for her. What mattered were the people in attendance, the company she was keeping, and her close proximity to the delicious taste of power.

The board of the Museum of Harlem was comprised of some of the world's most elite, and not only black elite, citizens. Sitting at the U-shaped table with Tandy were the African-American wife of a famous white multi-millionaire crime writer; an executive vice president of a leading consumer-products company; the wife of the head of an investment bank; an investment banker who ran his own firm; a white billionaire's wife; a lawyer who had helped to bring down corrupt corporate officers; a former baseball player whose earnings could finance a small country; and of course Ed Thomas. Yes, Tandy was very comfortable and happy in these surroundings. She was momentarily outmoneyed but not outclassed.

Today's meeting was especially good for her. As head of the committee that was researching the feasibility of adding a children's wing to the museum, she was about to be the center of attention, the star of the meeting, as she made her case before the board.

"Our committee reviewed the issues of exhibition space, storage space, acquisition resources, and curatorial leadership. Before I give you our conclusions, however, I want you all to know that the general issue for us is space. Presently, we barely have enough room for our current exhibits, and our storage facility is overflowing to the point where we've begun renting storage space elsewhere."

Tandy had to make her case for a new building without divulging her interest in or knowledge of the real estate transaction that she was proposing to cure all of the museum's exhibition and storage problems. As she finished her spiel, the chairman of the board, a retired entertainment executive whose passion was collecting art, thanked her for a thorough report and a passionate call to help the children in the Harlem community. He then announced a fifteen-minute break so everyone could stretch.

Heading back from the ladies' room, Tandy noticed Ed speaking rapidly into his cell phone. She slowed to a halt and brought her own phone to her ear, pretending to have a conversation. She was in a position where she could watch Ed but he wouldn't necessarily suspect she was spying on him. Plus, he never glanced in her direction.

Ed was bona fide fine, she thought. Like Ed Bradley, he was the kind of good-looking man who seemed to get better with age. He was also the type who made a good suit look even better with his tall, slim, manly build. Damn. She was getting carried away. But she could not stop thinking what a stunning pair the two of them would have made, the same age and both so beautiful. Timing, unfortunately, was everything. By the time Phil was dead, Ed had been married to Lauren for three years. If only things had been a little different.

He snapped his phone shut, and Tandy leaped to his side. "Ed, how are you? You look great!" She smiled, tossing her smooth black hair, giving him her best angles.

He seemed unimpressed. "Fine. You look good, as always." He was making his way back to the meeting.

"You are always so gracious. Listen, Ed, I wanted to talk with you." Tandy stopped him with her hand on his forearm. "I need some help on this estate business. I am totally overwhelmed. Can we have lunch sometime, sooner than later?" She gazed at him with longing in her eyes. She was thinking about their trysts in the Vineyard, when Phil was on the golf course and Ed's first wife was at home tending to their boys. They would get a room at the Harbor View Hotel in Edgartown, with a view of the Atlantic Ocean, seagulls, weathered shingled mansions, and green marshy lands, and they would spend lazy afternoons making passionate love. Tandy licked her lips at the image of his powerful body thrusting in and out of her. It had been such a long time since someone made love to her that way.

Before Ed could answer, the doors to the meeting room began to close. He looked anxious to get back to his seat but told her, "Sure. I promised Phil I would look after you and Deja should anything happen to him. Call Margaret this afternoon, and we'll make sure to get together before the end of next week."

"Thank you, Ed. You don't know how much that means to me." Ed was practically in the room before the last word left her mouth. Tandy, however, was unfazed. She had a promise from Ed for lunch before the end of next week. Who knew what might be on the menu for dessert? Something to look forward to, for sure. She knew Ed liked his cake.

As the board meeting worked toward the final items on the agenda, Ed chimed in on the discussion about the lease termination and renegotiation. As a member of the finance committee, he was responsible for making sure the museum was efficient in spending.

"I respectfully ask the board to wait until the next meeting, in two months, to decide the course of action regarding the lease. As Tandy reported earlier, we are short on space, and as you know, our landlord wants to increase the rent. My wife and I are investigating a situation that might solve our space problems and the rent increase. We are still eight months away from needing to make any significant decisions. I believe the museum will benefit tremendously by holding off on this decision. Thank you."

Again Tandy smiled big at Ed, even though he wasn't looking in her direction. She was pleased that she had read him well. The building would be purchased, because he wanted Lauren involved in his philanthropic goals. What a shame Ed had laden himself with such a naive little girl. Old men believed young pussy was better. They realized too late that the younger the girl, the more work was required in developing a truly valuable asset. Tandy allowed herself to believe that somewhere beneath Ed's gruff demeanor, he still had feelings for her and was simply frustrated with himself because he had missed the opportunity to rule New York with her.

TWENTY-TWO

As Tandy sashayed through the doors of the Four Seasons, she doubted her choice of clothing yet again. She had worn a powder-blue cashmere sport coat, a matching knit silk mockneck, and a black pencil skirt with her pointy-toed Jimmy Choo shoes, to give the ensemble a sexy finish. She'd planned it so Ed would get a good view of her legs via the daring slit that exposed her right thigh. He had always liked her calves.

Tandy had considered dressing down in a style similar to Lauren's casual, laid-back bohemian look. But she quickly dismissed the idea. She was in a different class from Lauren, she had to remind herself. True, Lauren had landed Ed, but she had youth and beauty working on her behalf. Those were temporary attributes, Tandy reasoned, ones that Ed would tire of once he realized he needed a real woman at his side. When it was all said and done, Lauren couldn't hold a candle to Tandy. Lauren's whole style went against Tandy's principles. No, for today's lunch, Tandy wanted to create a different image, one with which Ed was not currently familiar. She would be alluring and mysterious, reminding him of the glory days. She would distinguish herself from the little girl Lauren Thomas, make him see what he was missing.

Tandy approached the maître d' and gave him her name, since she had been the one to make the reservations. Walking through the crowded restaurant filled with out-of-town businessmen, ladies lunching, a smattering of music executives, and several VIPs, she began to feel confident again. She recognized a few faces from around the neighborhood, but more importantly, she knew she was recognized by the various nods and polite waves, and once Ed arrived, her table would be included in the VIP category. Tandy was pleased that their table was not directly next to a window. Despite her monthly facials and La Mer antiaging cream, she still did not want Ed staring at her in direct sunlight. The softer light of the corner table was ideal.

Taking her seat, she quickly checked her face for shine, smudges, food in the teeth, or any other unsightly thing that might be a turnoff to Ed. Muttering "Perfect" under her breath as she closed her compact mirror, she glanced up to see him moving toward her in what seemed like slow motion. Her breath caught. Every time she saw him, she was struck by his good looks. He was still such a specimen of a man. And the best part was, he was richer than ever. She imagined running her fingers through his curly salt-and-pepper hair and caressing his strong neck, touching the body he kept in such amazing physical shape. Phil had never been able to keep up with Ed Thomas on the tennis court or in business, Tandy morosely thought.

"Tandy," Ed said as he reached the table. "You look lovely."

"Thank you, Ed. You're looking quite well yourself." Tandy was happy that things were getting off to such a good start. Before sitting down, Ed leaned in to Tandy, giving her a gentle kiss on the cheek. He was such a gentleman, Tandy thought. If only things had been different, she might be Mrs. Ed Thomas instead of Lauren.

Tandy adjusted the diamond pendant around her neck, willing herself not to get nervous. Having finally gotten the nerve to ask him to lunch, she did not want to blow the opportunity of having his ear. Despite many years of knowing Ed, she recognized the value of having a single moment with him. She noticed several of the businessmen and -women casually glancing over at their table, whispering to one another. Ed was a celebrity, constantly covered in *The Wall Street Journal, BusinessWeek,* and *Fortune,* and a frequent guest on MSNBC, Fox, and CNN financial shows. Not only was he a billionaire, he was also considered a business guru. And if Ed Thomas was having lunch with someone, she *had* to be significant.

"What are you having, Ed?" Tandy asked as the waiter approached, deciding to take his cue on the tone of the lunch before ordering for herself.

"Black Label, straight up," Ed matter-of-factly told the black-and-white-clad young waiter, as if he should have known. Power gave one that authority, Tandy marveled, wishing she could bottle some of it for herself.

Tandy ordered a glass of chardonnay. She waited for the waiter to leave before saying, "I see you still like your Black Label." She was thinking of how they used to share tumblers of the rich Scotch before making love. She seductively stared Ed in the eyes, willing him to share the memory. She laid her hand lightly over his on the table and let it linger there for a moment. She even allowed herself the thought that they might get a room upstairs after lunch.

"Yes, I still like my Black Label."

"Those were good times," she said, rubbing his hand.

"That was a long time ago."

"Oh, not so long ago," Tandy said flirtatiously, but he didn't comment. Instead, he merely looked uncomfortable. Tandy wondered if there was a part deep inside him, despite his distance, that felt the same about their lost opportunity at a life together, but she dared not press him. Ed had never been the type to like scandal or disruption. Tandy firmly believed that had his first wife not left him, Ed would have been satisfied with screwing around on the side and having the stability of a wife at home. If only Ed had informed Tandy when he was going through his separation and divorce, she would have dumped Phil without a second thought. The fool would not have known what hit him.

When their drinks arrived, Tandy lifted her wine to his Scotch, took a deep breath, and said, "So, I bet you're wondering why I asked you here today." She beamed, trying her best to sound light and cheery.

Ed nodded. He never was a man of many words, even when fucking. He would simply give her a few seductive looks before suggesting they meet at a designated spot. Tandy was reminded how difficult it could be to get him to communicate. But she was determined. She was in dire straits. The Sugar Hill Building sale was not finalized yet, and she had bill collectors at her door.

Tandy put on her widow's face and then began, "You know, it's been difficult for me since Phil died."

Ed nodded and said, "I know. How've you been?" He seemed genuinely concerned.

"I have my good days and my bad, but you know me, Ed. I'm a survivor." Tandy was quick to include one of her many attributes. The last impression she wanted to leave him with was that of a desperate woman. She had to be careful to balance all of her statements. Now that she had his attention, she needed to make him feel as if her proposition would benefit him as well as her.

"I've been taking inventory of several of my pieces of art, and I happen to know that Lauren loves my W. H. Johnson folk-art series. I wondered if you'd like to buy the five paintings for her." There, she had said it. She felt relieved just getting the question off her chest. Not that she was feeling any better, because Ed was staring at her quizzically.

"What's the extent of your financial problems?" he said without blinking an eye. Tandy felt her face burning. He had never been one to mince words, but she had not expected him to be so blunt about such a delicate subject.

"I wouldn't say I have financial—"

Ed cut her off. "Have you thought about selling your co-op?"

"Ed!" Tandy said with as much mock indignation as she could muster.

"Tandy, listen, we've known each other a long time. I don't see any reason for pretense here. I know the situation you and Phil were in before he died."

Tandy was mortified. So he knew more than she had about Phil's predicament. If she had known what financial shambles she and Phil were in, she would have made many different decisions, many. She wondered how Ed had known; even worse, she wondered who else knew besides Ed. The shame of the moment was almost unbearable. She was beginning to regret ever asking Ed to lunch. She certainly had not expected him to read right through her.

Ed glanced at his watch and then downed his drink. "So, Lauren really likes the W. H. Johnson series?"

"Yes, yes, she does, but if you're not interested, I know several people who are. I just wanted to give you the first opportunity." Tandy held tightly to what little pride she had left.

"How much for each?"

"They should really be sold as a set." Tandy sat back in her chair. She was playing a dangerous game, risking his total loss of interest, but she did have an image to uphold, even if he was attempting to shatter it. "I'll sell you the set of five for two hundred and fifty thousand."

Ed looked at his wrist once again. "I'll give you one hundred and seventy-five. I have another meeting now; let my assistant know if we have a deal." He stood up and left just as the waiter was bringing their menus. He had not even given her the respect of staying for lunch. And then he had the nerve to bargain with her over her museum-quality paintings for a lousy seventy-five thousand dollars. He paid more than that in taxes for one day's work. Tandy was outraged. And to think he had known about her financial problems and had not even offered to help. What kind of friend was he to Phil? First fucking around with her, his so-called friend's wife, and now this. Ed Thomas was a selfish, narcissistic bastard.

Tandy fumed as she ordered another drink from the bewildered-looking waiter. Screw the chardonnay. This time she got the hard liquor. But maybe Ed had done her a favor. His actions were affirmation that she was doing the right thing, orchestrating this deal for the Sugar Hill Building. She couldn't rely on anyone except herself. Screw Ed and Lauren! Why should she care if they paid ten million more for the building than Dana actually wanted? That extra money would be much better spent by her. Ed and Lauren were becoming a self-absorbed couple, anyway: He didn't seem to give a shit about anyone but himself anymore, and she didn't even know how to properly spend her husband's money. They would never miss the extra ten million dollars Tandy and Manny would pocket. Sometimes the rules needed to be bent. And sometimes they didn't apply at all, especially in this town.

TWENTY-THREE

As serious and avid art collectors, Ed and Lauren had developed the habit of changing the paintings on the walls of their apartment every four to six months. Ed believed that walking past art for a while, one ceased to see the image. Thus, two to three times a year, the couple would head down to their vault to rummage through their collection. The safe was a temperature-controlled converted studio apartment on the ground floor of their building. Typically, apartments of the stature that Lauren and Ed owned came with a separate maid's apartment located in a remote spot in the building. Ed and Lauren bought their accompanying maid's apartment and turned it into a warehouse for rows and rows of narrow stalls in which the artwork was kept. In the middle of the room stood a large table flanked by two Stickley spindle chairs. On the one empty wall was a long built-in shelf that functioned as an easel whenever the need to study a painting arose. Extra security, including cameras, motion-sensor detectors, and sprinklers, had been installed. Together, Ed and Lauren would go through the racks and decide which paintings would adorn their walls. While they collected all types of art by various artists, their collection of

African-American work was spectacular, rivaling that of any mainstream museum.

Going down to the storage facility was always an adventure for Lauren, and it usually brought out the child in Ed. Searching through the works he had collected over the past twenty-five years made him giddy, showing the silly side that most people never witnessed. Also, it seemed to Lauren that he returned to a state of near-innocence, resembling a blank canvas anxious for new life to be brought forth in the form of art. And whenever they went down to the room, Ed would get a little frisky. He would flirt with her, touching her or flashing his stiff, hard dick. They often made love in the vault. But tonight Ed was not in a good mood. For the first time in their relationship, he did not make a pass at her in that room. Rather, he behaved antagonistically toward her. He was probably stressed with his latest project, Lauren reasoned, wondering what she could do to get his attention. This dry spell would not deter her from working on their marriage.

She said to Ed, "You know, as we go through all of this stuff, I can't help but think about the Museum of Harlem and their children's wing. We can give them their first show with our work. I can select about fifteen pieces that I think might be interesting to children. What do you think of this Jacob Lawrence? His color and graphic images would speak to kids, don't you think?" She held up a painting.

Ed stared through Lauren and then at the painting. "I'm so glad you're finally showing interest in the museum," he responded without much concern for Lauren's actual question or thought. He returned his attention to the rack in front of him, reading the label on the side to see what piece was stored there.

Lauren began again. "The more I speak to Tandy about the museum, the more clear I become. The museum, the children, the community. It's such a good cause. And to work with someone like Tandy, whom I've admired since I was a little kid—I'm actually excited."

"I don't know why you are so enamored with her. Tandy is fine, but you shouldn't get so carried away. She doesn't walk on water, you know." Ed's tone sounded impatient to Lauren. She felt he really did not want to be with her at this moment, as if her presence was annoying him. The discomfort between them was painful.

"All I'm saying is that Tandy is a legend. She's gorgeous, smart, and together. Ever since I was a child, I knew that she was a special lady. She has done so much charitable work for New York. She's raised millions. Maybe to you that's not a big deal, but for her to take me under her wing, to show an interest in what I do, makes me feel very special."

Ed pulled out a painting and placed it on the table. He stared at the work intently as he spoke. "Sometimes I don't understand you, Lauren. Tandy is a crazy, desperate relic. She has no moral fiber and is probably holding whatever it is that you think she has together with Scotch tape and paper clips." Ed chuckled lightly at his own joke, still studying the art.

Feeling protective of her friend and slightly defensive, Lauren wanted to know why Ed was being so snippy. "You probably know more about Tandy than I do. But I don't know why you have to be so mean about it. Tandy has been through a lot."

"Mean? Tandy Brooks drove my friend Phil into the poorhouse, and truth be told, she also drove him to his grave with all of her fake socialite crap. She only cares about herself. If she weren't the widow of someone who was such a good friend, I wouldn't give her the time of day." Ed had finally turned his gaze on Lauren.

Lauren took a deep breath and gathered all of her strength. "I brought up her name because, as you know, she has convinced me to get involved with the museum. With everyone trying to pressure me into their philanthropic agendas, the children's wing at the museum can buffer me from the vultures and leave me time for my work." By now Lauren had lost interest in going through the racks. She leaned against one of the shelves, needing all of her energy to focus on the conversation.

Dismissively, Ed continued, "I don't know why you don't do more, anyway. What are you afraid of? You have nothing but time. You could do a lot for the city philanthropically. More than Tandy, that's for sure. We have all the money you'll need to buy a place onto any charitable board in this city—your little Style Channel projects are okay, but I believe you could be more effective doing charity work."

She responded defiantly to his condescension. "I've told you. I want to work. I'm trying to build a career. It's hard, with everyone making so many demands on me. Once I'm done with the Style thing, I really want to do a documentary on women living in shelters. I hate it when you try to suggest my work is unimportant." Lauren's voice had risen. She was not quite shouting, but she was speaking louder than usual.

Equally filled with emotion, Ed faced Lauren and lit into her in a way that took her completely off guard. "You *want* to work? Lauren, this idea of your working creatively is fine. But how are you going about doing it? It seems to me that you're dabbling, doing a little piece here and a little piece there. I haven't seen you pound the pavement or hustle for a job." He paused to catch his breath. "Let's be honest, Lauren, you don't really know what hard work is. The charitable—"

"What?" Lauren interrupted. She hadn't known until this moment that people could hear, as well as see, red. She felt perspiration begin to sprout under her arms. "So you don't think I worked hard through school and at Thomas Industries before you forced me to quit? I thought I made a significant contribution before we began fucking. At least that's what Dennis, my boss, said. And do you honestly believe I don't take my producing seriously? I would be out there hustling more if I didn't have so many goddamned obligations to you!"

"Forget it." Ed was returning the art to its original place. "Let's do this later."

"I'm not forgetting this conversation. I may be many things, but I am not a dilettante. I'm starting a new career. It takes time to build. I would appreciate a little more support from you." Lauren tried to calm herself, but she felt a deep-seated frustration. Ed was typically more patient and certainly more loving. He was treating her like a spoiled brat.

"Look, baby, like I said, let's do this later. It's been a long day. I'm tired, you're tired. Let's go have a drink upstairs." This was Ed's usual strategy whenever they had an argument. He would blame the argument on fatigue, overwork, or underwork rather than legitimate emotions.

"I'm not tired," Lauren retorted. Her feelings were hurt, and a panicky feeling was creeping into her subconscious.

Tilting his head, Ed gave her a sloe-eyed, sideways grin. "Hey, you know what? You turn me on when you get all hot and passionate like that. Come on over here." He stepped toward her and pulled her close to him, hugging her tight.

"You may think playing with my feelings is cute, but I don't." Lauren pushed him away and headed out. Ed locked up the room, threw on the alarm, and quickly followed.

"I'm sorry. I didn't mean to hurt your feelings. You know I love you. You're my baby. Nobody can touch you. Especially not Tandy Brooks. I get mad when I hear you compare yourself to her. You are already way ahead of her."

Softening at his compliments, Lauren began to relax. In the elevator, she allowed Ed to hug her from behind, pressing his hardness up against her backside, sliding his large hands from her hips up her body, cupping her breasts as he gently tugged at her nipples.

"Stop! The doormen will see from the cameras." She giggled.

"I don't care! You're my wife. I can do what I want," came his response as he kissed her cheek, leaning his head down. Feeling her body respond to his touch, she was happy when the door opened onto their apartment. She was not interested in giving the doormen a show. Plus she was confused. Ed had seemed so terse. Maybe it was as he had said—he was simply annoyed at her admiration of Tandy—or maybe there was something else. But as they walked into their living room, Ed grabbed Lauren's hand in his and pulled her toward the staircase. At the base of the steps, he placed his mouth over hers and gave her a kiss that was delicious, with the extra spice of his soft tongue dancing over her lips. As all of the anger and anxiety left her, her body and spirit trusted his touch, temporarily forgetting his formerly harsh demeanor.

TWENTY-FOUR

THE pain in his stomach was almost unbearable. He sat on the toilet retching as sweat poured from his armpits and his forehead. He was clammy and sick. *Making money should not be this hard,* Manny thought.

Tandy had called with the date for him to meet Dana Trip's spiritual adviser. For five million dollars, a day at the spa would be worth it, Manny had thought. He had no idea what was in store for him.

When they arrived at the very exclusive spa on Fifty-seventh Street at the corner of Madison, Manny was actually looking forward to the day of pampering. A sauna and a massage were just what he needed to relax his overworked muscles. The spa itself was decorated with warm woods and soft lighting. There were no windows, and a multitude of fragrant candles contributed to a sexy, relaxed, calming atmosphere.

Together, Manny, Tandy, and Dana sat in the lounge area sipping a warm, bitter tea. When Manny first sampled the concoction, he was repulsed by the unpleasant scent and taste. He quickly returned his cup to the table. Dana, however, drank hers down. Tandy also had no problem swallowing the drink. The two women then turned to Manny and waited for him to follow suit. Thinking again of the money he was about to make, he took a breath and choked down every drop. Their toga-clad hostess then instructed them to go into private rooms and change into a fluffy terry-cloth robe. Manny noted that this was how the truly rich lived. He had visited ritzy spas like Bliss and Elizabeth Arden. This place was on an entirely different level. Even his five million wouldn't buy dollars this long, though he would definitely be moving up in the world.

When he got out to the next room, a communal massage area, Dana was already seated, waiting for him and Tandy and the masseuses. Dana was not a bad-looking woman, Manny thought. She was in great shape for fifty years of wear and tear. She clearly took care of herself with the gym and the surgeon's knife. She had explained to Manny that she did not want to discuss any business until their day had ended and they were all clean. She also wanted to reserve her thoughts until Shuram stopped by, which would be after all of their treatments. Whatever. Just as long as she signed the net-exclusive, as Tandy had promised, Manny didn't care if he had to be massaged all day and meet the Dalai Lama.

Manny had not understood, however, exactly what a Shuram Alita cleansing was. Tandy had told him he would spend a day in the spa getting rubdowns and sweating on Dana's tab. But the massage, even though it was full-body, had focused in large part on the abdominal area. After a good five minutes of rubbing, the gases in his stomach began to churn. He felt hot bubbles move around, and then he felt gripping pains. The masseuse continued rubbing, despite Manny's protests that he was not feeling well.

"You are fine. This is how it begins. Just relax," came the response.

Dana offered comfort as well: "Manny, you will feel better after you go to the bathroom. Just be sure to sit there and wait until you are all cleaned out, otherwise you will have to go again and again."

Manny was in for a colonic, and Tandy had not told him. Was she aware that this was what they would be doing? Judging by her cool demeanor, this was a regular day for her. Had he known he was to participate in a group colonic, he never would have come.

Finally, the massage was over, and he was able to go to the bathroom, barely in time, to relieve himself. Oh, the pain of his grumbling stomach. It felt like there was glass buried in his colon. He couldn't believe Tandy had fooled him into this sick ritual.

At last he had nothing left to expel from his body. Weak and spent, Manny made his way toward the next treatment, hoping he would be able to truly relax and rest and gather his strength. To his dismay, the next course was not rest but yoga. His initial thought was *Good;* a nice stretch would keep his tummy calm.

Dana and Tandy contorted their bodies this way and that, looking very serious as they followed the lead of their instructor. Manny tried to joke about how hungry he was and how his legs wouldn't follow what he was telling them. Neither Tandy nor Dana laughed or appeared amused. "Manny, please try to focus" was all the instructor said.

"Okay," Manny remarked sullenly, thinking that everyone here besides him was crazy. Again he had to remind himself that this sacrifice was for a good cause. Five million dollars was worth any insanity.

The final treatment of the day was a communal aromatherapy seaweed wrap. Despite the fact that these three people were fully naked in the same room, they were unseen by one another as each of their technicians rubbed them down with warm green goo. The fragrant scents of oil and spice filled the room, then they were covered with warm electric blankets and told to remain like that for twenty minutes.

After five minutes, Manny had had enough. Even though he was lying down, he was beginning to feel lightheaded and weak all over again. How these women went through this process without seeming to suffer in the least was beyond him. They were made of a different cloth, tough and strong. The cleansing process seemed to be more of an endurance test than anything else, and Manny thought he was sure to fail. He could not take one more wacky treatment or drink. He needed food. A Big Mac and a large order of fries were all he could think about. Tandy and her crazy concepts. What if he just bolted? He knew the answer to that. Dana would not sign a net-exclusive if Manny could not survive a cleansing. And besides, who did he think he was, trying to play in the big leagues? He really was just a salesman. He was beginning to consider the possibility that his life, as simple and ordinary as it was, might be his destiny, his fate. His thoughts were interrupted by the spa attendant, who told him that after they showered off the green goo, they would be served lunch and be joined by Shuram Alita. Food!

Manny wanted to get a moment alone with Tandy, to see how she thought things were going, but she was always with Dana and gave him no indication that she, too, thought the whole production was overkill. He was amazed at her ability to act completely engrossed in the process. Dana probably believed that Tandy bought into this type of spa treatment—spiritual supervision. Tandy was good at playing different roles. Manny just wanted to go home.

"Shuram. Blessings." Dana bowed and showed great deference to her guru, who turned out to be not only a Westerner but a six-foot-tall middle-aged man sporting a slick precision four-hundred-dollar haircut who, beneath his long mauve tunic, was, Manny could swear by his accent, a native New Yorker with the gravelly voice of a smoker, or at least a former smoker. But Dana either saw past the man's artifice or was completely out of her mind and desperate to believe in something.

"My Dana. How was the cleansing?" He spoke to her from his pillowed seat at the table, set for four, as if he were her father.

"So satisfying." Dana beamed. She truly looked refreshed and glowing. Manny knew that he was not glowing. He probably looked ashen, and he felt dehydrated. He had tried to drink water after every treatment, but it had not been enough.

"Shuram, please meet my friend Tandy and her friend Manny." Dana held her arms out toward Manny and Tandy like Vanna White pointing at the Wheel of Fortune.

"Ahh, Tandy, so nice to meet you. Dana speaks so well of you." Shuram almost seemed to be flirting. Maybe he was one of those fake gurus who slept with all his female idolaters, Manny thought.

Shuram turned his gaze on Manny. "Did you like the cleansing?"

Yeah, right, how ironic, Manny thought, since his stomach muscles were still strained from the morning's gripping pains. "Well, I've never done anything quite like it before. And I must say, I am a whole lot cleaner than when I came here this morning." Manny chuckled, trying to keep the mood light. Shuram studied him a moment and then laughed along. With this approval, Dana allowed herself to laugh. Tandy gave Manny a smirk that said, "You'd better not fuck up this deal." Manny heard her, loud and clear.

Much to his disappointment, lunch was not extensive. They had a clear broth that tasted like hot water flavored with cilantro or basil or some other unidentifiable herb, and a plain salad with lemon. They were also served water with a slice of lemon. Manny was famished and cranky. He wanted real food. He had been at this spa for six hours and had had enough of Dana and her weird guru guy, who did not speak to anyone after the introductions. Following his lead, Dana did not speak, and falling in line behind her, Tandy didn't say a word. Manny knew from the looks Tandy was giving him that he was not to say anything, either.

After Shuram finished his meal, he asked if Manny had brought the papers that Dana needed to sign. Manny excused himself and ran quickly back to his dressing room to retrieve the net-exclusive agreement that he and Tandy had drafted, along with the power of attorney. Shuram studied the papers, whispered to Dana, and left the room. One glance at Tandy, and Manny knew her facade was about to crack. She looked desperate to know which way the day had gone. Dana did not hold them in limbo for long. She announced that Shuram had felt the energy was good among Tandy, Manny, and herself. She was permitted to sign. Clearly, he was a fake, Manny realized, if he thought Tandy had good energy. But Tandy was a pro, Manny reminded himself.

Dana signed every page that Manny pointed out for her. She hardly read a word. Apparently, Shuram's blessing was really enough for her. Contract in hand, Manny hurriedly got dressed. In his haste to leave the spa, he did not hear the warning to eat small, light meals and broth. He went to the nearest McDonald's. As soon as he finished his burger and fries, he was sick all over again. But Manny was feeling no real pain. Step one of his plan to jump from salesman to real estate developer was in place. Getting the net-exclusive had not been all that bad. Now he had to make sure Lauren came through for him.

WHO would have thought that little Lauren Martin would one day be in a position to purchase anything for forty million dollars?

But here Lauren was, inspecting the five-story prewar building that she intended to buy for a museum that would carry the names of her and her husband. However, instead of feeling elated, she had a sense of dread and emptiness. Despite the fact that Lauren would do all of the work in purchasing the building, leasing or transferring it to the museum, and organizing the new children's program, she still felt she wasn't in charge of her own life. How had she ended up here? Notwithstanding her efforts to avoid spending time and energy on the causes of others, she had still been roped into working on the museum. Well, she'd try to look at the upside: She would be able to work with her idol, Tandy Brooks. And at least she could feel good about the cause: She would be helping the children of Harlem for generations to come.

"Lauren, this is the inspector, Charles Dugitt. I found him inside, already going through the property." Manny was always so helpful. He was more than a broker; he was an escort, a decorator, an assistant, a buffer, whatever Lauren needed at the moment. With her dwindling list of friends, she appreciated Manny's southern-gentlemanly companionship, as well as the part of him that was her hanging-out friend.

The inspector said, "Mrs. Thomas, the building is in pretty good condition. There are a few items I should mention to you. I'll put everything in the report, but I should show you the basement. There has been some recent water leakage in there."

"That's not good. We need the basement for storage of art. If there's a chance that the works could get damaged down there, then we will have to find something else."

Manny spoke up quickly, in his role as Mr. Helpful. "I wouldn't worry too much about that, Lauren. We can always have the walls sealed and protected."

"Sure, the walls could be protected, but I'll show you so you know what you're up against," the inspector insisted.

Manny handed Lauren a layout sheet of the building as they entered. The first floor had been a large retail space. Lauren began envisioning the museum in the vast open area, eighteen-foot ceilings with original dentil moldings and plaster relief work of flowers and cherubs. As they moved up the stairs, she saw room for art geared toward children, including interactive exhibits. On the floors above were residential tenants. Their presence would give the museum a more community-based feeling, at least initially. The rent would go to the museum. The space was perfect. But if the basement had water issues, there would indeed be a problem. As if reading her thoughts, the inspector suggested they head downstairs.

"You see this white mark. This is where the water reached sometime within the last six months." He was pointing at a white line on the wall that was about waist-high.

"You're saying the water came that high?" Lauren questioned.

"For sure," came his reply.

"But to seal the walls and floor, they could use special sealant, or even go over the walls and floors with concrete, couldn't they?" Manny asked.

"Fixing problems is not my specialty, but that sounds all right, depending on the underlying circumstances. If the unseen foundation erodes, then eventually, the water would break down the new concrete. You would have to watch the sealed area regularly and carefully."

"But there is a solution to this issue," Manny continued.

"Seems possible." The inspector shrugged.

Once he was gone, Lauren and Manny lingered on the first floor, Lauren memorizing the interior's details.

"I am so proud of you, Miss Lauren," Manny offered. "I think this is the perfect platform for you."

"Do you?" Lauren slyly responded. "And what's your platform? What's the perfect one for you?" She was getting sick and tired of everyone thinking she needed something to do, when in fact she had a plan for herself that was already in motion. She had not foreseen the huge net that her marriage would place over her.

"Oh, I'm just a lowly real estate broker, I don't need a platform," Manny joked in his usual self-deprecating fashion.

"Your false humility is not cute," Lauren retorted as they exited and got into the chauffeured Suburban. Manny instructed the driver to head back toward Lauren's neighborhood, to Sixty-third and Madison. "Let's go to Bilboquet," he suggested to Lauren. "I feel as though we should celebrate."

"Celebrate? Celebrate what? How do we know she will even accept our offer?"

"I have a good feeling about this. You will buy that building. I know this deal is going through."

"What makes you so sure?" Lauren asked as she watched Park Avenue change from empty trash-filled lots and boarded-up tenements to swanky, well-kept apartment buildings and manicured medians.

"I just am," he said, smiling.

MANNY sat in the ostentatiously decorated living room. The grotesque sounds coming from the bedroom made him want to squirm. He could only assume the "Aww, shit! Damn, baby!" noises were from Ed, though the guttural sounds clashed with everything Manny knew about Ed and certainly ran counter to anything he had ever heard escape Ed's mouth. Manny wished he had waited downstairs in the car while Alyssia and Ed said their good-byes in the temporary apartment where Ed had put her up and apparently enjoyed visiting. But when Manny had called to tell her he was waiting downstairs, she insisted that he come upstairs and let himself in. Now, he realized with a sick feeling, she was purposely flaunting her relationship in Manny's face.

Fifteen minutes later, Ed ambled into the foyer. Manny wondered if Ed even realized he was sitting across the room in the diminutive Louis XV chair. Ed stood adjusting his tie in the gilded mirror, still warm from his romp. Funny, Manny thought, Ed was the one who had just been in the next room fucking his mistress while his wife's best friend was listening a few feet away, but somehow Manny was the one who felt like disappearing into the shiny goose-down pillows. Ed had that effect on people. Manny was certain Ed knew his power, since he behaved like a shepherd with the rest of the world as his sheep. After all, hadn't he shepherded Manny into betraying Lauren? He certainly had fed Manny that crock of shit about Alyssia being a nice, hardworking kid he was just trying to help. Yeah, she worked hard, all right. She worked her body hard fucking Ed. Manny averted his eyes when Ed noticed him. He briefly looked surprised, but that expression quickly turned to one of composure as he said, "Hello, Manny."

Manny returned the greeting.

"Lauren was impressed with the Sugar Hill Building. How's that going?"

"Mrs. Trip accepted the foundation's offer," Manny lied. Dana had never received the forty-million-dollar offer from Ed and Lauren's foundation. He had simply conveyed to Dana that she would receive the thirty million dollars she was seeking.

"Good, good," Ed said, buttoning his navy three-button suit coat. "This project should keep Lauren occupied."

Manny stared straight ahead, biting his tongue to keep from saying, "Yeah, so you can remain occupied with your sidepiece." But Ed was smart. He had raised the subject of the big real estate deal to remind Manny that it could blow up in his face if he did not handle matters with Alyssia discreetly.

"I have to get to another meeting now. We'll speak later," Ed said over his shoulder as he headed out the door. Manny wondered if Ed was completely delusional, claiming he had to get to *another* meeting. As if what he had just been doing with Alyssia were business. Did he think Manny was a complete idiot? Or maybe he simply did not care. Why should he? Manny had, after all, agreed to do Ed's dirty work. For a flicker of a second, Manny wondered if he was playing himself for a fool, but he did not have time to give it much thought.

Alyssia bounded into the living room, obviously fresh from a shower and half-clothed, wearing only skintight lace-up brown corduroys and a tan silk bra. Manny marveled at her rippling stomach muscles and bulging biceps as she pulled a white Lycra T-shirt over her head. She smelled like she had just scrubbed herself with Zest, but something about her still seemed unclean, almost seedy. What she had just been doing with Ed hit too close to home for Manny in more ways than one. He regarded Alyssia and tried to figure out what struck him as odd. Maybe her lopsided mouth and her hard jaw were the culprits, or maybe it was the green scrunchy she used to pull her dripping-wet hair back into a ponytail that left the ends hanging like a rat's tail. She should have been beautiful, but something rang false. Again he could not help but think she was tacky. Lauren had so much more class and beauty. What was Ed thinking? Why was he risking everything he had with Lauren for Alyssia? Why was Manny, for that matter?

"I told you I'd look you up," Alyssia began with a self-satisfied smirk as she pulled on suede stiletto boots. "Well, I had Ed contact you."

Her commanding manner was not lost on Manny. All he could do was glance at his watch once again and see that they were thirty minutes behind schedule.

"We're a bit late for the first appointment, and I haven't been able to reach the broker on her cell, so we should probably get moving," Manny said as gently as possible.

The way Alyssia rolled her neck and eyes at him, one would have thought he had cursed her mama's name. "Get moving? Get moving?" She began in a high, screeching voice. "My man is paying three million dollars for my apartment, and you're tellin' me to get moving? I'm no fool. Ed told me the real estate market was flat now. Shit, whoever is waiting for us should stand there all day if it means a sale."

Manny took a deep breath. "Take all the time you need. I did not mean to pressure you."

"Hmmph, I didn't think you did." She pulled a pack of cigarettes out of a large suede sack and lit one.

Alyssia the dancer smoked. That was like a distance runner smoking. How disgusting. Manny watched her take a long drag. Suddenly, dragging on the Marlboro Light, she looked so much older than her twenty-two years. Manny knew she was from the streets of Compton and was considered a prodigy, but he wondered what her days had been like before her dancing skills catapulted her out of the ghetto. Her hardened gaze gave him the sense that she had seen a lot more than most people would understand. There was something familiar in the dark brown eyes, something he saw in the mirror, something he did not like.

After taking her sweet time filling her lungs with smoke, Alyssia sauntered over to Manny and looked him up and down like she wanted to fight. She said, "You might as well lose the uptight Negro act with me. You're not foolin' nobody. You and I are one and the same."

"Excuse me?" Manny was taken aback. True, he was doing Ed a favor, but that did not translate into him being a punching bag for this gutter rat. He didn't care if she was a prima ballerina.

"I think we both know what I'm talkin' about. You sitting up here looking at me like you're so much better. Like I'm so beneath you just 'cause you've latched on to these rich people. Anybody can look at you and figure out inside of ten seconds that you're not one of them."

Manny could not believe the way this girl was reading him. And what the hell did she know about him, other than what Ed may have told her? Furthermore, what had he done to bring on her wrath?

"Listen, I'm simply here to show you real estate. If you have a problem with me, we can cancel."

"No, I think you're the one who has the problem with me. Ed told me you're his wife's friend. And now you're here giving me looks like I'm in the wrong. If Lauren wasn't so damn stiff and took care of her daddy's needs, he wouldn't be beggin' on my doorstep. So don't look at me like I'm at fault. Ed Thomas chased me. Ed had me move here. You get it? He came after me, and I give him what he needs. Not his wife, your friend." Alyssia was acting like he was a personal proxy for Lauren, bound to repeat verbatim anything she said.

"Well, since you brought it up, Lauren is a friend. But what you and Ed do is your business."

"A business you don't have a problem profiting from, friend or no friend of the wife, I see. You're no different than me."

Clearly, Alyssia was trying to get a rise out of Manny, but he refused to allow her under his skin. "Do you feel uncomfortable going to look for property with me because of my friendship with Lauren? Is that what you're trying to tell me?"

Alyssia moved inches from Manny's face. He could smell the disgusting smoke on her breath as she spit out, "I don't ever feel uncomfortable with the help."

No, she did not! Manny's fist involuntarily formed into a ball. He put it in the pocket of his fitted navy blue raw silk jacket to keep it under wraps. This bitch wanted to get clocked. He had to control himself. How could he show her property after the way she'd talked to him?

But she wasn't finished. "The only difference between me and Lauren is the Mrs. in front of her name, the MBA behind it, and a few more dollars in between." And then she had the nerve to break into a smile. "So, you ready to find me my castle?"

What the hell had he gotten himself into? Manny thought about the way his house would look when the renovations were done to calm himself. No one would treat him this way when he had money in the bank. But first he'd have to tear out another piece of himself to pay his high-society dues.

Roxy Nixon sat in Tandy's living room, busily taking notes as Tandy threw ideas her way.

"Tandy Brooks has spearheaded the revival of art in Harlem, U.S.A., with the introduction of the new children's wing at the Museum of Harlem." Tandy stood, her hands flying as she spoke, her energy high. "How do you think that sounds?"

Roxy looked up from her notepad. "This is a great position for you. I like the idea of you working for the children of Harlem. We can link this to your past work with women and children, indicating that you were working toward this goal all along."

"With the museum's limited funds in the past, we were restricted to only a few programs, but now that my dear friends the Thomases have come on board, we can add the children's wing, something I've personally wanted to do for years. And you can quote me on that." Tandy laughed. She intended to receive lots of publicity for her work on the museum, leaving no room for Lauren's public relations. Lauren hated publicity, anyway; at least that was what she claimed.

Life was looking up. It seemed ironic to Tandy that after so many years of working for the museum, giving tens of thousands of dollars and count-less hours of her time, it would be the catalyst to put her back on the map.

"I'll send out queries to *Essence, Glamour, W, Town and Country,* and *Vogue.* Again, I think the local magazines and papers like *The New York Observer* or *New York* magazine would be ideal for you. Helping children and reviving impoverished neighborhoods is always good press. Everybody feels good. Everybody looks good. We will definitely get coverage." Roxy continued to make notes.

Tandy's thoughts were coming fast. "The photo shoot should capture me surrounded by children from the neighborhood as we do some kind of messy art project. I want to give the impression that not only do I give my money and time, I get involved as well. You know, not afraid to get my hands dirty. The public eats that up."

"That's really good!" Roxy could not write fast enough.

This past year had been difficult. But what doesn't kill you makes you stronger, Tandy thought. She was feeling strong. Though life had presented a few obstacles, by staying true to herself and her solid instinct to survive, Tandy would once again come out on top. Nothing and no one could hold her down for long.

TWENTY-EIGHT

MANNY's cell chirped once again as he was set to begin his second set of abs, an area he never overlooked during his rigorous workout regimen. He was poised to kick his legs into the air, and Lauren would push them back toward the ground. He would do twelve repetitions, never allowing his feet to touch the ground. He could not stand when a man reached his mid-thirties and developed a pouch and a slouch. Those traits equaled a lethal combination. Abruptly, he pulled the phone from underneath his gym towel.

"You're not going to answer that, are you?" Lauren probed. "You begged me to come all the way up to your gym, and all you've done is talk on your phone."

Manny ignored her annoyed tone. He was too embarrassed to tell her the real reason he was so pressed to answer his phone—he was waiting for Trenton to call him back. His boyfriend had supposedly spent the night out at a buddy's place after drinking too much, and Manny was worried. Despite the fact that Lauren obviously had issues in her own relationship, Manny never liked to appear insecure. Part of his appeal, he thought, was that he was always pulled together. He had learned during his years of sell-ing real estate that no one really wanted to hear about anyone else's prob-lems, especially from someone who was supposed to be servicing them. It was always better to be the listener than the complainer. He also did not want to seem dependent on anyone else, even if he was in the business of service. He had too much pride to admit that this young boyfriend had him strung out like a crack addict waiting for the next hit.

Anxiously flipping open his phone, he expected to hear Trenton's raspy voice. His hopes were dashed as soon as Coffee said, "Hey, Manny!"

Attempting to match her enthusiasm, Manny returned the greeting and waited for her to get to the point quickly, as she usually did, since she had such a busy life being a socialite, philanthropist, and all. "Darryl and I really like the Olympic Tower penthouse, but as Niche mentioned, we're going to need our psychic to view it before we make a final decision."

"When do you want to come?" Manny did not even bother to ask for an explanation about the psychic. Between the personal photographer, feng shui specialist, and traveling publicist, the Rayes' antics had ceased to sur-prise him.

"As soon as possible," Coffee said.

"How about later this afternoon, early evening?" Manny suggested, hoping she was as anxious to close the deal as she sounded.

"No, we have our Read to Achieve fund-raiser fashion show tonight. Aren't you coming to see your man?"

"My man? Trenton?" Manny was confused.

"Yes, he's in our show."

"Oh, yeah, yeah, that's right. I forgot. I'm not sure if I'll be able to make it," Manny lied, knowing full well he wouldn't miss the show for anything, especially since Trenton had purposely neglected to invite him.

"I'd love you to come as my guest. I'll have my assistant call you later and fill you in on the particulars. Oh, and could you maybe bring Lauren Thomas? We sent her an invitation, but I'm not sure if she received it. Any-way, how's tomorrow to see the apartment?"

"That's fine, let's talk in the morning to figure out a time." Manny said his good-byes and, without a word to Lauren, put his phone back and began the ab exercises. Of course Coffee wanted Manny to bring Lauren. Mrs. Lauren Thomas was a true socialite, and her mere presence at the Rayes' undoubtedly urban event would bring credibility. But Manny was not going to mention the event to Lauren. When he showed up tonight, he didn't want anyone who was close to him present in case some drama popped off with Trenton.

Lauren was doing crunches on the mat next to him. Exercise was the last thing on Manny's mind now. He wanted to know where Trenton was and why he hadn't told him about being in Coffee and Darryl's fashion show.

"Manny? Manny?"

"Yeah."

"You all right?" Lauren asked as the sweat streamed down her temples.

"I'm fine." Manny put a smile on his face. "Just these crazy-ass clients. You know Coffee and Darryl Raye? They want to bring a psychic back to an apartment I showed them." How small New York was, Manny thought: the apartment Coffee and Darryl were interested in was across the hall from Lauren's husband's love den.

Lauren stopped. "A psychic?"

"You heard right," Manny absently said. His mind was still on Trenton.

"What for?"

"Huh?"

"Why do they want a psychic?"

"I didn't even ask. I'll just be glad when they close."

"Didn't Tandy tell you they were a little nutty?"

"Yeah, she did. Maybe I should've listened to her." Manny felt tired, despite the four Diet Fuel energy pills he had ingested only an hour before. He had to get in touch with Trenton. He stood up abruptly, leaving Lauren on the mat. "Come on, let's do the ab machine."

Lauren glanced at him oddly. "You sure you're okay?"

No, he was not okay. He had visions of Trenton snuggled in bed with another man. Even worse, he had pangs of guilt about Ed cheating on Lauren and the role he was playing in the whole affair. Strange, how you could be oblivious to the pain of others until that pain settled on you. Was this the self-absorption of people in general, Manny wondered, or only New Yorkers? One thing was certain: Manny had indeed become a New Yorker, and hadn't that been his goal? Not to be called a skinny country boy with flood pants and chipped yellow teeth. To blend in, to dine at the tables of the African-American elite.

Lauren extended her hand to Manny, and he pulled her to a standing position. They silently headed to the ab machine, amid the array of gay black men who congregated at the Harlem International gym, where Manny had been working out for over a decade. Manny hardly noticed the various men staring at him. His thoughts were far away from this high-tech mirrored meat market. He could not even enjoy the coup of having convinced Lauren here to show off in front of his queen friends who loved rich, beautiful Upper East Side women.

"Just think, Manny, after the closing of the Sugar Hill Building, you might find a new calling," Lauren offered in an obvious attempt to lift Manny's spirits.

The mention of the Sugar Hill deal at that moment made Manny skittish—another questionable endeavor in his life brought about by people he had long admired and whose favor he wanted to win.

"You know what I mean, Manny?"

They approached the steel apparatus. Manny sat down on the small, elevated leather bench and adjusted the weight to a hundred pounds. He then made sure the cushioned bar in front of him rested firmly above his abdomen and directly below his chest. Thrusting forward, he wanted to shut out the world. He hated these feelings. He would not be able to concentrate fully until he spoke to Trenton, got an explanation for his lover's behavior, heard whether or not the story rang true.

"Earth to Manny!" Lauren said before popping him in the back of his clean-shaven head.

"I'm sorry, I'm just dreading having to deal with the Rayes and their damn entourage again."

"Maybe after the Sugar Hill deal, the door will be open for you to broker more commercial deals, bigger deals. Then you won't have to deal with folks like the Rayes anymore. You could spend half your time down in South Beach and summer in the North. Isn't that what you wanted, to be a true man of leisure?"

"Maybe so," Manny said. She knew him well, if not as well as she thought. She did have a point, though. She was articulating what he was hoping would be the result of this deal, but he wanted to downplay his plan until after the closing. No need to bring any unnecessary attention to it.

Lauren pushed Manny off the seat, took her place at the ab machine, and adjusted the weight to forty pounds. "'Maybe so?" she incredulously asked. "Manny, do you realize what a big deal this is? Not that you weren't already successful, but this is going to firmly put Marks Realty on the map. You'll be taken seriously by the heavy hitters in the real estate world, the business world, and the cultural world. This means so much to the museum, not to mention to Ed's and my charitable arts trust. So don't stress over the Rayes."

Manny suppressed the lump forming in his throat. Lauren really seemed happy for him. Despite his occasionally feeling like her personal gofer, she had been a true friend. She had always looked out for him, tried to help him whenever the opportunity arose. He glanced at her and then averted his gaze. He couldn't look her in the eyes. He toyed with the idea of breaking down and telling her everything—about Alyssia, the illegal net-exclusive deal that would give him and Tandy ten million dollars of Lauren's and Ed's money. He wanted to tell her all of it, but that wouldn't accomplish anything. Ed would lie his way out of the whole mess, and Tandy would never speak to Manny again. He had reached the point of no return. Besides, he was betting that Lauren would never find out. And once he found the apartment for Alyssia and the Sugar Hill deal closed, he would be on the straight and narrow path. Once they got through this period, he would never do anything else to jeopardize his friendship with Lauren, would never do anything that would make it difficult for him to look another person in the eye.

TWENTY-NINE

MANNY felt ancient standing amid the hip-hoppers, rappers, and twenty-one-year-old music executives. He had arrived moments before at Coffee and Darryl Raye's Read to Achieve benefit fashion show at Chelsea Piers on the Hudson River. He felt queasy. If Coffee had not reached him on his cell, he never would have known about Trenton's involvement in the event. When Manny had impulsively called Trenton to find out why he had not been invited, Trenton had the nerve to act like it was no big deal. "I didn't think you'd like the crowd, but you know if you want to come, I'd love for you to be there." Manny desperately wanted to believe he was being truthful. The alternative was more than Manny could handle.

Hurt feelings aside, Trenton had been right about the people at the event, Manny thought as he was shoved aside by an obese Hawaiian man who resembled a sumo wrestler, obviously someone's bodyguard. "Comin' through, comin' through. I got Dime Dog here!" the big fellow was shouting to the restless crowd. "Yo, pops, yo, pops! I got Dime Dog here. I asked you nicely to step aside. Could you please clear the way? You know who

I got?" the large man said again, this time looking directly at Manny. Yes, Manny knew who Dime Dog was. Everyone who owned a radio or a television was familiar with the diminutive reigning rap king, record-label owner, film producer, and now clothing designer. But what Manny was not used to was being called "pops." Sure, he may not have been attired in urban gear—baggy pants, Timberland boots, and NBA jersey—but he certainly did not look old enough to be anybody's daddy. He was a professional man. He had arrived straight from his office wearing a shirt, tie, and overcoat, and at best he looked out of place. But he was sharp. These people were the ones with no style. Still, as Manny looked around, he realized they were probably thinking the same thing about him.

Manny distastefully watched the king of rap, Dime Dog, bounce by inside a circular wall of moving body armor. He was over the top, with his crew of protection escorting him front and center of the standing-room-only crowd. Manny wondered if the rapper was on the program. He had enough people guarding him to make up a whole band—hell, a whole orchestra.

Across the warehouse-sized room, Manny spotted Coffee and Darryl Raye. As usual, they were surrounded by flashing bulbs and an entourage. Was that what truly "making it" meant? Being acknowledged by the media and then the public? Inventing a persona in New York City could be easy for some, and for others a most difficult task. Coffee and Darryl had made a career out of creating themselves, their image. They navigated between two worlds, hip-hop fabulousness and the African-American bourgeois; and though they seemed to fit in nowhere, remaining on the surface of each, their money gained them access to both. Manny wondered if public adoration made them happy.

Coffee was wearing a burgundy jersey halter minidress that clung in the right places. Manny watched her silhouette in the New Jersey skyline as the sun continued its descent. She reminded Manny of Nefertiti, with her long, graceful neck and smooth ebony skin. She turned away from her fans for a moment and peered out the window. This was the first time he had seen her guard come down. He was curious about what she was thinking. Her view was west of the Hudson, but that horizon did not count, in Manny's opinion. East of the Hudson was the world that mattered. Everyone in this room, Manny surmised, was working to live east of the Hudson, on the island of Manhattan. The small rectangular piece of concrete, steel, and man-made green parks was unlike any other. Here, anyone could re-create themselves with a good hustle and the right acquaintances.

Manny surveyed the room again as the lights were dimmed, then turned back up, then dimmed again, an indication that the overdue fashion show was about to begin. He wondered what all of these people wanted, what they were looking for. Were they so different from him, despite their appearance? He spotted five or six young men and women who looked like extras for rap-video shoots feverishly typing away on their two-way pagers. Several others were bobbing their heads to the rap music. Some were on cell phones, some socializing, but they all looked lost to Manny, as if they were running in a hamster's wheel, chasing a plastic carrot. One thing was certain: Manny's life was starting to feel like smoke and mirrors, and discerning what was real had become increasingly difficult.

Manny thought about his own risky climb just to get where he was: how Alexander had taken him in and helped him carve a niche for himself, and how he was now helping Trenton. Alexander had basically taken Manny out of the gutter when he was only twenty years old. Manny had an epiphany right there, in the middle of a hip-hop scene—he was replaying what Alexander had done for him, only this time he was in Alexander's role, and Trenton was the young lover. Trenton, so much like Manny all those years ago, seemed poised to move on once his modeling career picked up and he got back on his feet. Maybe Manny deserved to be left behind.

Alexander's apartment was one of two on the seventh floor of the Sixty-eighth Street and Fifth Avenue prewar building. Manny heard Marvin

Gaye's silky voice in the hall as soon as the elevator doors opened. He dreaded entering the apartment after the blissful day he'd had selling exquisite items at Tiffany, a job Alexander had set up for him when the modeling and acting did not pan out. Manny had come a long way from the skinny eighteen-year-old who had shown up in his cousin Tommy's stairwell. He half wondered if he simply didn't have what it took to make it as a model—or had Alexander, the half-assed agent, screwed things up for him? Shortly after moving into the plush apartment, Manny learned that the talent agency was just one of Alexander's many bright ideas that his trust-fund money financed. Apparently, he had a new business venture every year. When the agency idea folded, Alexander convinced Manny that he could turn himself into a totally new person with the right clothes, attitude, and charm. After extensive etiquette tutoring and a new wardrobe, Alexander told Manny that Tiffany was the perfect place to start fresh.

Manny discovered that Alexander was right, especially since he gave Manny a jump start by referring several Upper East Side friends. Manny also realized that he was a natural for Tiffany, charming people with his southern drawl, engaging smile, and sharp wit. Of course, the crisp custom-made shirts and suits that Alexander had insisted on buying him didn't hurt, either. Things were working out so well for Manny. One of his regular clients suggested that he try selling real estate at her boutique firm. She had more business than she could handle, and if he took the short real estate course and passed the state exam, he could make a lot of money. Manny was grateful to Alexander. That was why he was dreading opening the door to the eight-room apartment, with its eclectic, elegant decor, that he had shared with Alexander for the past three years, first as his client, then his lover.

"I ordered suuuushi!" Alexander sang out before Manny had the opportunity to remove his coat. "Then we can watch *My Fair Lady*," he excitedly continued. Alexander had turned into a perverted housewife. Once he shut the doors of his talent agency, and their relationship turned intimate, he had focused all of his energy on cultivating Manny. But tonight Manny couldn't muster up enough enthusiasm to respond. The last thing he wanted was raw fish. Then Alexander would want to top off the evening by giving Manny a blow job. And that damn movie! They had been watching *My Fair Lady* once a month since he moved in with Alexander. Manny had only recently convinced Alexander to stop calling him his little Eliza Doolittle. Alexander found the pet name cute, especially when they were in the presence of his Faulkner- and Byron-reading prep school friends.

Manny pretended not to hear Alexander as he went into the bedroom and removed his clothes and threw on some sweatpants and a T-shirt.

"Maaanny, Maaanny!" Alexander called as he appeared in their bedroom, pale and dewy, pouch protruding from beneath his turquoise kimono. His face was shiny, and his brows furrowed when he saw Manny. "Didn't you hear me?"

"No," Manny lied as he searched for a pair of matching sweat socks in the bamboo dresser Alexander had picked up during one of his many overseas trips. He had so much time on his hands and so little drive to do anything other than dote on Manny and sit on his shrink's couch. Manny often wondered if Alexander was acting out any remaining remnants of ambition through Manny.

Ignoring Manny's indifferent tone, Alexander said, "Well, I've got sushi. And where's my kiss, mister?" He tapped his wooden-clog-clad foot, looking like a shadow of the person Manny had fallen for three years before. His once fair hair was limp and lifeless; his bright eyes had become resigned and possessive; and his thin physique had become thick around the middle: the picture of a man who had let himself go.

The last thing Manny was thinking about was giving Alexander a kiss, or anything else. He wanted to get to the gym, Man Country, and meet up with the fine brother he had been flirting with for the past two weeks. He was getting horny, and Alexander was no longer his first choice. Manny needed someone more masculine, stronger, sexier.

"Hey! You're not going to work out now, are you?" Alexander whined.

"Yeah. It's been kind of stressful at work lately. I need to get to the gym. Work off some tension."

"Stressful? At Tiffany?"

Clueless, Alexander strutted toward Manny like the sexiest man alive and said, "We could skip the movie if you want, and I'll help you work out your tension."

"I'll take a rain check," Manny said as he tried to move past Alexander, who looked like he was going to cry.

"You don't love me anymore, do you?" Alexander wailed. This was his line every time Manny went somewhere other than work. "Suds and Jack tried to tell me you're just using me until someone better comes along," he said, the tears coming fast now. Alexander also never failed to drag the opinions of his uptight older friends into every emotional encounter they had, as if Manny gave a damn what they thought.

"Have you taken your medicine today?"

"Oh, great! Now you want to drug me up, too. That's the same trick my parents always used to push me away." Alexander pouted and threw himself on the bed.

Manny shook his head at the formerly vibrant man sprawled across the white mink comforter, crying about his childhood. He had to get out of this relationship.

"I even put on *your kind* of music, and you can't stay with me," Alexander said, referring to the Marvin Gaye floating from the speakers.

Manny rolled his eyes and left the bedroom, but before he had made it halfway down the long hallway filled with Andy Warhol prints, Alexander was at his back, grabbing him around the waist.

"Don't go, Manny, please don't go. I didn't mean anything by the music comment. I would have bought Marvin Gaye even if you weren't black. Please don't go, Manny," he begged, holding Manny as if his life depended on the feel of his torso.

"Listen, I'll see you later tonight."

Even more desperate, Alexander asked, "Could I just give you a blow job before you go? Could I? I was thinking about you all day. God, I miss you so much when you're gone. You're going to leave me, aren't you? I know you are. I know you are." Alexander sank down to the floor in a jumbled heap.

"I'll see you later, Alexander."

"Should I even bother to wait up for you?"

Manny mouthed "No" as he reached the front door.

The next day, while Alexander was at his therapist's office for one of his thrice-weekly visits, Manny packed up all of his belongings and moved into a large studio on West End Avenue and Ninety-fifth Street. No amount of money in the world could have made him stay with Alexander one more day. Besides, Manny knew that with his success selling jewelry at Tiffany, he could just as easily sell the same people real estate. He was going to make his own money now, on his own terms. Manny felt a little guilt, but he had been in New York long enough to realize that it was about survival of the fittest in this town. And Alexander had lost his usefulness for Manny's evolution.

"Bitch! She a bitch, not my boo, she a bitch, not my boo!" One of Dime Dog's songs blared as the first models began walking down the runway, wearing leather and furs from—what else—Dime Dog's clothing line, Dimin'. Perfect to kick off a Read to Achieve fashion show, Manny thought. Keeping in step with the motley crowd, he bogarted his way closer to the stage, anxious to spot his "bitch." He wanted to have a perfect view of Trenton strutting his fine ass down the runway. Just as Manny got within a few feet of the fiberglass red-lit stage, Trenton walked out. He looked incredible in a pair of beige leather pants and a fox coat over his bare chest, pectorals oiled to perfection. Manny smiled proudly, watching his man work the crowd. He waited for Trenton to notice him and give a wink or some sign of recognition. That hope was quickly doused. When Trenton arrived at the tip of the runway, the only man he seemed to notice was Dime Dog. And if Manny was not mistaken, Dime Dog was eyeing Trenton as if he were wearing pork-chop underwear.

Survival of the fittest, Manny thought. He couldn't compete with Dime Dog even if he brokered fifty big deals in Harlem. Maybe Trenton was moving up the food chain, or maybe he had simply outgrown Manny. Whatever the case, with what little faith Manny had in God, he prayed that he still had his man's heart. The thought occurred to Manny that Alexander had felt the same way about him.

THIRTY

L AUREN had decided to find office space outside of her home. With the many philanthropic requests, the amount of work the museum would require, and her desire to build the film-producing business, she felt that working in an office would help her stay focused. She did not need a large area, just enough room for herself. When she mentioned this to Manny, he promised to find her the perfect place. After a couple of weeks of not getting a response from him, Lauren decided to pay him a visit and go through his computer database of listings herself. Manny was happy to oblige. When Lauren arrived, he was there with coffee, bagels, and the database ready to go.

"This one looks good: four hundred square feet, twenty-five hundred a month with shared switchboard, conference room, and other office services." Lauren read from the computer, taking small bites from her bagel. "How big is four hundred square feet?"

"Oh, probably about as big as this room, with a bit of the reception area out there," Manny answered.

"That's all I need," Lauren said thoughtfully.

"Why don't you get a space in Ed's building? I'm sure there is something on one of those forty-plus floors that he could let you have for free," Manny said.

"Oh, please. I would not want to be up under Ed. I need my own identity, my own space. If I were in his building, I would feel like he had yet another leash on me. Sometimes I just need to be free from anything connected to Ed Thomas. Sometimes I need to simply be Lauren. You know?" Lauren spoke earnestly. Lately, she had been feeling like she needed to strike out on her own more. Ed was hardly around, and when he was, he didn't act very nice or very interested. Lauren rationalized that if she threw herself into her work and separated it from home, she would not feel so alone. She had been married for four years. The honeymoon was over. They were entering into the phase during which they would settle down and things would not necessarily be as exciting. Now was the time for her to build her own career. Despite her occasional twinges at the sight of radiant pregnant women and angelic newborns, Lauren had convinced herself that not having children was okay, at least for now. Besides, it wasn't like Ed would have much time for a child, even if he did want one.

Lauren had learned a lot from Ed about hard work and tenacity. She aimed to put all of her smarts into becoming a successful producer. She would gain respect for her career and make a difference to society. She would not remain completely dependent on her husband for everything.

Lauren continued going through Manny's computer as he perused additional listings his assistant had pulled from the newspaper. They compared notes and made a list of properties for her to view.

The phone in Manny's office rang constantly. The assistant was busy taking messages, occasionally interrupting to see if Manny wanted to take a call from a particular client or broker. He was generally denying most calls, giving Lauren his full attention. One call disrupted the flow.

"Manny, Alyssia Banks is on the phone for you. Shall I put her through?" The chubby, redheaded, freckled assistant, Patrick, leaned through the door. Manny never had to worry about competition with Patrick. He served only to make Manny look better.

"No. Tell her I am out of the office and won't be back until tomorrow. I'll call her later. Do not give her my cell-phone number." Manny spoke quickly and with force, making it clear that he did not want to speak to this woman today under any circumstances.

"That's Alyssia Banks the dancer?" Lauren asked curiously.

"She is a dancer," Manny responded shortly and returned to the listings.

"We saw her picture in the paper, remember? She dances with the New York City Dance Company?" Lauren was surprised Manny did not recall this. He was usually on top of who's who.

"Oh, right." Manny was still tight-lipped.

"Remember, I told you Ed was on the board of the dance company?" Lauren did not understand how Manny could recall some things and totally forget others.

"Vaguely," came his empty response.

"Are you showing her apartments?"

"Yes."

Lauren wanted to know the entire story of how Manny had hooked up with Alyssia, how long he had known her, and what he thought of her. "How did you meet her, Manny?"

"We met through a mutual friend who works in costumes at the ballet," Manny lied.

"What kind of place is she looking for that you would take your time to show her?" Lauren knew that Manny dealt with only a certain caliber of property if he could help it. A dancer's salary would not put this woman among Manny's typical clientele.

"She wants something fairly modest in a fun part of the city. But I'll be glad when she finds a place. She can be demanding." Manny finally seemed to thaw a little.

"Hmph. That does not surprise me. Ed was consulting for the San Francisco Ballet a few years ago, and we met her out there. I don't mean to be nasty, but Alyssia is kind of crass, or she was back then. She acted like a diva, but she has no class." Lauren rarely disparaged anyone, but Alyssia had made a bad impression. "She was so rude to me and sidled up to Ed. I don't forget these things." As she thought about it, Lauren got more irritated.

Manny did not say a word. In fact, he seemed completely disinterested. He held the paper up to his face as if concentrating really hard on the listing.

Then Lauren had another thought. For Manny to deal with her, Alyssia probably had someone bankrolling the new purchase. "Ooooh, I bet Alyssia has a sugar daddy. Come on, Manny, you know I'm right. She can't afford your listings. No, she's got someone taking care of her. Hmph, hmph, hmph."

"As far as I can tell, she's taking care of everything herself. Can we talk about your office space? Here's a good one."

Lauren at last took Manny's cue and left the topic of Alyssia alone. "You're right. I want my office space so I can get to work." She did not have time to gossip or worry about what other people were doing. But in the back of her mind, she had an unsettling feeling. Something was not quite right.

WIDE-EYED, Tamara and Eric Jones seemed to study each word as it dropped from Manny's lips: "And don't ask any questions. Just be prepared to answer whatever they ask of you."

The Joneses had implored Manny to accompany them to their co-op board interview. When he explained that he would not be allowed to attend, they begged him to at least escort them to the building. They behaved like nervous teenagers on a first date. The co-op interview process had that effect on most people trying to get into the exclusive buildings of Manhattan. When Manny began showing the Joneses apartments, he had to explain what a co-op was. People outside of the city generally did not understand this special breed of real estate.

"As Barbara Corcoran, New York's real estate diva, has said, a co-op is what makes New York so special," Manny had explained on the afternoon the Joneses fell in love with the Central Park West apartment they were now trying to buy. "Yes, you do actually own your apartment, but everyone else in the building has a lot to say about pretty much everything you do with it. They can determine what appliances you put into your home, and to whom you can and cannot sell your apartment. Co-op boards have actually rejected potential fiscally able buyers because they don't approve of the clothes they wear to the co-op interview. Image is important to these people."

Once the Joneses understood that the co-op owners were interested in maintaining a respectable lifestyle for their families in the close quarters of an apartment building, they appreciated the purpose of co-op boards. They were conservative people themselves.

"We certainly wouldn't want someone like that rapper Dime Dog as our neighbor. What's that song? 'You're my bitch, not my boo'?" Eric had said, turning up his nose.

"I heard some buildings restrict blacks and Jews," Tamara said, pulling her trench coat tight around her thick midsection while glancing upward. She seemed to be protecting herself from the cool fall wind, or perhaps the gesture was an effort to stave off the harsh co-op boards. They were standing on Central Park West, almost mesmerized by the decorous old buildings, most with limestone gargoyles and bas-reliefs.

"Traditionally Upper West Side apartments are more open than East. They don't want the perception that they are racist."

"Why? What do they care?" Eric and Tamara were highly interested in race and class issues as relating to entry into a New York co-op, as were most people when they learned that a co-op board had the power to reject anyone without having to provide a reason. These buildings were privately owned and could be as restrictive as Augusta National Golf Club, and nobody could do a damn thing about it.

Manny knew his history of the city and enjoyed sharing his knowledge. "When Jews found themselves unable to get into the WASPy Fifth Avenue and Park Avenue buildings, they turned to the Upper West Side, most notably Central Park West, and developed it into their own gold coast. Then some African-Americans followed suit. In fact, Harry Belafonte went so far as to buy his own building on West End Avenue and turn it into a co-op."

The Joneses nodded in understanding.

"Still, a couple of the buildings on Central Park West are as racist as the East Side apartments."

"I heard Satchel Jackson, the soul singer, got rejected from a building on the West Side," Tamara said.

"Aren't *you* doing your homework." Manny smiled. "Yes, you are right. She tried to buy Barbra Streisand's apartment. When she showed up at her co-op interview with two armed bodyguards, the building thought she was a bit flossy."

"Now, I wouldn't mind her as my neighbor, heh, heh," Eric chuckled as Tamara rolled her eyes.

Judging by the way they had dressed—Eric in a conservative navy suit and yellow tie and Tamara in a skirt suit with her hair in a neat up-do—the Joneses had listened to Manny's advice.

Manny believed the Joneses would have no problem getting into the San Remo. After all, the building had let Madonna in, when no others wanted her screaming fans outside or her wild sexcapades inside. Plus, there were already a few black families in the building. The Joneses had the required 50 percent to put down on the three-million-dollar apartment and were financially sound enough to receive financing and keep up with maintenance payments.

"I don't know why you guys are so nervous. You'll be fine. This is easy. You have only this one interview, as opposed to three, if you were moving into some stodgy East Side co-op. And since you don't have a dog, you don't have to worry about a poorly behaved animal ruining your chances of moving into the home of your dreams." Manny checked his Cartier tank watch, eager to leave the Joneses to their interview and return to his office.

"Are you serious? Dog interviews?" Eric seemed amazed.

"Dog interviews do happen in New York City co-ops." Manny smiled his best smile, thinking all the while that soon he would no longer need to coddle people in order to make his money. In the future, he would say no to needy clients like the Joneses. But today their commission check was precious.

As Manny bade the Joneses farewell, leaving them in the good hands of the uniformed doorman, he had a moment of positive reflection. Despite his overwhelming desire to be rid of neophyte buyers in New York, he was proud of the role he played for the black people who came his way. Having been in the business for over fifteen years, Manny knew that there were not many black brokers who really knew the ins and outs of prime real estate in Manhattan.

Too often, white—and even some black—brokers faced with wealthy African-American clients, whether they be athletes, entertainers, bankers, or businesspeople, could not get past skin color. Instead of allowing the co-op board to decide whether they wanted certain people to be their neighbors, some brokers simply steered well-to-do, respectable, classy black people away from apartments these brokers could never afford themselves. They directed their clients to places where they thought they should live.

Manny prided himself on being the type of broker who would take his clients to any building that met their requirements, as long as they could pay for it. He would then coach them through the co-op board process, allowing the delicate relationship to unfold naturally.

Walking down the wide Central Park West sidewalk, Manny thought about potential buyers who would be missing out on what he had to offer. *Oh well, they will survive without me somehow,* he thought, nearly laughing out loud at the prospect of his financial freedom.

The Joneses would be in their interview for at least an hour. Just enough time for Manny to run to his office, check on things, and return to take them to lunch for debriefing and hand-holding while they awaited official approval.

THIRTY-TWO

LAUREN stood in the back of the industrial studio, watching her crew get the lighting ready on the next model she would interview. Sipping her Starbucks vanilla latte, Lauren regarded the thirty or so people milling about the darkened room. She felt fulfilled, finally at work on an interesting subject that the mainstream media typically overlooked.

"How do you like the orange and red background?" the thin, ponytailed set decorator asked her.

"I like it. Do you think you can do something to add some texture? The background looks a little flat," Lauren responded.

"Ooh. I have just the thing. I have something that looks like a large black fishnet. I'll get it." He hurried off.

Lauren walked over to the goateed director of photography. "I checked the shot in the monitor, and he looks beautiful. How much longer before you're ready to go?" Lauren totally respected this slightly older man, who had a vast amount of experience. At the same time, she had to make sure he stayed on schedule and didn't get caught up in perfectionism. She and Samantha Burns, her Style Channel producer, had agreed on him as their photographer after interviewing several. He was great at his job and had shot documentaries, important pieces of work, for celebrated directors. Most importantly, he understood Lauren's vision.

"We should be ready in five minutes, if that set designer doesn't take too long," he informed her.

"Great! We'll go to lunch after this shot." Lauren was beside herself with happiness. She loved working with a talented group of people. Samantha, a mid-thirties stocky African-American woman with dreadlocks, had been with Style Channel for eight years and was a sister interested in getting more work about her people on television. She knew to whom Lauren was married but never mentioned Ed, unless it was in the context of dealing with "couple issues," as Samantha was newly married. She lent experience and guidance, making sure Lauren's vision and the aesthetics of Style Channel matched. Though they had been working together only a month, they were like old girlfriends.

"You got everything covered?" Samantha asked Lauren.

"I think so, but if you think of anything else, let me know," Lauren responded sincerely.

Lauren moved across the room to take her seat behind the camera. She started light and easy talk with Bradley, the man sitting in the light. He would discuss overcoming stereotypes of being stupid and gay. She wanted the discussion to be upbeat, even though he also wanted to talk about turning down advances from powerful gay photographers and how it had almost hurt his career.

"The background colors and the light really compliment you. You look great, Bradley."

"Thanks, Lauren. I want you to know that I think this piece you are doing is sublime. There is so much we go through that no one knows. Thanks for caring." Bradley smiled, revealing beautiful teeth against flawless mocha skin. His slim, muscular build was apparent through his slightly fitted sweater.

"Well, if our photographer is ready, we will get started letting folks know the real story." As she turned her head to check on her photographer, who was also acting as director, Lauren caught a glimpse of her mother coming through the sound door just before it was locked. She was lugging two large bags filled to the brim with what looked like fabric. Lauren waved from her spot as her mother dropped the bags and looked at Lauren with her brows slightly furrowed and pointed to her watch. At that, the director shouted, "Action," and Lauren returned to the task at hand, hoping the tension that had crept into her shoulders with her mother's arrival would disappear as she began her questions.

"Hi, Mom." Lauren and her mother greeted each other with a kiss on each cheek.

"Hello, dear."

Lauren was discomfited by her mother's surveillance, knowing Grace was taking note of the sneakers, nondescript jeans, and black tank top she was wearing. Before her mother could say a word, she said, "I know, Mom, but this is what I wear to work. Comfortable and practical. I don't care if this stuff gets messed up. You never know when you might get called on to move a piece of equipment." Lauren chuckled, trying to make light of the situation.

"I didn't say anything, I didn't say anything," Grace replied, smoothing out her navy Armani pantsuit but staring at her daughter with concern.

"What, Mother, what?"

"Nothing. You just look tired to me, that's all."

"Well, I've been working a lot of hours," Lauren said, hoping to fend off any unsolicited advice.

"Fine, fine. I just worry about you." Lauren gave her mother a sharp look, and for the moment Grace seemed to take the hint. "Well, are we having lunch here?"

"Yes, I told you. We only have an hour, and that's not enough time to go out and come back. But the caterer did a great job. There is salmon and Caesar salad. We can eat in the back over there. We'll have privacy."

"I'll set up all of this stuff I brought to show you," Grace said as she picked up her bags.

"Fine. I'll have a PA bring us our food. I don't know why you had to bring all of that stuff, anyway. We could have simply had a meal together, you know." Lauren was trying to tease her mother.

"You're always so busy, but you really need to get your home together. I've been trying to get you to look at fabrics for the windows in your bedroom and living room for a year now. We will get this done, one way or another," Grace said resolutely.

"Great," Lauren said dourly. "I can't wait. I'm in the middle of setting up my career, and you want to go over window treatments."

Grace leaned in to her daughter so only Lauren could hear. "You had quite a career before you and Ed got married. *That* was why your father and I sent you to Wharton." Lauren ignored her mother and moved her along with the bags of fabrics to a quiet, removed corner so that the crew would not know she was picking through fabrics for her living room. She thought, *How could anyone take me seriously as a producer if I'm busy tending to home business with my mother during the shoot?*

As Lauren joined her mother in the makeshift office a young PA brought two paper plates filled with food. "Thank you. I'm starving. I haven't eaten anything since five this morning," Lauren said before shoving bites of salmon in her mouth. "This is really good. You might enjoy it too if you didn't have so much laid out there." Lauren indicated the mounds of wallpaper and fabric on the table in front of mother.

Grace began, looking like she was ready to get to serious business. "Don't worry about me. I'm not that hungry, anyway. I also brought wallpaper, in case you're interested in redoing your walls." Lauren's mother was not an interior decorator, but she had done all of the design work on her own homes, which were beautiful. She was a professional without a license. A she was clearly on a mission, so far as Lauren's apartment was concerne

"Look, Mom, I really don't have the time or the focus to go throu of this and decide right now. I'll tell you what, why don't you do it

How about that?" Lauren was feeling overwhelmed and frustrated by her mother's demands. "How's Daddy?" she asked, changing the subject.

Looking over the top of her glasses, fabrics in her hands, Grace started, "Focus? Lauren, really. Is *this* what you're going to focus all of your time on? And, and . . ." Obviously, something was on her mind. "How's Ed?"

The question seemed odd to Lauren, as did the manner in which her mother asked, as if something else was behind it. But Lauren was in no mood to discuss Ed at any great length with her mother. So she told her he was fine.

"Oh?" her mother said, sifting through some more fabrics. "I saw his picture in a magazine."

"What are you talking about?" Lauren had no idea what her mother was getting at. "Ed is constantly photographed."

"I'm not talking about a business photograph, Lauren."

"Well, what are you talking about?" Lauren said, losing patience.

"I'm talking about a picture of Ed and that new ballerina in *New York* magazine."

Lauren shook her head. That night a few weeks ago had been a sore spot for her. She tried to push it out of her mind. And now that her mother had brought up this subject, a familiar sick feeling was appearing in her gut. "That's no big deal, Mom. Ed is on the board, there were a lot of pictures taken that night." Lauren knew she sounded defensive.

"Well, where were you when Ed and that dancer had their picture taken?"

Lauren had been front and center watching the events unfold, paralyzed. The evening had started off in the usual way. Ed came home to change into his black-tie wear and to pick up Lauren. Typically, as of late, Ed had seemed preoccupied but was cordial enough. He complimented her on her dress and held the car door for her as she stepped in.

At the ballet, Ed had been flitting about before the curtain went up, schmoozing with other board members and associates of the ballet. Lauren knew a few of the members but not well, and she was in no mood to make

small talk. She waved across the room at some familiar faces, remaining alone while Ed worked the room. He then settled into his seat next to Lauren just before the orchestra began to play. For Lauren, the ballet consisted of waiting for Alyssia to appear onstage and then watching only her dance. She scrutinized the dancer's perfect body and pretty face. Comparing herself to the dancer, Lauren felt flawed, fat, and awkward. At the end of the performance, Ed jumped up with the rest of the audience to give the company a standing ovation.

The afterparty brought about feelings Lauren would have preferred not to have endured. She prided herself on not being a jealous woman and believed in her marriage. She and Ed had spoken about how fate and God had brought them together. But Ed's recent introverted behavior and Alyssia's appearance on the scene from San Francisco, where Ed had had so much business, made Lauren feel uneasy.

The evening went from bad to terrible. Lauren's already unchecked insecurity had thrown her off balance. As much as she tried to get her confidence back, she still felt out of her element in the crowd of wealthy ballet patrons and young dancers. She and Ed rode over to the Hudson Hotel in the Rolls-Royce. They were among the first to arrive in the courtyard, which was designed like a Moroccan casbah. There were pillows scattered on the mosaic marble floor, intricately woven blankets thrown across chaises, little stools, and tiled tables. There was even a wrought-iron bed that sat low to the ground, which many people relaxed on after an evening of too many French martinis. With the rich colors, warm lighting, and Indian-summer breeze blowing, the feeling was sensual. Ed ordered drinks, Black Label for him and an apple martini for Lauren. As they finished their first round, the room began to fill up.

Lauren wished she had brought Manny for company. Once people started arriving, Ed was at it again as the host of the party. He left Lauren sitting alone at their table, and in her insecurity, she could not rise from the table to be social or even go to the bathroom. From her perch she saw Alyssia walk in with a few other members of the cast, statuesque and taut-bodied, and her heart skipped a beat. The room exploded into applause. Alyssia smiled a big fire-engine-red lipstick smile as she took a bow. She was clearly happy and looked gorgeous in a form-fitting black gown with Belgian lace barely covering her perfect breasts. It looked more like an expensive nightgown to Lauren than a dress.

Ed had been standing near the door when Alyssia and her colleagues arrived. Like everyone else, he applauded and beamed, looking like nothing so much as a bantam with its chest stuck out. Or so it seemed to Lauren. Alyssia waved to the crowd, then headed straight for Ed, wrapping her arms around his torso and giving him an exaggerated kiss on the lips. She playfully wiped the remaining red stain from his mouth with her fingers and tossed her head back in laughter. Ed looked taken aback and a little uncomfortable. Lauren had to turn her head away, and she felt her face burn with a combination of embarrassment, jealousy, and anger. Then Alyssia grabbed Ed's arm and stood close to him for the photographers, busy snapping pictures. After the photos were taken, Ed moved quickly away from Alyssia and continued to make the rounds. Lauren spent the evening alone in a booth that had been reserved for her and Ed. After her third apple martini, she wobbled to the ladies' room. On her way back to her post, Ed grabbed her arm.

"Ready to go?" was all he said.

"You bet," she replied.

Lauren did not mention Alyssia, and neither did Ed, despite the fact that he was still wearing a smudge of red on his face. The night had raised suspicions in Lauren that she did not want to address.

"All I'm saying, honey, is that you need to keep your eyes open, and you don't need to let Ed disrespect you with that tawdry dancer hanging all over him in front of the cameras."

Grace's tough love was something Lauren could never grow accustomed to. "What am I supposed to do about other women out there?"

"I can't tell you what to do. And I realize that you can't tell Ed what to do, either. But you are a flower in Ed's lapel. He needs to be honoring you, not posing for pictures with these young girls, cuckolding you and this family."

"Thank you, Mom. Sorry my husband embarrassed you and Daddy. Thanks for coming down to visit my very first set with your enlightening advice. I have to get back to my job. Please stay and watch. You might have fun." Lauren struggled to stay calm, holding back tears and pain. She needed to remain composed to finish the day. Heading toward the bathroom to splash cool water on her face, she promised herself that she would not allow Grace's comments to crush her. But the damage was done. Grace had pulled out of Lauren what she wanted to suppress. Now Lauren could not hide from herself the fear that Ed could be fucking around.

For a moment she thought she couldn't return to work, until Michael, the light-skinned, blue-eyed model who would be the next interview, sneaked from behind to give her a huge hug. She allowed herself to enjoy the attention and regain focus. And for all her comments, Grace seemed to appreciate the presence of the models. Lauren looked over Michael's shoulder and saw that her mother, glasses down on the tip of her nose, was checking out one of the hotties. She gave Lauren a look and a shrug that said, "Hey, he's kind of cute."

But it was too late to stop the suspicion and anguish that had been set in motion. Lauren felt her life beginning to come unglued.

THIRTY-THREE

THE glowing green alarm clock read 1:10 A.M. Ed had been out of town working the last two nights. Lauren had thought he was in Dallas until he called to tell her he had been there only for the day and had gone on to Atlanta. He didn't even call until the second night. She could never get used to Ed's frenetic schedule and not knowing exactly where he was, but that wasn't what had been so upsetting to her.

Lauren's troubles had been brewing for a while, but yesterday things had escalated to new heights. She had been looking through their dry-cleaning hamper for a skirt, and besides her own clothing, she found one of Ed's French-cuffed shirts, with his monogram on the cuff—E.A.T.—which Ed always thought clever, Edward Albert Thomas, since his business involved eating other companies. On the collar of this shirt, Lauren discovered smudged foundation and lipstick. She stared at the stains and turned the collar this way and that, holding the shirt to her nose, inhaling his musky odor. She began to feel queasy. There was pain in her heart and anger in her mind. How could he?

She called him instantly but got his voice mail. She left a message. "Ed, it's Lauren. I need to ask you a question. Please call me as soon as you get a chance. Thanks, honey." She tried to sound upbeat so he would return the call without hesitation. Hanging up the phone, she sat in her chair staring at nothing, not able to make sense of the events unfolding before her. Thankfully, there were no pressing appointments for the day. She would cancel the lunch she had unwillingly scheduled. The documentary was in good hands with her editor, who was spending the next day or so loading all the footage onto the Avid editing machine. After canceling lunch, Lauren told Mr. Francis that she was not feeling well and would be taking a nap. She asked him not to disturb her unless Ed called. She then got under the covers of their big bed and began flipping through TV channels. She stopped at an old black-and-white movie, *The Women*, about a woman whose husband was having an affair with a girl who sold perfume in a department store, and how the gossip of the affair traveled among their social circle. Lauren watched the film with dread, hearing her mother's criticism that she had created the situation by not demanding respect from her husband.

Until the phone rang, she was unaware that she had fallen asleep. Ed's voice drove away her grogginess. He was in a good mood but sounded busy, without much time to talk.

"Hi, baby. What's going on? I got your message. Just got done talking with the owner of the Hawks. Who knows, your man may soon be part owner of an NBA franchise. Heh, heh."

"Oh, that's great. Listen. I uh, found your shirt . . ."

He was impatient. "What? What are you saying, Lauren?"

"On your shirt collar, I found makeup and lipstick, Ed. Whose is it? It certainly doesn't belong to me."

"Makeup? I don't know what you're talking about. It's probably food or something."

She was getting angrier. "Food? Ed, do you think I'm a complete idiot? I know the difference between food and hot-pink lipstick."

He got real cool. "Okay. Wait. Let me think. Hmmm . . . Oh. It must have been from that San Francisco trip. I told you, some of the clients I deal with out there like to go to strip bars or have dancers come around, especially those Wall Street money guys. One of the girls must have gotten too close doing a dance or something. You know how it goes."

"Ed, I don't really know. Why do you have to go to those events, anyway?"

"Lauren, you know how the business is. I have to be social."

She realized he would not get honest. "This incident aside, I feel like something has changed. You don't seem as interested in me as you used to. I feel like we're growing apart."

With seeming sincerity, Ed said, "Lauren, I am just floored. I can't believe you feel that way. I've been feeling like we've been getting along better than ever."

Confused, Lauren replied, "Really? You've seemed so preoccupied. I feel like I haven't been able to get through to you; you're always so busy. And now I find out you're going to strip bars without telling me."

"The strip-club thing was business. Honestly, I forgot about it. Do you think I would have left my shirt for you to find if I was trying to hide it from you?"

"You know I don't usually see your laundry, Ed. Stop insulting me."

In a conciliatory tone, Ed replied, "Look, maybe I have been obsessed with work lately. I'm trying to expand. I've got plans to take the company bigger and possibly public."

"Oh."

"And as I told you, I might buy a part of this NBA team. But you're right, we need to spend some special time together. Maybe plan a trip somewhere. What do you say?"

"I don't know. I guess."

"You guess? Come on, baby. I love you. And about the makeup, trust me, I would never mess with any of those skanky strippers. Not even when I was single. I'm sorry you had to find the shirt like that and get yourself all worked up."

Still unsure, she replied, "Okay, Ed."

"I'll try to be home early tomorrow," he said. But later, he called to say that his meeting had run much longer than expected, and he wouldn't be able to get home until very late. "Don't wait up" was what he had told her.

At 1:13, Ed slipped into their dark bedroom with his shoes in his hand. He changed his clothes in the bathroom and slid under the covers of their king-size bed. All the while Lauren pretended to sleep.

As recently as a few months ago, Ed would have wrapped his arms around her, spooning her body into his. Tonight a deep ocean lay between them as they clung to their lonely edges of the bed.

Once she heard the heavy breathing of Ed's slumber, Lauren quietly climbed out from under the covers, tiptoed out of the bedroom, and headed downstairs into his study.

She stood at the threshold of his private room, hesitating. She had never gone through the pockets of his pants, much less the drawers of his desk. This was new territory. She felt guilty yet entitled. Tonight she would go through all of his personal belongings, looking for what, exactly, she did not know. Her heart beat fast and hard in her throat. She was afraid of what she knew she would probably find.

She began with his mahogany desk, which was remarkably organized. A stack of mail sat in its center. There were piles among piles neatly put together across his leather box organizer. She picked them up and put them down, looking at the writing on the front, the return address, sniffing them. She opened the drawers and looked through papers and faxes. She then turned to his cell phone. She sat in a corner of his office on the floor, listening to all the saved messages. Before each voice, her heart skipped a beat, but when nothing untoward turned up, she returned the phone to the charger and focused her attention on his Palm Pilot. She tried to search the myriad of names in his phone book, but there were too many for her to discern the business colleagues from friends or lovers.

She then went into his calendar and looked back two weeks, then scrolled forward day by day until the end of the current week, which was where she saw it. The entry for Friday read, *12:30—One if by Land, Two if by Sea.* Her vision blurred, and her mouth went dry. Her hands shook uncontrollably as sweat from her palms covered the gadget. She knew the restaurant well. Ed had taken her there on numerous occasions for romantic afternoons and evenings. The elegant eatery was not a place for business. It was a place for lovers to lunch.

She felt sick. Her first instinct was to run upstairs and pull Ed from bed to curse him out. Gathering herself together, Lauren decided an immediate head-on confrontation would not be the best course of action. She needed to cool down. She needed to get more information so that Ed could not lie his way out, as he had about the makeup on his shirt. She needed to figure out who he was meeting at the restaurant. Thinking about the shirt, she felt her face burn. She had been so stupid, and Ed had made her look like such a fool. The lipstick obviously belonged to the woman he was seeing.

Friday was two days away. She would go to the restaurant and witness them herself. And then she would take action, whatever that action may be. But at least she would no longer be in the dark.

Tonight Lauren would not return to bed. Instead she would stay in the television room, hugging her legs to her chest, spacing out before Lifetime movies and music videos. Images of Ed and some faceless woman locked in a passionate kiss replayed in her mind. She had a sick suspicion who it was, but that was too much information for her to process right now. She kept envisioning bodies intertwined, destroying all that was sacred between the two of them. Her body felt weak. Her mind was numb. She was heartbroken, alone, and more scared than she had ever been in her entire life. If only sleep would come, she could escape back to Geneva, when love was new and Ed was hers alone.

THE rotund, middle-aged woman with chafed red cheeks, strawlike blond hair, and a floral muumuu paced the oversize galley kitchen. First her eyes were closed, and then they were half-mast. Manny, Coffee, Darryl, and Niche stood back while she conducted her business. After all, she was the professional. Judy Miller was a world-renowned psychic, or that was what Manny had been told. The Rayes were prepared to make an offer on the Olympic Tower duplex penthouse, but first their personal psychic had to assess the apartment to determine whether or not there were any "undesirable spirits." Whomever this woman was in Coffee and Darryl's lives, Manny thought, she had a powerful influence over them. She had convinced them to leave their entourage in their custom stretch SUV, even though (like their American Express card) they never left home without them—publicist, photographer, personal assistant, and all. Judy did not want any interference during her reading of the home. Manny had even gotten the impression she would prefer he not be inside, but he could not leave them alone in the apartment. They may have been multimillionaires, but he did not know what these crazy people were capable of doing.

Suddenly, Judy stopped pacing and spoke to no one in particular. "I need to go to the center axis."

Niche nodded as if he knew exactly what she was talking about. Steel beams and concrete came to mind for Manny. He didn't know what kind of spirits she was going to find in this apartment. The condominium board had paid an architectural firm to build the penthouse on spec, and no one had lived here yet. And no one had been beaten or killed in this space, as far as Manny knew; quite frankly, he felt like the entire spectacle was a waste of everyone's time. But hell, he reasoned, if it translated into a sale, perhaps the whole sideshow would be worth the extra trouble. Besides, his days as a real estate broker would be coming to an end soon.

"Follow me," Niche instructed. "I know where the center axis is." He scurried away, his drawstring pants and burlap poncho flapping behind him. Manny noticed Coffee and Darryl glance at each other as if waiting for some monumental discovery. They appeared so impressionable, like two small children buying into the magic of fairies, wizards, and bad guys. Manny was having a difficult time reconciling the shrewd businessman Darryl Raye was with the naive image he presented, waiting to hear the predictions of this haggard hoax of a woman.

Many of Manny's perceptions about this world were starting to crack. He had always assumed that once a person achieved a certain amount of financial success, autonomy would follow. Manny did not think perfection would ensue, but he believed empowerment would come with the territory. Coffee and Darryl seemed to have given all of their power away, whether it be to the latest trends or the public's perception. They, too, seemed to be on a treadmill, sweating and laboring on a level-ten incline, moving, moving, but going nowhere.

Curiosity getting the best of him, Manny worked his way to the rest of the group, congregated in the alcove between the dining room and the formal living room. They were standing beneath the arched ceiling, which was painted like a faux sky with faint white clouds, à la the Sistine Chapel.

"I think the center point is right here." Niche maneuvered his body in a semicircle around one empty spot, as if he were feeling some unseen energy.

Judy walked in a small circle around the mosaic marble floor, carefully placing one red loafer in front of the other. She then began walking backward and forward. "*This* is the epicenter," she said as if making a proclamation. Then her eyes began to roll into the back of her head. *This woman cannot be serious with this ten-cent act,* Manny thought. He tried his best not to laugh. Coffee, Darryl, and Niche stared at Judy as if in a trance themselves. These people could not honestly believe that the so-called psychic was sensing something from "beyond." Manny felt embarrassed for them. Judy seemed like a carnival freak show, and they had all paid to get a glimpse of her.

The woman's hair was practically standing on end, and she was beginning to convulse. She looked as if what little life was left in her were being sucked out. Lord, Manny hoped she didn't drop dead in the middle of the floor. A dead psychic would almost certainly be a deal-breaker. Then she started groaning. That was it. He was going into the hallway.

Manny slowly backed out of the alcove into the living room until something invisible stopped him. His stomach felt like a hundred pounds of lead had settled in the bottom. Then the room began to spin, and the floor beneath him shook. His mouth became dry and itchy, as if acid were prickling his tongue. Then he was on a high-speed elevator hurtling down, so quickly, the lead in his stomach was now in the roof of his mouth. Blackness. Silence. Grayness. Streams of light stabbed at Manny's eyes as he fought to regain consciousness. He couldn't figure out what had happened to him. Maybe he had ingested one too many fat burners. They sometimes made him lightheaded.

When he opened his eyes, the psycho psychic was inches from his face, and her hands were on either side of his head. Manny tried to free himself from his confusion and fear. She was regarding him with her wild eyes. In a raspy voice so small Manny had to strain to hear her, she said, "Others can't see this, but your time here is limited. Leave before your soul does."

Still disoriented, Manny jerked away from the madwoman as Coffee, Darryl, and Niche hovered around.

"Manny, are you okay?" Coffee asked, kneeling beside Manny.

"Yo, you all right, man?" Darryl chimed in.

Manny stood up, self-conscious. He felt disheveled and out of control. He still did not understand what had happened, and apparently, neither did anyone else. That is, other than Judy. She stared at him again and mouthed the word, "Leave." No one else seemed to be aware of their exchange. But Manny was all too cognizant as he regained his composure and straightened his shirt and tie. Sale or no sale, he was leaving this apartment. They could stay all day and chant to the rain gods, for all he cared. But these crazy people were trying to make him lose his mind.

THIRTY-FIVE

"BARROW, between Seventh Avenue South and West Fourth," Lauren told the cabdriver through the heavy haze of her mind. She was on her way to One if by Land, Two if by Sea to spy on Ed. Like a private investigator, she was tracking the case of a married man involved in an adulterous affair. This scenario would be funny to Lauren, dressed in dark shades, baseball cap, and nondescript sweatshirt, if she weren't going to spy on her own husband. As she lingered on that thought, she reached into her large bucket bag and pulled out the bottle of Jack Daniel's she had been nursing since ten o'clock this morning. She noted that the bottle was over half empty. Hadn't it been brand-new when she began drinking? She thought so but couldn't remember drinking so much. She capped it and returned it to her purse.

From the window, she watched people carry on their happy regular lives as hers unraveled. She could not believe her perfect husband would ruin their perfect relationship. She had worked hard to be something other than a housewife, someone who would make him proud. Lauren looked at her long, capable fingers. She touched her face. She was attractive and smart. She would do anything for Ed.

But none of that mattered. Right now she felt she couldn't keep her husband from straying. She was weak and pathetic. She took out her friend Jack again, put the bottle to her lips and swallowed hard. Her head began to throb, and the Middle Eastern music the cabdriver was playing seemed to get louder. She put her head back on the seat and dropped the nearly empty bottle into her handbag. She could barely move. The music sounded ancient; the whining beat repeated the same refrain. She pictured beautiful women dancing in colorful scarves of pink and green, seductively moving around a dark room of rich colors as men began to clap.

"Lady, lady. We here." A harsh voice brought her from her reverie. She opened her eyes, blinking at the unfamiliar face. "You okay?" he asked, concerned. "That nine-twenty."

Without saying a word, Lauren handed him the crumpled twenty-dollar bill she had been holding in her hand throughout the ride. At a snail's pace, she opened the door and stumbled to the curb. She stood on the corner in a stupor well after the taxi pulled off. She was operating more on instinct than will. The restaurant was familiar enough that she wouldn't have to think about where she was going. She thought this place had belonged to her and Ed. Now she realized he took all of his women to the same restaurant. He probably gave them all the same gifts.

Her legs were so heavy. To lift one she needed to swing her arms, which felt weighted down as well. But once she got going, she moved swiftly. At the entrance of the restaurant she stopped. She had a horrible taste in her mouth. Of course she had a bad taste in her mouth—Ed and his mistress had put it there. But just in case her breath smelled, she popped a Listerine strip on her tongue and drank some of the water from the bottle she always carried. It was one o'clock, and she figured Ed and his woman were almost midway through their meal.

She wanted to go inside, but she could not bring herself to cross that threshold. Patrons of the restaurant went in and out, staring at Lauren as they passed. She had thought to wait outside, but it dawned on her that if she wanted to witness their romancing, she would have to go in. Now she wished she had dressed for lunch rather than detective work.

Lauren removed her cap and shook out her hair. She hadn't combed it for two days, feigning sick with Ed and Mr. Francis, and she was certain it was in an unruly Afro. Lauren then pulled her Black Dog sweatshirt off to reveal a white wifebeater, which looked more fashionable with the jeans she was wearing. Still, she was obviously not dressed to dine at such a fine establishment.

She walked, or rather staggered, over to the host's podium. The man and woman standing behind it looked up with prefabricated smiles. At Lauren's appearance, the smiles quickly dissolved.

The man spoke up first. "May we help you?"

"Yes," Lauren began. She had intended to smile, but the weight of the moment was too much. "I'm Ed Thomas. I mean I'm here to see Ed Thomas. He told me to meet him here."

"I'm sorry, ma'am, but there is no Ed Thomas here," the man responded without checking his reservation book.

"Yes. He is here. I'm his wife. He told me to meet him." Lauren was having trouble getting the words out. She realized, standing there, that she should have practiced what she was going to say. She wasn't prepared. And these people were acting like they were protecting Ed from her.

"Ohh, Mrs. Thomas. I'm sorry. I didn't recognize you. You've changed your hair," the hostess said. "I'll go tell Mr. Thomas you're here." She left quickly.

Fuck that! Lauren did not wait for an invitation. She followed the blond ponytailed hostess, not wanting Ed to be warned about her presence. She wanted, no, *needed*, to see what was really going on; if he rubbed the nape of the woman's neck the same way he did with Lauren, if he smiled lovingly at her in the same way. But when Lauren reached the same table where she and Ed used to dine, she was shocked by the scene before her. Ed and Alyssia Banks were gazing into each other's eyes and holding hands across the table as only a couple deeply into each other would do. They were cozily in front of the fireplace that was big enough for a ten-year-old child to stand in. Alyssia wore a large smile, her nose scrunched up, gazing at Ed like the only man in the world. Ed appeared equally enthralled.

If someone had taken a jagged-edged knife and ripped into Lauren's guts, it would not have hurt like this. "No, no, no, no . . ." Lauren cried, slumping to the floor in tears. "You are. You are having an affair. You liar, you fucking liar." Ed froze for just a moment before racing to Lauren's side, picking her up from the floor. He seemed to temporarily forget Alyssia as his wife had a very public mental breakdown. "Lauren. What? How? Oh, baby. Let's get you out of here," he said. The staff of the restaurant and the other diners looked on. Lauren's meltdown was providing them entertainment about which to gossip when they returned to their offices and homes.

But Alyssia presented the coup de grâce as she stood up from the table. Her words did not match her elegant appearance. "Um, Ed. Since Miss Princess now knows, I guess the jig is up and we can move on." She stood with her hands on her hips, looking down at Lauren. Her body was perfect in a tight red A-line skirt with a soft black sleeveless top and a plunging neckline, revealing two size-C breasts that stood naturally erect with no bra. From Lauren's position on the floor, at the bottom of the pit of her life, Alyssia looked like a Goddess of Love. "Are you going to tell her, Ed? Or should I be the one to let her know that we are moving—"

"That is enough, Alyssia!" Ed's voice boomed loudly as he got Lauren to her feet. Actually, they make a good-looking couple, Lauren thought. Her husband looked so dapper in his navy pin-striped suit. The two of them obviously enjoyed dressing and primping to please the other: a stark contrast to Lauren's broken-down neglected-wife look, her fashion statement of the moment.

"What? You're yelling at me when *she* comes in here causing a scene, drunk out of her mind, ruining our lunch? You need to put her in check, Ed!" Alyssia's shrill voice oozed antagonism.

The staff was overtly anxious. "Mr. Thomas. Is there anything that I can help you with?" the host offered.

"No. I apologize. We are leaving this instant." Ed guided Lauren out of the restaurant as he called his car from his cell phone. In the short time it took them to reach the curb, the car was there, door open, and Ed poured Lauren in.

Standing at the curb, peeking into the car as though ready to get in, Alyssia cried, "What am I supposed to do?"

"Taxi it!" Ed said briskly as he handed her a fifty-dollar bill from the roll of fifties and hundreds he pulled from his pocket.

"You're just going to leave me to get a cab and toss me a fifty like I'm yo' ho?" Alyssia remained in the same spot on the sidewalk as Ed climbed into the car next to Lauren and shut the door. He seemed oblivious to Alyssia, who continued to shout an array of expletives at the tinted window. The next thing Lauren heard was Ed mumbling into his phone about changing meetings. She was exhausted. He had placed her head on his shoulder, and even though she was hurt and angry, she had no strength to alter her position. She remained leaning against him, semiconscious, throughout the ride home.

At their building, Ed, the driver, and Mr. Francis helped Lauren upstairs to her bathroom, where Ed undressed her and put her into a cool shower. He then dried her off, dressed her in a silk gown, and placed her in their bed, pulling the blanket and bedspread up to her chin. "Rest, love. I'll be here when you wake up."

Lauren tried to open her eyes, but they felt like they were glued shut. Her sleep was restless, broken by Ed's distant voice talking into the phone. She dreamed of Ed and Alyssia making love, Alyssia still wearing her billowing red skirt as she sat on top of Ed, humping up and down, up and down, in the center of the restaurant with everyone standing around applauding and laughing. Everyone except Lauren.

When she awoke for real, day had turned to night, and Ed was sitting on the bed next to her.

Ed and Lauren silently stared at each other for a while. She remained under the covers with her head on the pillow. Ed sat on top of the bedspread, propped up by several pillows.

He spoke softly. "How are you feeling, baby?"

"I feel like shit," she said.

"I guess you do. You almost drank an entire liter of liquor," he said, holding up the empty bottle of Jack Daniel's.

She stared at her husband with as much resentment as she could muster. "The booze isn't what has me feeling so bad." She turned onto her back and closed her eyes. The truth was that the alcohol had left her feeling more tired and strung out than she remembered ever feeling. She would not concede that fact to Ed. As her mind became clearer, she reminded herself that he had no idea how she knew they were at the restaurant. As far as he was concerned, she might have had a private investigator following them around. Lauren wanted the truth about Ed and Alyssia's relationship. She would say as little as possible, hoping that Ed would reveal himself. But Ed was a genius at lying and covering his tracks, Lauren now knew. Getting the full story from him would be difficult.

"Of course, the drinking is only symptomatic." Bowing his head, Ed continued, "But Lauren, my lunch with Alyssia was truly about business."

"Right. And the lipstick on your shirt was food. Why don't you just get out and leave me alone?" Lauren snapped. "I am so sick of your bullshit. What's the point? Go have your girlfriend. I won't stand in your way."

Grabbing her hand, he said, "You're not in the way of anything, baby. I love you. I don't want a girlfriend."

Pulling her hand away, she said, "You are so fucking full of shit. As Alyssia said, the jig is up. The princess now knows. Oh yeah, I may have been fucked up, but I heard that!"

Ed stared blankly at Lauren as if deciding what new strategy he should take. Lauren guessed he hadn't anticipated her remembering the specifics of the earlier scene.

"I don't know why Alyssia said that stupid shit," Ed said, sounding somewhat defeated.

"I do. The jig is up! I know that you and Alyssia are an item. She's ready for you two to get together and be a couple. And you should. Be with her, and leave me the hell out of your bullshit lies!"

"Lauren, I don't want Alyssia. I know this looks bad, but I only want you. Alyssia is nothing. She's just a pebble in the sand."

"Oh! That's supposed to make me feel better. How many more are there, Ed? 'Pebble in the sand' implies there is an entire beachful of women."

"No, you took that wrong."

"I've been taking many things the wrong way when it comes to you."

"No. Lauren, you can believe in me." Ed got up and came over to her side of the bed. Getting down on his knees, he placed his face close to Lauren's, trying to force her to look at him. "Listen to me," he began. "I made a lot of mistakes in my first marriage. I told you, there were lots of other women when Claudia and I were married. When I met you, I instantly knew I wanted you to be my wife. I vowed that we would have a pure relationship. I love you, and I have always wanted things to be right between us." He held his head down in what appeared to be legitimate shame. "I made a mistake, a mistake in acting on old habits. Without you, Lauren, I have nothing. I have no future. You mean everything to me. Please. Please forgive me. Nothing like this will ever happen again. I promise," Ed said, his voice choked with tears.

Lauren had never seen a grown man cry before. "What about Alyssia? Do you love her?" she asked, teary-eyed herself.

"Hell, no! In fact, I'll prove it to you. I'll call her now." Eager to show Lauren he meant business, Ed jumped up, wiped his eyes, and ran to his cell phone. He pressed in some numbers and returned to the floor beside Lauren, who was sitting up in the bed.

When Alyssia answered, Ed held the phone so Lauren could hear. He said, "Alyssia, you and I are over. I don't want you to call me anymore, and don't expect to hear from me again."

"Excuse me?"

"It's over, Alyssia."

"Why? Just because wifey-poo busted you? That's some weak shit, Ed. I thought you were more of a man than that."

"I *am* more of a man. That's why I'm going to do right by my wife. I love her, and our marriage deserves a chance. My relationship with you was a mistake."

"You can't do this, Ed. What am I supposed to do now?" Alyssia sounded angry instead of indignant.

"That isn't my problem. I love my wife, and I plan to have a long, happy relationship with her, if she'll have me. Good-bye." He turned his phone off and returned his attention to Lauren. "You'll see, Lauren. I will do right by you."

Lauren spoke slowly. "I don't know, Ed. I need some time to think this through." The entire episode was almost too much for her to bear. She didn't know what to believe. Who was to say that Ed would not call Alyssia back when he was alone and apologize?

Lauren needed someone to talk to whom she could trust. Oh, God. She couldn't talk to Manny. Even he had been playing a part in their affair: He was working for Ed, showing Alyssia apartments. "You were going to buy an apartment for you and Alyssia!"

Ed fell back and burst into more tears. "I know it was sick. I am sick. I . . . I . . . don't know what to say. There is no excuse. I am pathetic."

Lauren was angry. "Cut your crying and get out of my fucking face. You parade around town with your whore, acting like the big man, buying expensive property down the street for your love nest, and then you cry? I don't want to see your face! You should be ashamed to be in my presence. How dare you? How dare you sleep with that bitch and crawl back into the bed with me. You're disgusting." For the first time in almost a year, Lauren spoke with a confidence that came from within.

"I understand. I'll leave you. I'll sleep in one of the guest rooms. You won't see me unless you ask for me. I'll get my things." Ed headed toward his closet for a bag.

"Ed," Lauren called out, and he turned around, hopeful as a puppy dog. "Ed, you've left me in a position where I don't know what I'm going to do, but I'll tell you this much—if you ever have any thoughts of us reconciling, don't come near me until you're ready to come clean about everything." With that proclamation, she dismissed him.

After Ed left the room, Lauren stood up for the first time in what felt like years. She put on the robe that Ed had laid out for her at the foot of the bed. She needed to get some clarity. No more booze to cloud her mind. Opening her closet, she slipped her feet into her slippers, then headed downstairs to the kitchen. She wanted strong, hot coffee. And she needed to talk with someone to get perspective. A therapist, a lawyer; which was more important, she wasn't sure. But the more she thought about it, the more she knew who would be helpful to her. Once she got ahold of herself, she would call Tandy. Tandy had been around a long while and had seen a lot. She would offer sound advice that Lauren could trust. Speaking with her friend would be the first step in figuring out where her life would go from this point on. Lauren could never face her family in such disgrace without a plan of action, especially since her mother had warned her about Ed. No, she would confide in the one real friend she had left.

THIRTY-SIX

TANDY barely recognized the disheveled, swollen-eyed thing when she opened her front door. Lauren looked like she hadn't bathed in days, and her face was puffy and contorted with pain; the emotional kind, Tandy realized within seconds. The girl nearly collapsed into her arms, as though Tandy were some sort of fucking oasis. Tandy instantly knew either something had happened with Ed or somebody had died.

As Lauren stumbled into Tandy's foyer, she began to whimper, "I don't understand, I don't understand." She seemed to be talking to herself. "How could he do this to me?" she asked with more naïveté than Tandy had possessed as a newborn.

"Why don't we go to the kitchen, get you a nice cup of tea," Tandy suggested, withholding that she was going to lace it with whiskey.

"But, but, I, I trusted him . . . I really, really trusted him," Lauren wailed, not moving from her spot in the entry hall.

"Calm down, sweetheart. You need to calm down," Tandy said in her best take-charge soothing voice. Lauren needed a friend to lean on. She had come to Tandy, and Tandy would appear to be there for her, no matter what.

She had a prepared demeanor for every occasion. She had even practiced the various appropriate expressions in the mirror. For shock, she knew the perfect size her mouth should open and her eyes widen. For sadness, she knew the precise placement of her lips, gently pursed together to create a pained expression. For elation, she knew to clasp her hands together and smile. But Tandy had never sincerely felt any of these emotions. Indifference had been the only prevalent feeling in her life for so long—that and rage, or jealousy.

Looking at Lauren slumped over, dabbing her eyes with tissue, Tandy knew that she had to give her everything she needed to get through this emotional moment and back on track with her husband—unbeknownst to Lauren, Tandy was also in need. Lauren and Ed could not break up yet. They had to work through their problems until the Sugar Hill building had transferred ownership. Tandy was determined not to allow this episode to interfere with the closing. Too much was riding on the deal to allow a simple act of infidelity to ruin all of Tandy's hard work. She needed a plan of action, but convincing this idealistic young woman that the fairy tale was over and real life was about to begin would not be easy.

Her wheels turned. First she had to restrain herself from slapping some sense into Lauren. What about her irritated Tandy so much? Was it her youth, her smooth fresh complexion, her unlimited wealth, her rising star to Tandy's flickering one? Or was it simply that she was Mrs. Ed Thomas? Snapping herself out of self-pity, Tandy reminded herself that today these thoughts were irrelevant. Her agenda was clear. After today's conversation, Lauren would return home, ready to work at keeping her marriage intact.

Though it made her uncomfortable, Tandy took Lauren's hands in her own. Lauren looked up as if thankful for human contact.

"You're going to be all right, Lauren. I don't know what happened, but you and Ed are going to be just fine. It may take some time, but I know."

"It's never going to be the same. I'll never be able to trust him again. Why would he even marry me if he wanted to cheat?"

Tandy stopped herself from shouting, "Because you're the perfect arm piece, with your family pedigree, Wharton MBA, and looks." Instead, she stood up to run water into the stainless-steel pot that sat atop the stove. She placed the kettle on the big Aga and took a seat across the table from Lauren. She managed a grim expression, calculating that this was the appropriate motherly demeanor. Looking Lauren dead on in her red-rimmed eyes, she began her pitch. "I'm going to tell you something that you're not going to like hearing. Lauren, all men cheat. *All* men cheat."

"I don't buy it, Tandy. Ed should know better than that."

"A lot of men should know better, but the fact remains that men need different validation than women. They have bigger egos than us, and they need their egos stroked. It has nothing to do with their wives. Men need to see themselves re-created in the eyes of other women. When women want to be re-created, we do something more sensible, like buy a new dress."

Lauren sighed, but Tandy went on. "Ed's rendezvous has nothing to do with his love for you. Anyone who sees the two of you together can see how much he adores you." Tandy added a fake smile, although her stomach churned at the thought. She was, however, getting a sick pleasure from thinking about Ed cheating on Little Miss Perfect.

"Nothing to do with me? How could Ed fucking someone else under my nose, lying to me, deceiving me, betraying me, have nothing to do with me? I don't understand."

"Listen, Lauren, Ed is a powerful man. Many women probably throw themselves at him, willing to do anything just to get his attention. He travels a lot. He probably gets lonely every now and then."

"Yeah, well, his affair with prima ballerina Alyssia was more than a case of loneliness. Not only was he buying her an apartment, he was using Manny as the broker."

Now even Tandy was shocked. "Oh, dear." *That dumb-ass, Manny.* She could kill the stupid bastard. How dare he do such a foolish thing and jeopardize their deal? She wanted to strangle the little faggot. Tandy needed to regroup, reorganize her thoughts. She went to the stove and removed the steaming pot and placed it on the clay holder. She then removed her porcelain teapot and teacups and prepared a tray, taking the bottle of whiskey from the cabinet and pouring a cup in the teapot. Lauren needed to be loosened up.

"Alyssia Banks from the ballet company?"

"Uh-huh," Lauren said through sniffles.

"Honey, listen. Women like Alyssia are a dime a dozen. I know. That woman is a bitch on the prowl. If it wasn't Ed, it would have been another woman's husband, as long as the pockets were deep enough."

"That doesn't excuse Ed's behavior." Sniffle, sniffle.

"No, it doesn't. But believe me, he would never ever leave you for her low-class, unrefined ass. It was a slip. Pure and simple. He would look like the biggest fool, taking her seriously, and Ed is no fool."

Tandy placed the tea service on the table and poured each of them a cup. Taking a seat, she changed tactics. "Look, no one can deny that Ed did a lousy thing. It was dishonest, hurtful, and painful. He's a real shit to have done this to you. A real shit. You truly deserve better; you do."

"Got that right," Lauren chimed in. She took her first sip of tea and scrunched up her face. "What's in this?"

"I thought under the circumstances, a little liquor was in order."

Lauren didn't seem to hear. She continued, "And you know, Tandy, I really thought he was different. I mean, he talks such a good game. But I knew something wasn't right between us. I even asked him if everything was all right, and his response was an overwhelming yes. Why couldn't he have just been man enough to tell me that he wanted someone else, that I wasn't enough for him? I certainly would have had a lot more respect for him. Instead I have to find the two of them cuddled up at the most romantic restaurant in the city, and the Negro still had the nerve to tell me I didn't see what I saw. He tried to tell me he was helping Alyssia out, that it was a business lunch. He tried to play me like a damn fool. That's almost worse than him cheating on me."

Tandy looked at the girl who had everything the world had to offer and wondered why the hell she would let a cheating husband ruin it all. But she was so naive. "What's Ed saying to you now? Does he admit to anything?"

"Yeah." Disgust tinged Lauren's voice. "He says he made a mistake, that he was acting on old bad habits. He never meant to hurt me, he loves me more than life itself, his life would be nothing without me."

"Did he say it was over?"

"Yes. He even called her in front of me and told her he didn't want anything else to do with her."

"Do you believe him?"

"I don't know. I don't know what to believe anymore."

"Understandable. But trust me, now that you know, Alyssia is looking more and more to Ed like the actual tramp she is. He sees that she is damaged goods." Tandy waited, looking for a glimmer of softening from Lauren. "What's the status between the two of you now?"

"Ed's sleeping in the guest wing. He told me he knew I needed my space right now."

"Have you thought about what you want to do?"

"I don't know, Tandy, I don't know. What do I do? I used to always think if my husband ever cheated on me, I would divorce him the instant I found out. But now that it's actually happened to me, I feel paralyzed."

"I know you do. And I know at this moment you can't imagine ever getting over his indiscretion."

"Maybe if I didn't love him so much, I wouldn't be so devastated, but I am. I feel like my best friend has died . . . like two of my best friends have died, when I think about Manny being in cahoots with Ed and Alyssia."

"Just get Manny out of your head, Lauren. Get him out now. He's been a weasel since we met him. You shouldn't have expected much of him. He's just out to make a buck."

Lauren shook her head. "I thought he was my friend."

"No matter how he tried to portray himself, he was your real estate broker first. You always represented a potential sale to him. Don't forget that. Do you think he would have acted like your personal gofer if you were married to Joe Schmoe?" Tandy had to make sure Lauren at least got back on the right track with Ed before she left. "Ed is a different story. Lauren, I know it's hard to realize this now, but he does love you, he adores you. And I truly believe he made a mistake. When I told you that all men cheat, I didn't mean that all men cheat all the time. I meant that all men, at one point or another in their marriages, make mistakes, little slips. Ed made a mistake. He was wrong. And it sounds to me like he knows he was wrong. Lauren, I think your relationship can grow stronger and more honest out of this whole affair."

"Does Ed have you on his payroll, too?" Lauren half laughed between tears, but Tandy felt hopeful. She was starting to break Lauren's resolve. She decided to go for the kill.

"You know, Lauren, I don't like to think of myself in these terms, and I hate these words, but well, after Phil died, I learned how tough it is out there without a partner to share your life with." Tandy began to blink, willing the tears to come. She thought about being forced to sell her apartment, and a solitary teardrop trickled down her face.

Now it was Lauren's turn to hold Tandy's hand. "I'm sorry, Tandy, here I am crying about my issues, and you're still dealing with the loss of Phil. I didn't mean to be insensitive."

Tandy waved her off. "No, no. I'm glad you came to me. I've always thought of you like my second daughter. It's just that I do know how hard it is out in the world on your own. And honestly, Lauren, you throw out a man with one bad habit, and you pick up another with five bad habits. I know you can't see it right now, but you and Ed have something special. I think he deserves another chance. Don't give another woman the satisfaction of becoming Mrs. Ed Thomas. Believe it or not, men need us to protect them from women like Alyssia. Women are smarter than men. Of course, men would never admit that. Teach Ed how to be the man he wants to be. Don't leave him. He would be nothing without you."

Tandy watched the tears roll down Lauren's face again. "God, Tandy. I want so much to believe you. I want so much to believe him."

Tandy fixed her lips to tell a lie on the dead. "I never told you this, Lauren, but when Phil was still alive, he told me that he had never seen Ed so happy as he was with you. And he said that Ed had told him he didn't know what it meant to be in love until he met you. Take your time, Lauren, but give him another chance. He's human."

THIRTY-SEVEN

As Manny waited in the large conference room with floor-to-ceiling windows boasting panoramic views of lower Manhattan and New Jersey, he had to remind himself that he was at the offices of Stonemark Forum, the same organization responsible for the sickening colonic he'd had to endure. Manny had expected candles in humble rooms and people walking around dressed in tunics. Instead he found serious corporate suites and people dressed to do business, to make money.

He had spoken to Dana's attorney, Daniel Graham, on the phone, and had surmised that he was a white queen. Graham had been pleasant to deal with, informing Manny in their first conversation that while he was an attorney, he hadn't practiced for some time and never did any real estate work. He said he trusted Manny to walk him through any difficult points. Manny was happy to oblige.

Stanley Allen, the attorney for the Thomas Foundation, arrived after Manny. He entered the room with presence and style, remaining aloof. The six-foot-three, fair-complexioned, sandy-haired black man with freckles and a sharp navy suit held out his hand to Manny, who grabbed it. Stanley then placed his left hand over Manny's, revealing a wedding ring. Manny felt his smile fade slightly. Oh well, he might not be able to attract a man today, but he would walk home with five million dollars. Nothing could dampen that feeling.

Nonetheless, Manny was beginning to get anxious. He had arrived twenty minutes early. He hadn't slept the night before and had had no appetite for the last two days, which was just as well, to help bring out that six-pack. But now he had been waiting a half an hour, and the buyer's attorney was present with the check in his briefcase. What was taking Daniel so long? And then, with the glamour that only a diva could command, Daniel entered. He was dressed more like an interior designer than a lawyer, with his long-sleeved black T-shirt and tapered black pants. His gray hair was spiky. He walked into the room, hands flailing all over the place. "Oh, my God! I am so sorry I've taken so long, but I was having the best reading, and she went over."

Manny and Stanley gave each other a look that said, "Is this guy for real?"

"Anyway, I'm Daniel Graham." He extended his hand to Manny.

"Manny Marks."

Throwing his hands to his face, Daniel said, "I had no idea I was talking to such a good-looking man on the other end of the phone. I would have come up with a reason for us to have a private meeting sooner." He laughed and eyed Manny.

Since Manny would be receiving the check from Stanley in escrow for Dana, he took control of the meeting. Everything went smoothly as they approached the actual handoff of the check.

"As I mentioned, Stanley, here is the notarized letter from Dana authorizing you to deliver the Thomas Foundation check to my company." Manny hoped the document did not tremble in his fingers.

"Good. This is my copy?"

"Yes, for you."

"Then I guess this check is for you." Stanley reached into his black leather case and pulled out an envelope.

"Allrighty then," Manny uttered, full of delight as he opened the envelope to view the check. This piece of paper felt so light, considering its hefty amount. The butterflies in his stomach danced as he longingly counted the zeros and read the word "million" after the "forty" on the face of the check.

"So, Manny, I guess you made out well in this deal," the loud, annoying homosexual chimed in.

Manny smiled. "Not as well as your client."

"Oh, what about the settlement sheet?" asked Stanley. Lauren and Ed's attorney was obviously used to doing more closings than Daniel.

"You don't need that for commercial property, do you?" Daniel was clueless.

"Actually, you do, Daniel. And I have it right here." Manny had made sure nothing would go wrong with this deal.

"And no commission invoice?" Stanley was crossing his T's and dotting his I's.

"No. That's all taken care of. That's why the check goes into escrow."

"But the letter from Dana doesn't mention a dollar amount."

The guy was beginning to work Manny. Dumb-ass Daniel just sat there staring at Manny, making stupid faces. He asked nothing. He offered nothing. This was just as well for Manny. He could handle the situation.

"Trust me, if Dana doesn't get her money, she will get me." Manny chuckled, keeping the mood light.

Stanley began to collect his things. "Okay, then. That's it. Take care, Manny; Daniel." And the attorney left.

Manny had his check. The deal was done. In under an hour, Manny had become a millionaire. He couldn't wait to deposit the money, wire Tandy's cash to the Caymans account she'd specified, pay Dana, and count his own money.

"Are you going to personally deliver that check, or should I come and retrieve it?" Daniel was actually trying to come on to him.

"Oh no, darling, my very trusted assistant will hand-deliver it to you later this afternoon."

"Too bad." Daniel sulked.

"Good meeting you, Daniel." Manny picked up his briefcase and patted his breast pocket, making sure the check was secure. He then walked out of the conference room, onto the elevator, and toward his new life as a millionaire. He couldn't wait to get home and celebrate with Trenton.

Now that he was five million dollars richer, Manny had decided that from this day on he would travel only by car and driver. He had his regular service pick him up from the closing in the black Mercedes 600. The driver took him to the bank to make the deposit and the transfer of funds to Tandy's and his personal accounts. He created three separate accounts for himself, not wanting to put all of his eggs in one basket. With all of the paperwork done and a prearranged appointment with the bank that always handled Manny's real estate transactions, he was able to do everything immediately. Next he returned Dana's check to her lawyer. Afterward, Manny had his driver stop off at Cellini, a jewelry store on Madison Avenue, where he selected a fifteen-thousand-dollar two-carat diamond stud for Trenton. On the ride uptown, Manny had tried to reach his lover, but Trenton hadn't been home, and his cell went directly into voice mail. Manny left messages in both places. Tonight would be a celebration like no other.

Manny also had the car stop off at Sherry-Lehman for two bottles of champagne. Only the best from now on. The salesman tried to talk Manny out of Cristal, suggesting he try something less known but more flavorful, but Manny heard Tandy's voice—"Cristal and Dom are the only champagnes to drink"—and knew that Trenton wouldn't appreciate another brand.

He was beyond excited. His payday had come. From this time on, he did not have to work ever again if he managed his money well. He would probably stay in the game and broker a couple of big deals a year. Maybe he would sell his firm. This was all too much for him to think about now. First things first: Time to celebrate.

When the car pulled up in front of his stoop, Manny noticed a maroon Bentley parked in front of the house next door, with someone sitting in the driver's seat and another person in the back, talking into a cell phone. The license plate read D.D. He had never seen this car before and was concerned that drug dealers might be invading his block. If they were drug dealers, they certainly were not your basic hustlers. Flossy Negroes always needed to call attention to themselves, Manny thought as his own driver opened the door for him.

He skipped up the stairs to his brownstone, opened the door, and yelled out, "Trenton! Daddy's home. Big Papa is back, and I bring gifts!" He singsonged as he went from the living room to the kitchen, "Trenton? Where oh where are you, baby?" He simply could not wait to share his good fortune.

Finally, he heard Trenton fumbling around in their bedroom. The door was cracked, so Manny could only see his lover's profile. When he entered, what he saw did not register. A duffel bag sat on the unmade bed, and Trenton was placing underwear, cologne, sweatsuits, and photos of his mother and sister inside.

Manny did not understand. "What's going on?" he asked, feeling as if he were moving in slow motion.

"Damn. Oh, Manny, I thought I would be gone before you got here. I mean, I felt that way would be easier." Trenton kept packing.

"Gone? Easier? I'm not following you." Then Manny put two and two together. The Bentley outside didn't belong to any drug dealer. It belonged to a rapper. "D.D." was Dime Dog. He felt his heart break inside his chest as the realization that he was being jilted sank in. "But Trenton, our celebration . . . I brought champagne, and this is for you." Manny tossed the box, wrapped in shiny silver paper, Trenton's way.

Trenton picked up the box and placed it unopened on Manny's bureau, which gave Manny a glimpse of the platinum Rolex laced in diamonds on Trenton's wrist.

Manny plopped down on the bed next to the packed duffel. He sat staring at the wall in a stupor. How could the best day of his life end up like this?

"I would ask why or what happened, but I already know the answer. You traded up. You traded up."

"Listen, man, don't think of it that way." Trenton paused after zipping the bag. He stood in front of Manny, obviously trying to soften the blow. "I actually fell in love. Dante—that's his real name—swept me off my feet. We love each other. It happens, you know." Trenton threw the bag over his shoulder as he took a step toward the door.

"I'm sure that watch and the Bentley outside helped soften the fall." Manny was someplace beyond anger. How could Trenton so selfishly walk out on his big day?

"I know you're angry, but I also know you'll be all right, Manny." Trenton headed out of the door and then popped his head back into the bedroom. "Oh, yeah, congratulations on your big deal. You dah man." Trenton flashed his big perfect-toothed grin, the white of his teeth beautifully contrasting with the brown of his skin, then left for good.

Manny remained sitting on the bed for many minutes, holding the cool bottle of Dom. Finally, he opened the champagne, jumping at the loud pop the cork made as it escaped the bottle. The bubbly poured over his hands and leg, but Manny didn't notice. He put the bottle to his lips and took a long swig. The clean, clear bubbles burned as they charged down his throat. The feeling reminded him that he was alive.

He reached for the telephone and dialed the number of his best buddy for some consolation, but quickly hung up, remembering that she did not want to talk to him. Ed had called Manny the day before to say he would not be helping Alyssia out after all. If she called, Manny should not show her anything else. He had not asked Ed, but he assumed that Lauren must have found out about the affair, which might explain why she had not returned any of his calls. Sadly, Manny realized, he had lost his two love relationships in one fell swoop.

Manny went to the drawer of his nightstand and opened the flat jewelry box that contained his weed stash. He lit the joint he had rolled this morning in expectation of the celebratory evening. He sat alone, listening to the sounds of the street and of the very old house, drinking and smoking. Today he had achieved what he'd wanted from the time he was a little boy. He was a millionaire. The saying "It's lonely at the top" had never rung truer than it did today. Manny had had no idea how lonely he could feel until this very moment.

THIRTY-EIGHT

SITTING alone at the bar absently munching peanuts, Lauren checked her Franck Muller rose-gold watch, given to her by her husband. Manny would not arrive for another fifteen minutes. One thing she could always count on was his promptness. Lauren had arrived early at this glamorous party, held in the duplex penthouse of a serious art dealer, to strategically place herself directly in view of the door. As always, Manny had been pleased to be included with this illustrious crowd when she called to invite him. Little did he know that tonight would be his last among this—or any other—group of New York's elite. Lauren was eager to see how he entered the room. Tonight was about reading his body language, looking into his soul. Despite having known Manny for years, she realized she didn't know him at all.

As she sipped her smooth Petron tequila on the rocks, Lauren reflected on the egregious deceptions Manny had perpetrated against her. She grunted out loud in disgust. It was sheer luck that had tipped her off to his second betrayal.

Sending over Dana Trip's file from Stonemark Forum had been a huge mistake on someone's part. Lauren had called Dana's attorney to ask for a copy of the closing documents; when she had called her attorney, he was away on business for a couple of days. In her eagerness to move forward, she tracked down Daniel Graham. He was so disorganized he could barely remember the closing, let alone the documents. Lauren had not expected to receive anything from him. When the disorderly original papers arrived at her apartment, she was surprised, to say the least. The fool of an attorney had sent over everything in the Dana Trip file, including the private-investigator reports of Dana's husband's comings and goings. He had also included the net-exclusive agreement between Manny and Dana that promised Lauren's so-called best friend a commission of anything above the thirty-million-dollar price Dana wanted. This agreement itself wouldn't have been so bad, but Manny had insisted that at forty million, Ed and Lauren were getting a deal. Further, Lauren knew that this type of contract between a seller and a broker was no longer legal in New York State. Manny had tried to be slick. He thought he had played them. In fact, he had attempted to play Lauren twice. As far as she was concerned, he would be all played out when she finished with him.

Her zeal to get the documents had come with an effort to stop feeling sorry for herself and take her mind off her problems. Before discovering her husband's affair, she normally would have waited to receive the papers from her personal attorney, but she had been restless since finishing her black-male-model documentary for Style Channel. Once editing was complete, she found herself depressed and without much to do. Now she was stuck with time to just sit around and think about her situation with Ed. Since he had moved out of their bedroom, they barely spoke, even though he contin-uously apologized. He had taken to moping around their home as if he were the one who had been lied to and cheated on. Ironically, he rarely went to the office, and in the last weeks he had not gone out of town. But Lauren had decided her conversations with Ed would be kept to a minimum until he came clean with her about everything and committed to couples therapy. His refusal to dig deeper and divulge all of the sordid details Lauren was obsessed with knowing had exacerbated the nightmare that had become her life. Sadly, she was beginning to accept what Tandy had told her, that philandering husbands—hers included—were the norm rather than the exception.

At this low moment, Lauren had become very introspective. She thought long and hard about how she might have contributed to Ed's cheating. She tried to go deep within herself to discover what Lauren Thomas wanted. She realized that she could no longer live to please her mother or her husband. She had to stop complaining about what other people wanted from her and decide what she wanted for herself.

In this new proactive mode, propelled by a need to take responsibility for herself, she had discovered Manny's betrayal. Initially, she felt pain at being taken advantage of over and over again. But that quickly turned to anger when the realization of Manny's trickery sank in.

Lauren turned her gaze toward the door and saw him standing there looking vacant, shallow, and pathetic despite his clear skin, fresh haircut, and impeccable taste in clothes. His armor, she realized, consisted of his exterior accoutrements and that dashing smile. But now, even from across the room, she could see the empty shell of a miserable human being.

Manny had been a bit ambivalent when Lauren finally called him and invited him to dinner. He reasoned that Lauren knew he had shown Alyssia property. He was embarrassed and ready to grovel at her feet. He thought it would probably take a while for them to get their friendship back to status quo. Maybe she would understand how he had tried to protect her.

He nervously walked through the dark crowd, turning this way and that to reach Lauren at the bar. He noted a few familiar faces throughout the room, which glowed in the warm light. They were all smiling, laughing, eating, and enjoying the high-pressure frivolity of Manhattan's upper crust. One would never imagine a recession was going on by using this room as an indicator. The price of Hermès bags and Jimmy Choo shoes alone could buy a small house in Jersey.

As Manny reached the bar, he could tell Lauren was angry and wounded. However, she looked beautiful, her naturally curly hair blown straight and resting on her shoulders. She was noticeably thinner, not gaunt, but very slim. She was decked out in all black, a form-fitting skirt just below the knee with an equally form-fitting one-shouldered top that accentuated her soft skin and healthy breasts. A pair of black stiletto sling-backs finished off the outfit. Lauren looked the best Manny had ever seen her. But the new severe look was disturbing to an old friend who knew he was in trouble. Manny had always appreciated Lauren's soft, carefree approach to life. Tonight there was nothing soft about her. Her posture, her movements, and the glint in her eye were all razor-sharp.

She was gracious enough to air-kiss his cheek, stiffly leaning forward, her lips pursed tight.

"What are you drinking?" Manny began, trying his best to be upbeat.

Lauren cut her eyes at him. "Tequila on the rocks."

"Well, allrighty then. I think I'll have a Black Label."

As Manny's drink arrived, he looked up to see his old nemesis, Gossip to Go Glo, waddle into the party with a surprisingly good-looking male companion. As he wondered about Glo and her friend, Lauren's abrupt voice broke through his thoughts. "Why did you do it, Manny?"

Manny tried to face her by leaning on the bar, but he was stuck between Lauren and a heavyset man who wasn't giving him much room. He was uncomfortable and would have preferred to sit down for this conversation. "You don't want to wait for us to get some privacy?"

"Why, Manny?" was all Lauren said.

He sipped his drink, letting it burn his throat. He searched Lauren's eyes for a soft place. "I . . . I . . ." he began, having a difficult time as a lump welled up in his throat. "Ed came to me. He explained to me that you knew what you had gotten into when you married him. He said that his arrangement with her had nothing to do with his love for you."

Her stare remained hard. "I didn't ask you why Ed did what he did. I asked why did *you*?" She sipped her almost empty drink.

"I was getting to that. I told him I didn't want to do it. But then he said he would use another broker, and I figured, as crazy as it may sound now, that I would at least keep any rumors quiet. I even rationalized that I might be able to break them up."

"Hmph." Lauren got the attention of the bartender and ordered another.

"I told Ed—I told him I didn't want the money. I refused to accept a commission. Whether you believe me or not, the whole thing made me sick. I felt terrible lying to you."

"I see." Lauren stared intently at Manny. She seemed to be searching for something. She was so cool. Like ice. He wanted to break through, but she was impenetrable. "You didn't want the commission?"

"No. I would never accept any money on those conditions."

"Oh, but you would take money that didn't belong to you in other ways."

Manny stopped short. He surveyed her carefully. "I don't know what you mean."

"No?" Lauren raised her eyebrows. "How about that nice commission you made from the Sugar Hill Building sale? The way you made that commission was acceptable to you?"

"I still don't know what you are trying to say, Lauren." Manny's palms moistened, his heart picked up a beat, and his mind began racing. She couldn't possibly know.

"Yes you do, you liar." She spoke quickly and clearly without becoming overly loud.

"Lauren, I—"

"Shut up! I know about that net-exclusive agreement with Dana Trip. In fact, I have a copy of it."

I can handle this, he rationalized. "Okay. Well, that agreement is private, between me and the seller. I don't know how you got it, but this was a confidential business matter. These types of agreements are commonplace."

Lauren chuckled slightly, looking at Manny, shaking her head. She took another drag on her drink. "It wouldn't be so bad if you hadn't told me and

Ed that we were getting a bargain at forty. We took your word. You lied to us. We were supposedly your friends, when the reality is that every time you looked at us, all you saw were big fat moneybags."

"No. That's not true. I love you, Lauren. But this was business. It wasn't personal."

"But Manny, is your business legal?"

Lauren stared through Manny, and he regarded her back. Fear crept up his spine. His professional life was potentially on the brink.

"What?"

"You and I both know that this is some shady shit. This document alone is enough to at least get your license revoked. How fucking stupid are you? I guess you thought you and Dana would be the only ones with the actual contract, and no one would be the wiser. She gets the money. She's happy. You get yours."

Manny continued to stand, but his legs felt weak.

"Manny, you look a little pale. You want some air? I know I do. Let's step out onto the terrace."

Gathering their drinks, Lauren and Manny slowly maneuvered their way from the crowded bar to the terrace, overlooking a beautifully lighted uptown Manhattan skyline.

Turning toward Manny, Lauren said, "You know, I really cared for you. I thought you were smart. I thought you were ambitious. I thought you had class. But what I see, Manny, is a weak, pathetic person. You think that making it is about fucking over the people who put you on the map in the first place?"

"Wait. Wait. Let me explain. I never would have done anything like this. Someone else convinced me that by structuring our deal, your deal, like we did, no one would be hurt." Manny was speaking fast as he followed Lauren to the cement and iron railing that guarded the terrace from the concrete streets below.

"Manny, for you to sit up here and blame some fictional person for your actions is despicable. You need to take responsibility for yourself."

"I do, Lauren. But you need to know the truth. Tandy introduced me to Dana Trip. She—"

"Tandy? Are you implicating Tandy? Someone who I know also took you under her wing? You are sick." Lauren leaned on the railing, her knuckles white from holding her drink so tightly.

Manny continued, "Listen to me. You may hate me with good reason, but you need to know the real story. Tandy introduced me to Dana. She then told me that she could convince you to take on the museum as your cause. She believed that Ed would support your wish to help the museum. She came up with the net-exclusive idea with Dana. I told her those types of arrangements weren't legal anymore. Hell, I didn't want to lose my license. But she insisted that Dana wouldn't know or care about the legalities of the situation. Dana only wanted her thirty million dollars. And Tandy was right." Manny paused and checked to see if Lauren was understanding him. "Tandy told me she put that forty-million figure in your head. You have to understand. Tandy is in dire straits financially. Phil left her broke. She is desperate. We split the money fifty-fifty. I sent her half to the Cayman Islands." Manny looked down. "I'm sorry. I know it's a weak thing to say, but I am sorry."

Without addressing anything Manny had said about Tandy, Lauren cut into him. "You are right about one thing: You are one sorry motherfucker. Let me explain it to you like this. New York is no place for you. This town is very small. And despite the millions of people who inhabit this island, when you have no friends, when there is no one to call to help you, when you have burned your last bridge, misused your last favor, there's nothing left for you here. And believe me when I tell you this: You have no more friends in Manhattan. You will never work again on any significant real estate projects. You won't even be able to broker a studio rental. My wings spread that wide and far."

Manny could not speak. He was afraid that tears would tumble out of his eyes. He stared across the island, beginning to understand that he was no longer a part of what he had come to love—the power players of New York City, of the world.

"I suggest you pack your shit. Pay me back my money and skip town. If you elect to stay here, I guess you could always manage to get a job delivering groceries from a neighborhood Food Emporium." Lauren was visibly shaking. "You know, on the real, you need to go somewhere and save what is left of your soul."

Moving from the edge of the terrace, Lauren started back to the party. "Manny, I hope the ride was a fun one for you." Stepping back so that only Manny could hear her, "Oh. And if you don't repay my every cent and disappear, not only will I embarrass you socially and professionally, making sure everyone knows what a lying sneaky snake you are, I will prosecute you and make sure you can no longer work and that you spend time in a federal prison. Are we clear?"

Manny looked into Lauren's dark eyes and saw a strong, fiery, powerful woman, no longer carefree. He realized that he was partially responsible for stripping her of innocence.

As Lauren headed back into the crowded party, leaving Manny alone on the terrace, he noticed Gossip to Go Glo fall in line behind her. He saw Lauren furrow her brow and then relax, smile and say a few words. Yes, his life in New York was truly over. Maybe Lauren was right. A little soul-searching might be in order.

THIRTY-NINE

L AUREN had called Tandy and invited her to Grace's Links gala bene-fit in Connecticut on a Saturday evening. Tandy knew most of the Westchester/Fairfield County African-Americans who would be in atten-dance. She had not been to a social function out of the city since Phil died. Going as Lauren's guest would be a nice way to reenter this world, she thought, and a good opportunity to begin talking, very casually, about what direction she intended to move the children's wing of the museum.

Tandy had a car service drive her up to the Greenwich Hyatt, since Lauren insisted they ride back to the city together. Lauren claimed she never had enough opportunities to drive her Porsche, and she wanted to show off to Tandy.

When Tandy arrived at the Hyatt, Lauren was nowhere to be found. Tandy checked herself in and found her table. She bumped into people she had not seen in years. They all raved about how wonderful she looked, bet-ter than ever. And not one of them had seen Lauren tonight.

Organizers of the event implored people to take their seats for what would surely be an excruciatingly long, boring program of overly self-important women glorifying their charitable contributions to the unfortunate. Still no Lauren. Tandy took her place at a table in the very back of the room. If she had been any farther back, she thought, she would be sitting in the lobby. Who on earth had put her and Lauren at this lackluster table? Her dinner partners wore cheap clothing, costume jewelry, and too much makeup. Most of the time Tandy could put on a good face and at least personify the meaning of class, but tonight it was all she could do not to ask these people if they really belonged at this event. She turned her nose up, sat in the seat that bore her name, and completely ignored the other guests, making no eye contact whatsoever. Tandy remained in no-man's-land while the program progressed. The president of the organization, an accomplished Ph.D. in her field of community development, droned on for what felt like hours about the importance of giving back, especially through their club.

Sipping the red wine in front of her, Tandy thought back to her conversation with Lauren. She knew she had gotten the story right: Lauren was supposed to be here, and they were supposed to ride back to the city together in Lauren's sports car. Checking her cell phone, Tandy saw that she had no messages. How rude. Even if there was some sort of emergency, unless she was either dead or lying unconscious, Lauren should have called to let Tandy know that she would be alone at this function. Grace, a cohost of the evening's festivities, did not look worried about her daughter's absence as she smiled from the front of the room and made transitions from one speaker to another, handing out awards to those who had helped to raise money in the name of the Links.

As soon as the program was over and Grace announced the band and dancing, Tandy started for the door. She had to get a car service to pick her up. It would probably take an hour for a car to reach her. Damn that Lauren. For someone who was supposed to be so together, so cultured—a woman born of the manor, so to speak—Lauren was demonstrating a serious lack of etiquette. Tandy would have to school the pitiful child once again.

"Oh, Tandy, there you are." Lauren interrupted Tandy's thoughts with a tap on her shoulder from behind.

"Lauren, I was beginning to think you had decided not to show up. I was about to order a car to get home." Tandy spoke lightheartedly, waiting for Lauren to explain the terrible situation that had kept her.

"Well, you know how these things go. I got here when I could" was all Lauren offered, looking sophisticated in her black pantsuit. "So, are you ready to head back to the city? I've already said my hellos and good-byes."

How strange, thought Tandy. Lauren could not have been at this party over ten minutes. Perhaps she was still mentally off because of Ed's transgression. *That must be it.* Women who allowed their marital problems to affect their judgment and behavior sickened Tandy. But tonight, to get a ride home, she would put on a friendly face and humor Lauren.

"I'm ready when you are." Tandy smiled and fell in step with Lauren, who was already heading to the valet parking and the midnight-blue Porsche with red leather interior. Tandy, in her evening gown, thought the car rather uncomfortable, but she pretended to be pleased as she settled back for the long ride.

"Strap in!" Lauren yelled over the revving engine as she peeled out of the parking lot. At eleven-thirty, winding Connecticut roads were pitch black, with no streetlights. Having grown up chasing around with her friends, Lauren had all of the hidden roads etched in her mind. She zipped and maneuvered the curves as though playing a video game.

"Whew! You sure are moving fast around these bends," Tandy commented with a nervous chuckle.

Lauren noticed Tandy was holding on to the side of her seat. "Don't tell me you're nervous. We haven't even reached the Merritt Parkway yet. That's where I really have fun."

"I can't wait." Tandy's voice was unenthused.

She doesn't seem so tough and sure of herself now, Lauren thought. And then she began Act One. "You know the real reason I arrived late? I've been so depressed, I didn't want to face any of my mother's friends."

"I figured as much. But Lauren, you can't let your marital issues affect your public face. People are counting on you. I'm counting on you." Being Lauren's personal cheerleader was becoming a bore. If Tandy hadn't needed her so much in the first place, she never would have taken on the role. After tonight her exposure to Lauren would be limited to museum talk. She needed a break from this poor child.

"I know you're right." Lauren was now heading the two-seater onto the dark, curving Merritt Parkway toward Manhattan. She had been driving the Merritt to and from New York for fifteen years. When she was a teenager, her friends would marvel at her skill with whipping around the turns at ninety miles an hour, singing along with the radio. Invariably, her passengers were nervous. But Lauren was confident. She liked driving and was great at it.

As she eased onto the parkway, she quickly changed gears, getting the Carrera 2 up to seventy-five in no time. Tandy was such a fake, pretending to give a damn about Lauren's social obligations. Lauren settled into her seat, feeling the car adjust to her slightest movements.

"It's just so hard dealing, because I don't know who to trust anymore, Tandy. Everyone lies to me. You know what I mean?" Tandy did not respond. "You know what I mean, don't you, Tandy?"

"Well, Lauren, as I've said to you before, you must be careful with whom you share yourself. You can't let everyone into your heart. I do know what you mean, and you are right. You can't trust everyone." Tandy could not wait to be out of this car and away from Lauren's reckless driving. The girl was like a maniac, going around the dark curves way too fast.

"But Tandy, my best friends, they let me down, too. Did Manny tell you about our discussion?"

Tandy had not spoken to Manny in days. She felt it would be better for the both of them if they laid low for a couple of months as the sale of the building in Harlem cooled off. Truth be told, she was tired of Manny, anyway. He was a little fish trying to be a big player. He would never be any-one of importance. Despite what she had told him over the years to bolster him for her own purposes, Tandy knew that no matter how much money

Manny made, he would always be a glorified salesman. As a gay man, New York society—Tandy included—would allow him to go only so far.

"No, dear. I haven't spoken to Manny in a while. But you told me he was showing Alyssia apartments. I told you to forget him."

"No. There's more. He stole from me."

Oh shit, thought Tandy. What with Lauren's strange antics of the night and now her wild handling of the car, Tandy was beginning to believe that Lauren might have actually lost her mind. But perhaps something else was going on. Maybe Lauren knew what Tandy and Manny had done. If Lauren could learn of Manny's betrayal over Alyssia, what was to say she didn't know about the other? If Lauren had confronted Manny, he would have sold Tandy out in a heartbeat. Whatever Lauren thought she knew, Tandy would deny, deny, deny.

"I don't believe that, Lauren. Manny is many things, but a thief?"

Spare me, Lauren thought to herself. Defending Manny did not suit Tandy.

"Believe it, Tandy. Manny told me everything. He told me about how he got Dana Trip to sign a net-exclusive deal with his firm and how she only wanted thirty million for the building, but he decided to make it seem like we were getting it for a bargain at forty million." Lauren had begun to cry. She had not been expecting this burst of emotion. She'd wanted to maintain her cool, to let Tandy know how strong she was. And now she was crying. Tears were streaming down her face, blurring the road before her. "He claimed he was my friend, and then he goes house-hunting for my husband's mistress and steals ten million dollars from me! I guess I was a simple fool to believe that he could want to just be friends with me. Why does everyone have to have an angle?"

Tandy sat as still as a deer listening for the sound of a hunter's footstep. The Porsche swerved around curve after dark curve, jolting Tandy's body from side to side. She assumed Lauren could not see through her tears. But Lauren picked up speed. Whirring past a humongous Ford Excursion, Lauren was nearly pressed up against the cement divider.

"Ooooh." Tandy's noise sounded involuntary to Lauren.

"And do you want to know the worst part of Manny's confession, Tandy? Do you?" Lauren took her eyes off the road to take a glance at a horror-stricken Tandy. Her knuckles were white from holding on to the sides of the seat so hard; her face glistened with a cold sweat. Lauren turned her attention back to the highway just in time to avoid hitting a car slowing down in front of them. Tandy remained silent.

"The worst part was that he said you were the mastermind behind the entire scheme. He said you came to him with Dana Trip. I said, 'Oh no, not Tandy. Tandy is my dear friend. I've looked up to Tandy all of my fucking life. I wanted to *be* Tandy. She wouldn't stab me in the back like that.' But then I thought about it, and I realized that the only way Manny could have gotten a listing from Dana was through you. And then you give me that speech on the golf course about me needing a platform, and how I would be doing such a service for the po' colored children in Harlem by paying forty million for the Sugar Hill Building. You had it all planned out. The only servicing I was doing was of your ass!"

Finally, Tandy's vocal cords became unglued. "I don't know what Manny told you. Yes, I gave him Dana as a referral. I've given him many referrals over the years. That doesn't mean I stole from you."

By now Lauren's tears had stopped. "True. True. I said the same thing to Manny. But then he showed me how the money was divided. See, Manny put his five-million-dollar cut in three separate bank accounts. He showed me the receipts. Then he showed me the receipt for the account in the Cayman Islands, the one you set up to receive your half of my money."

"That is preposterous. I've never taken anything that didn't belong to me." Tandy was livid. "After all that I've been through, you dare accuse me of such a thing! You don't know anything about living."

"I know one thing. It's not about fucking over the people who love you to get what you want," Lauren shouted.

"Love? What's love got to do with anything? Either you survive or you don't."

"Don't sit there and continue to lie to me, Tandy!" Lauren said. "I know goddamn well what you did. I have the proof. Manny told me he would testify against you if I decided to prosecute. You have nothing." She zoomed along, crossing the Connecticut border, entering Westchester, New York, and the Hutchinson River Parkway.

"Lauren, I am sick of your sniveling. Sometimes in life you have to make the best of your situation. After that husband of mine left me broke, I've had to struggle to make ends meet. But you wouldn't know anything about that. You went practically from your mother's womb to marry a man who became like another father to you. You need to grow the fuck up and stop crying about what everyone else is doing to you!" Tandy was beyond herself with anger. "This is the real world. This is how people survive. Get a clue and get with the program. If you want to make it in the big leagues, you need to learn how to play the game."

Lauren shifted down from fifth gear to fourth, getting more power to go faster. The speedometer read ninety, and she was climbing faster. "If playing your game is the only way to make it, as you say, then maybe I don't want to live in this world anymore. How is that living, if you are always gaming your friends and loved ones? What's life if you can't trust anyone?" Lauren edged up to a hundred miles an hour as she took a turn, sending Tandy into the passenger door. The car raced onto the shoulder, branches from trees brushing up against the vehicle.

Tandy was fed up with this child playing Speed Racer at the amusement park. "ALL RIGHT! YOU STUPID LITTLE BITCH! Life is tough. Get over it. If you want to kill yourself, go ahead, but let me out. Your money is better served in my hands. You don't know how to live." In her fear, Tandy had made a subtle admission. At this point she no longer cared what Lauren knew; she just wanted out of the car before Lauren killed them both.

The Porsche slowed to sixty miles an hour, which felt like twenty. Tandy calmed down and tried to clean up her last statement. "I'm sorry. I had no choice" was all she could muster.

"You had no choice? No choice. The thing is that I would have helped you. I would have done anything for you. You are such a narcissistic person. You never cared about me. You only cared about yourself. When I came to you about Ed, you weren't consoling me. You were making sure your payday came. You make me sick. And to think about all the years I wasted idolizing you." Lauren was not yelling anymore; nor was she driving like a maniac. She was remarkably calm.

Tandy gave a slight chuckle. "I make you sick? Let me tell you about yourself. I may have wanted that deal to go through, but what I told you about Ed was true. All men cheat. All men are dogs. Some are just good dogs. Of course Ed is going to have other women. You aren't a woman yet. He needs someone with strength of character. He needs someone with a vision of herself. He needs to know that his wife is holding the house and his image in order while he is out there blazing trails and making history. Instead you whine about not having a career, about everyone's expectations of you. You, my dear, will never be enough woman for him, unless you grow up real fast. And trust me, I'm not telling you this out of any desire to get anything from you. This is the truth."

"That may be true for you, Tandy." Lauren made the left exit off the Hutch into a Mobil station in the middle of the parkway. "Ed and I have had many a long talk since the day I visited your home. We have talked about Alyssia and his past affairs. He cheated often on Claudia. He no longer wants to be that man who leads a double life. He wants honesty. He longs for clarity and true love. And I plan to give him another chance."

Again Tandy chuckled. "Ed wants true love now, huh?"

"Oh, you think that's funny, do you?" Lauren stopped the car by the minimart.

"Yes, I do. I've known Ed since before you were born, and a dog doesn't change his spots."

"Oh. Are you referring to the affair that you and Ed had?" Lauren looked so composed and controlled. She suddenly seemed much older under the neon lights of the gas station.

"What? I don't kn—"

Putting her hand up as if telling Tandy not to waste her time trying to deny this one, Lauren said, "Ed told me about the fling you two had when he was married to Claudia. He mentioned the days spent at the Harbor View Hotel when she thought he was playing golf."

Tandy's mouth dropped open.

"He also told me what a lousy lay you were. How he had to have several cocktails before he could rise to the occasion, pardon the pun. Anyway, he wishes those days had never happened, and he felt guilty about doing that to Phil. How did Ed put it? He said you were a pebble in the sand." Lauren enjoyed the sour look on Tandy's face. "Why don't you listen to me very carefully," she continued. "This is about our money. I want you to pay us back every cent. If we do not get every cent of our money back, I will press charges, and believe me, I have more than enough evidence to secure a conviction. Ed and I have decided to give you fifteen days to return the money. We also expect you to disappear off the map of New York society. We don't want you taking advantage of any of our friends. Frankly, I would think you'd want to leave New York and move out west, somewhere like Santa Fe, where the cost of living is cheap and the weather is always nice. Better yet, why don't you relocate closer to your daughter? Learn how to love. Give her something besides your coldness to feed off of so she doesn't turn out like you. Either way, we'd better not see your name on any invitation or your face at any event. If we do, I promise I will tell everyone what a cheating, scamming fraud you are. Do we understand each other?"

Tandy was in shock. "But what if I can't afford to move or sell my apartment?" She had never been so busted before. Lauren said Ed knew. Ed was in agreement. Ed was giving these marching orders. Her life truly was over.

"What you can and cannot afford is no longer my business. I would have helped you out before you stole from me. Now you're on your own."

Tandy stared out at the dark, desolate gas station. A lone man worked behind bulletproof glass inside the minimart. Then it dawned on her. Why had Lauren stopped?

"You can get out now."

Lauren couldn't be serious. She wouldn't leave Tandy out in the middle of nowhere in the middle of the night by herself in her evening gown.

"Go ahead. Get out," Lauren persisted.

"You want me to get out here? By myself? But how will I get home?" Tandy stared at Lauren, looking for some compassion, but there was none.

"Once again, that's not my problem. Now, get the fuck out of my car!"

Tandy gathered her purse and pulled out her cell phone as she exited the car, disentangling the train of her gown. As soon as she shut the door, the Porsche zoomed off, leaving Tandy staring at the back lights. She suddenly wished Lauren had crashed them both into the cement guardrail.

Lauren never looked back. She gathered up speed as the car zipped onto the highway. Driving always made Lauren feel powerful. Being in control, manipulating every move, anticipating the motion of traffic, surviving through the elements were also the fundamentals of life.

FORTY

MANNY asked the brown-skinned driver of the black Lincoln Town Car to take the scenic route to Newark Airport. There was plenty of time before his flight out this dark morning, and he wanted to go through the streets of the city one last time. He checked his face in the vanity mirror, exasperated by the crop of red bumps that spread across his once bronzed, now yellow-toned face. The dark circles under his eyes further revealed the anguish of the last six months of his life. He could not get over how haggard he looked.

Returning his portion of Lauren's money had not taken long. He hadn't had time to spend much before Lauren confronted him. When he brought the check to her home, in hopes of seeing her, he was prepared to get down on his knees. Unfortunately, Mr. Francis was her proxy; Lauren refused to see him. To convince Lauren that total banishment from New York was too extreme, Manny left messages and wrote many notes apologizing for his selfish behavior. He knew he had done wrong, but to take away seventeen years of hard work? He hoped Lauren would understand that he was truly sorry, maybe forgive him in some small way, once she had a moment to get over her initial anger. But she remained steadfast. After six months of groveling and dragging his feet on selling his brownstone, Manny bumped into Lauren in front of the new Museum of Harlem. She assured him she would prosecute if he did not leave New York by the end of the year.

Manny gave serious consideration to whether she would actually have a case against him, since he had returned the money. He realized, regardless of whether he would be convicted—which he probably would, since Ed and the district attorney were buddies—that his career in New York was over. Even if Lauren had forgiven him, Manny would have had to deal with the lack of referrals. Darryl and Coffee Raye had been his last clients. By the time Glo had publicly made him persona non grata, he had closed with the Rayes, but the damage was done. Glo had quoted Lauren in her column: "When I need a real estate broker, Manny Marks would no longer be my choice." Glo went on to editorialize, adding that while she did not know exactly what had transpired, from the looks of it Manny Marks had betrayed not just a client but one of his best friends. If you can't trust your friend, you surely can't trust him to be your broker, she said. And that was the end of Marks Realty of Manhattan. Lauren was right about one thing: There was no place left for him in this city. Coming to that realization had almost broken him. He would have to devise a new plan for survival.

Manny did not want to leave New York. Every time he stepped out of his home, he was exhilarated by the pulse of the city and excited by what the new day might bring. Manny Marks had been able to come up from the South, an anonymous character with a few dollars in his pocket, and turn himself into a respectable man who provided an important service to the upper crust. He had been on the cusp of ultimate success when his life spun out of control. As he thought about the mess that his world had become, he had to consider who was at fault.

Manny looked out of the window. The car eased past Lincoln Center before most people were up and on their way to work. He had spent a few evenings at the prestigious theater, listening to Wynton Marsalis and his jazz band, or watching independent films at the New York Film Festival, or the occasional dance performance by Alvin Ailey or the New York City Ballet. The events themselves were never what had thrilled Manny. For him, the people in attendance were always the most important, the most interesting. He was coming to see that he had made a terrible mistake. He had believed that all of these glamorous, wealthy individuals knew more than he did. He had thought he should follow their lead. What he now appreciated was that he was just as smart and capable as the rest of them. He didn't need Ed Thomas as a client to be successful. He didn't need referrals from Tandy Brooks to survive. He had done well before they entered his life. They had convinced him that he needed them when in fact they needed him. As he pondered this idea more, Manny knew he had to take responsibility for the damage that he had done to himself. At the same time he recognized that they, too, were liable. He had not created the game. The difference in who survived and who didn't was about a billion dollars. If Manny had Lauren and Ed's money, he wouldn't be moving anywhere. It would merely be checkmate.

Anger and sadness rested firmly in his gut. Life for him in New York had really come to an end; his hard-earned reputation was no longer intact. He forced himself to consider the positive aspects of his life. He still had a real estate license, about two hundred and fifty thousand dollars, and the ability to win people over with the flash of a smile. He was leaving New York with more knowledge and lessons learned than money could buy. Yes, he had socialized with important people and would forever remain in the archives. But most important, he had learned how to play the game of life with the best of them.

Moving to a new location would be difficult, yet if he could create himself out of nothing in New York, he could do even more with a little cash and seventeen years of experience in the toughest town in the world. He had decided to go out to San Francisco; Oakland, actually. Manny wanted to live in a warm place: no more cold harsh winters or cold harsh people. Oakland, where all the cute boys were. They would all be amateurs compared to Trenton, who had turned out to be smarter than Manny had given him credit for. The ex had worked his way into the enviable position of spokesmodel for every product in Dime Dog's enterprise, from the cologne to the designer eyewear. Yes, Manny would replenish his soul in a new home. No one would care about what had happened in New York, a different planet as far as the people out west were concerned. He would make his way in San Francisco, get his California license, and be the king of real estate in the second hottest market in the country.

Once again he would re-create himself, and this time he would not make the same mistakes. Never again would Manny allow another person to use him to accomplish sordid goals. He would always remain true to his convictions, no matter how unconventional they seemed.

The Town Car rolled down Ninth Avenue through Chelsea, a neighborhood that had grown and changed, as Manny had, over the years. He felt a pang of melancholy. He had grown to love New York for its energy, its flavor, its diversity, its acceptance of most things, and its ability to make people dream. But he was not sentimental about his heartbreak. Part of his being had been truly altered. He might be an old man before he ever set foot on this island again.

Most everything about the city had been what he expected since the day he arrived. But he had learned two lessons that would prove invaluable wherever he traveled. Lesson one: Convince people that they cannot survive without you, and that they owe all of their success to you and your efforts on their behalf. Tandy had taught him that one. She had been a great disappointment. Manny should have known she was no good by the way she played Lauren, so friendly to her face yet so conniving behind her back. When she had finally spoken to Manny, after the deal unraveled, she cursed him out with venom. No one had ever spoken to him with so much hatred. She blamed Manny for the whole scheme blowing up in their faces. Manny had ruined her life, he was nothing, not worthy of the friendship of a bum off the street. She was so cruel, calling him names that ranged from "country" to "faggot." Her tirade went on and on. Were it not for her, she said, he never would have been anything in New York in the first place.

Tandy was wrong. Manny had flourished long before he met her. In fact, Lauren had introduced them. But life was taking care of Tandy. Word on the street was that Tandy had finally sold her apartment and, with whatever little money remained, went to visit friends in London. *Good riddance,* Manny thought as the car took him through the Village down Seventh Avenue, past Two Boots Pizza, reminding him of Tommy and the good times they had shared.

He looked up at a billboard advertising a new movie starring an A-list Oscar-winning actor. He smiled. He had heard rumors that Alyssia, still dancing with the City Dance Company, was having a torrid affair with this married leading man. It hadn't taken her long to get over Ed.

Approaching the Holland Tunnel, Manny felt a lump in his throat. His reign was truly over. New York was moving quickly behind him. His friendship with Lauren was already becoming a blurry memory. He had trusted that she was a genuine friend, not wanting anything except his companionship. But his guilty feelings allowed him to think that he had been mistaken. In trying to let himself off the hook, he told his conscience that he had been used by her. A true friend would find room for empathy and forgiveness. Lauren had taught him lesson two: Never let anyone know your life's true desires.

Cynically, Manny believed that all along, Lauren had acted unaffected by the world around her to gather more interest in herself from her friends and the community. While Tandy had blasted Lauren for being a youngster unaware of how to manipulate her own publicity, she was working her situation just right. The sweet, innocent girl was not so naive. Lauren was clever. She seemed to realize that public adulation and money were the all-important aspects of survival in New York City. Tandy did, too; she just didn't have enough money. Lauren had married a billionaire. And though he had caused her public humiliation, she had recovered and remained with him. She would not banish Ed Thomas from her life. No, she needed him and all of his worth. She had told Manny so many stories, convincing him that she was enamored of Ed and that her relationship had meant so much to her, when she was the one who saw dollar signs. Why else would she stay with a philandering husband? Angrily, Manny pondered Lauren's phoniness. She would stay with Ed, forgiving him, and toss Manny from her life without a second thought. Ed would have other affairs, Manny was certain. And Lauren would tolerate them. His rage at her double standard allowed him a flicker of pleasure at the lifetime of heartache Lauren would surely endure. At the same time, a twinge of shame came over him. He had to admit that he had abused their friendship, and she could have done worse to him. She could have dragged him through the criminal-justice system.

Over the course of the year, Lauren had embraced the public, calculating her way into the spotlight with more intention than ever before. Manny had seen her picture everywhere, in local papers and national magazines, especially promoting the work she was doing for the children of Harlem. Lauren appeared in one fashion magazine surrounded by children. They were all covered in clay and laughing—even Lauren's head was tossed back in apparent joy—while making clay pots. The caption read, *Lauren Thomas takes time out to enjoy an art project with the children of Harlem.* She was a pro. She would be fine.

Once he was situated on the airplane, Manny looked out of the window. As the aircraft climbed past the clouds, he watched the island grow smaller and smaller. He felt he could still see all of the people populating the cracks and crevices of the streets, busy with their lives like ants working an anthill with a focused purpose—to be someone important in some way. His sadness dissipated somewhat as Manhattan completely disappeared from sight. Sitting back in his seat, he closed his eyes to ponder the fruitful life in the sunshine that lay before him. Perhaps stepping out of a world in which people lied to and cheated their closest pals would be good for his spirit. A simpler life. A quieter existence, where people had solid, old-fashioned values like his mother had tried to teach him. Where kindness to one's neighbor was paramount. Everyone drove his own car. Doormen and butlers didn't exist. Hundred-dollar lunches happened only on very special occasions. Designer wear was purchased at outlet stores, and celebrity was truly captivating. As Manny considered easy living, he looked down at the gold Rolex on his wrist, which lay on the armrest of his first-class seat. He knew deep down that for him, simple would never be the answer. Manny needed energy, style, and drama. This next go-round, he promised himself, armed with all of his new knowledge, he would be bigger, better, wealthier—but, most important, smarter.

LAUREN breathed in the cool, moist ocean air. She wrapped her arms around herself as the evening chill began to settle in. Even though it was mid-July, the nights at Martha's Vineyard could get cool and windy. Lauren gazed at the array of fishing boats, motorboats, and sailboats, assembled like a collection of fluttering white flags bobbing in the water. She watched them from the beach as they gently swayed from side to side. Their rhythmic motions soothed her bruised soul.

Lauren had been on a slow climb from hell over the past year. She was amazed she had come this far. After confronting all of the people who had betrayed her, she had been left emotionally depleted and was bedridden for a couple of weeks. Initially, she told her parents she had a bad flu, but she eventually confessed to them about Manny's and Tandy's betrayals. To Lauren's surprise, her mother was not totally shocked by Tandy's actions. Grace had known all along how much Tandy hated Phil. She also knew that Tandy was not a faithful wife, though she neglected to mention if she knew of the affair with Ed. Lauren didn't mention it, either. Over the course of many conversations with her mom, Lauren learned a lot about Tandy, as well as the many scandals that had plagued her mother's other friends over the years. These talks suggested to Lauren that maybe she should have been listening to her mother all along.

But despite the heart-to-hearts, Lauren avoided telling her parents about Ed's infidelity, fearing an "I told you so." Although, over time, Lauren came to realize that her mother had tried to warn her about Ed's behavior out of concern—not out of negativity, as Lauren had believed.

Lauren may not have found peace of mind, but a calm was descending upon her since her arrival at her East Chop home with unobstructed views of the Atlantic Ocean. Lauren loved summers on the island, and this year felt particularly therapeutic to her. Something about the cape made her feel safe. Perhaps it was the absence of towering concrete buildings, or maybe it was the untarnished air. Or, maybe, maybe, it was simply being in the place where she had met Ed, when the promise of honesty was a reality.

Even with magical moments like the one she was experiencing this perfect evening on Menemsha Beach, the past was never too far behind. Even with all of Ed's efforts to make things right between them, forgiving and forgetting were two very different things.

"We couldn't have a better night for watching the sunset," Ed told Lauren while nuzzling her bronzed shoulder with his lips. "I'm glad you brought us all out here."

Lauren turned around and looked at the four couples spread out on woven Mexican blankets alongside wine and cheese, lobster, and salad ordered fresh from Homeport Restaurant. Sunsets on the Vineyard were always a good occasion for friends to come together. Lauren had invited Rhonda Williams—her friend who used to work at Style Channel but had taken a bigger job at Buena Vista Films, in acquisitions—and her husband, Clarence. Lauren had also included another nice young couple, Rick Belser and his wife, Patti. Lauren had decided to reach out to Ella Johnson also, an attorney who managed the career of her husband, Cole, a jazz musician. They lived in New Orleans when they weren't traveling the world on tour, and they kept a summer place on the Vineyard. They were happy people with positive energy. Lauren found herself laughing and smiling when she was around them. The other couple was Rose Sanderson and her husband, Milton; they lived in Cambridge, Massachusetts, where he taught African-American studies at Harvard and she worked in biotechnology at MIT. Both the Johnsons and the Sandersons had become Lauren's Vineyard friends over the last few years. They would run into one another on the beach, in restaurants, and at the homes of mutual acquaintances. But this year was the first time Lauren had taken the initiative to reach out and meet new people. Her soul was rewarded by the interaction with other intelligent, free-spirited folks. It felt good to start opening up to people. She was learning how to trust again—both the motivations of others and her own judgment.

"Yes, thank you, Lauren. You and I have been talking about getting together longer than I can remember. Finally, you made it happen," Rhonda added.

"I'm glad we could all make it," Lauren told her friends. She was pleased that everyone had accepted her rather spontaneous invitation. Looking past her own party, she surveyed the throngs of people seated on their own folding chairs and picnic blankets, packed together in anticipation of one of the most glorious shows—an unobstructed sunset on the horizon.

"Hey, ladies, anyone up for the rock-skipping lesson I promised?" Rick said before finishing off the last of his beer. He had been a high-powered attorney in the Clinton administration, and now his unofficial job was in political fund-raising. Lauren had met him and Patti at a dinner party in Oak Bluffs three summers ago and found them both interesting. She was particularly intrigued by the vast philanthropy of the couple—their passion for indigent children and poor artists.

"Shall I grab my own rock, or are you going to teach me how to do that?" Lauren teased. She and Rick had quickly developed a brother/sister rapport.

"Just pick one that's flat and smooth," Rick began as he headed toward the water. "Anyone else up to learning something new?"

"I'll join you guys." Rhonda gathered her slightly overweight bottom off the blanket to follow.

They walked toward the shore, navigating among the guitar players, straying toddlers, and kids tossing balls. A small blue ball landed at Lauren's feet just as she reached the edge of the water. She noticed a toddler scurrying toward her, determined that she not steal his toy. "Is this yours?" Lauren asked, picking up the ball and handing it to the anxious child.

"Yes, that's mine. My dada is playing with me," the three-year-old emphatically told her, as if half expecting her to run off with it.

"Well, you and your dada have a good time," Lauren told the little guy, suppressing a grin. He marched off like he was returning to his official duties. His little chubby arms possessively embraced the ball, and he glanced back at Lauren a couple of times just to make sure she knew who was in control.

Lauren was reminded of Ed's latest proposal—one about which she had mixed feelings. Over the last few months, he had begun expressing interest in starting a family, reversing his earlier pronouncement. He now claimed he wanted to carry on his lineage through her, to leave behind a tribute to their union. As Lauren watched the little boy toss the ball, now between his mother and father, she considered what Ed had suggested. A child? It seemed ironic to her that at one point in the relationship, she had thought she would have to convince *him* to change his mind. At this juncture, Lauren wasn't sure she wanted to bring a baby into a relationship that was not built on a foundation of trust. She did not want her children to suffer the whims of their father's indiscretions. *She* did not wish to suffer from Ed's indiscretions again. How could she ever be sure?

But Lauren was determined to press forward, with truth illuminating her path. She refused to allow Ed's infidelity, lies, and dysfunction to become the norm in her relationship—she was beyond that. She also had no intention of settling for a mediocre marriage, which was why she and Ed were seeing a professional to help work through their issues. In her heart, Lauren believed Ed was capable of becoming a better man—a lifetime of lies and cheating was more than she could bear to think her future held. During the rehabilitation process, Lauren was discovering how complex a marriage really was. Over the years, she had heard women in passing describe marriage as being "complicated." With regret, she finally understood what they had meant. More than anything, she wanted to believe that Ed would never cheat on her again—that thought gave her hope—but the fact remained that he had betrayed her. The potential for him to do it again hung in the air like stale cigar smoke.

"Hey, Lauren, you're missing my patented move. You taking notes?" yelled Rick as he wound his arm and hurled a rock just beyond the break of a small wave. After Lauren's failed attempt at replicating his move, she decided to return to the rest of her guests before embarrassing herself anymore.

As Lauren reached their blanket, Ed was at her side with a fresh glass of chardonnay. She was trying to appreciate his newly revived attentiveness, but it was hard, very hard at times. She wondered if his gestures were genuine or simply the actions of a man trying to get out of the doghouse. Could he always appreciate her, or would his eyes wander again as soon as some hot, new young girl caught his attention? Lauren had thought about this question many times. She decided not to drive herself crazy worrying about what Ed would or would not do when she wasn't around. She could not live under those circumstances. She had goals of her own that needed her attention: validating work that brought her personal gratification, with or without his acceptance. Although she was Ed Thomas's wife, she refused to be defined by him or defeated by him.

To bring herself out of depression, Lauren worked out every day. She also decided to throw herself into her work. She began a project about women giving birth in prison, financed by the foundation she and Ed had created. After her Style Channel piece, she had no problem accessing a crew and resources. Rhonda had assured Lauren that once the documentary was completed, she would introduce Lauren to possible distributors or get the work into festivals for exposure.

"Lauren, how is your film coming along?" Milton asked.

"So far so good, but we still have a long way to go," Lauren responded.

"Well, I've already seen some of the footage, and it looks damn good. She captures some very touching moments," Ed interjected.

Lauren smiled at his compliment, though she still felt insecure about all of his admiring comments. Something about them felt a little self-serving, like he was trying to prove his love. She was lingering on the thought of his disingenuousness when Ed leaned in to her ear and whispered, "I love you so much."

Lauren ached for the love she wanted to accept, but her heart was resistant. With time, she hoped to be less conflicted about his purported love. In the meantime, she knew that relearning self-love was most important. With so many betrayals, Lauren had had to ask what about her had invited such disdain. In her first few months of self-imposed seclusion, she beat herself up, thinking she was ugly, stupid, naive, and unworthy of love. With much digging, she had stopped feeling sorry for herself.

"Don't you love me, too?" Ed whispered into her ear. Lauren did not respond. She just looked at her hands. "I understand, but I know you do," Ed continued, hopeful. If nothing else, he was persistent.

But what Ed did not understand was that Lauren had to be sure she fully loved herself before she could admit to loving anyone else. For the time being, she was working toward fully appreciating herself and trusting her judgment.

"It's on the horizon!" one of her guests shouted excitedly. Everyone looked toward the ocean to watch the sun begin its descent.

The round ball of fire loomed large above the water as if an artist had spent months painting it. Watching the sun eagerly make its move toward the eternal straight line, the revelers looked on as if observing a master at work. Lauren reflected on a lifetime of summers coming to this same beach as a child, as a young adult, and now as a woman—as a wife. The sun always made an appearance, unless it was a cloudy night. But eventually, it would show up again, bright and brilliant.

Like the sun, Lauren was returning to the world after a dark, cloudy period. She was approaching the vast horizon that held the promise of a long and fruitful life.

ACKNOWLEDGMENTS

There would be no me without the work, encouragement, guidance, support, and love of my mom and dad, Lillian and George Lewis. Thanks so much for nurturing me along this journey. I also must thank my sister, Dr. Tracey Lewis Elligan, for her support; her hard work is an inspiration to us all.

My dear husband and children have put up with me for years as I worked on this book and other ventures. Their continued support and belief in me and my work has propelled me to be the best that I can be. Spike, Satchel, and Jackson, thank you for understanding when Mommy "had" to write and for always cheering me on. Your love is priceless. And thank you, Kettely, for your assistance and dedication.

To my family and all of my friends from everywhere, especially the goddesses—I haven't named you all because I don't want to carelessly leave anyone out—because every one of you feeds my soul.

To Cole and Ella, thank you for letting Mommy work with me even when you really wanted her attention. And thank you, Greg, for your brotherly love that included lots of support and encouragement.

I must say a very special thank-you to Spencer David Means—a good friend who not only gave us important details on the real estate business but whose spirit brightens anyone who comes in contact with him. A class act all the way. Thank you for being someone we all can count on . . . I feel fortunate to have you as a friend. And to David Daniels, thank you for all of your wonderful support and encouragement.

To Dale Harris, the only writing teacher who taught me you can't write what you don't know or feel. You showed me that I could write when so many others told me I couldn't. Thank you for making me dig deeper. RIP.

To Sandi Gelles-Cole, whose tutelage was so helpful. With just a few words you helped to pull out what was lying under the surface. Your encouragement throughout the process meant so much to me. Thank you.

David Wirtschafter, for your sustained encouragement and guidance.

To Suzanne Gluck, thanks for taking us seriously and for nurturing, guiding, and believing in us. You, too, said just a few words that helped us to see how to really make *Gotham Diaries* come alive. You are formidable. Thank you. To Emily Nurkin and Christine Price, thank you for all of your assistance.

To Ellen Archer, Leslie Wells, and the entire crew at Hyperion, your contributions to and your passion for *Gotham Diaries* has been like a dream.

Crystal, we've come a long way, baby, from our days in Cannes . . . I am so glad you got on that plane . . . the ride has been interesting thus far, filled with lots of fun, good humor, and introspection . . . every step continues to be a joy . . . you go, girl! Your friendship is precious.

And most important—thank you, God, for all of the many blessings in my life and for the opportunity to be creative.

—T.L.L.

Greg—thank you for all of your inspiration, but more than anything, thank you for helping me create the greatest gifts of all—our children.

My sister, Ruthie—every time I talk to you, I feel like I've had a triple shot of espresso and just stepped out of a "You can do it!" seminar. Thank you. And thank you, David, for making Ruthie so happy.

My muse—Spencer Means—thank you for your friendship, wit, integrity, charm, and for finding me a home amidst my terrible case of sticker shock. And David Daniels, thank you for always being so kind and helpful.

To my University of Michigan English professors, Enid Zimmerman and Ralph Story, for teaching me free writing and encouraging all of my creative endeavors.

To my whole family, who has offered me a sense of belonging and grounding. For that, I thank all of you.

First, the McCrary side—Monga and Kid, your spirits live on in us. Vikki, my mother, you are truly one of a kind. Aunt Toni. Joe Nowell. Richard, Melva, Michelle, and Steven Nowell. Aunt Dores. Kathleen, David, Aaron, and Sarah Lewis. Wade, LaVerne, Lauren, and Justin McCree. Karen McCree—I can't wait to read your book! Aunt Winnie. Mitchell, Kelen, and Megan Duncan. Shelley, Roger, and Camille. Renee Lee. Morgan Duncan. Aunt MoMo. Russell Smith. Kim and Andrew.

Now, the Barrington side—Grandmother Bernice and Hugh F. Barrington, your spirits live on in us. Auntie Fran and Uncle Arthur. Art, Romayne, Avery, and Amara Raines. Albert, Karen, Allison, and Ashley Raines. Uncle Hugh and Pat. Aunt Loretta. Nancy and Chasen. Karon. Linda, James, Austin, Carter, and Lyndon Whittacker. Hugh F. Barrington III.

Pat and Mama, you will always be loved and missed.

Aunt Webby—you are a treasure and a phenomenal human being. Aunt Evelyn—I'm looking forward to you coming East to "hold your babies."

Charlette "June" Topsey—thank you for taking such loving care of my babies. I always know they are in good hands with you.

To my original Detroit crew—nobody can do it like we do it in the "D"—

Leslie Danley and Wil Bennett, Nicole Doss, Nikki Skalski, Dominique Sims Lash, Carla Diggs Smith, Dena Dodd Perry, Marcia Mackey, Shaun Robinson, Keith Kelley, Lanier Covington, Mike Evans, Marty Jones, Dennis Archer, Ben Smith, and Byron Pitts—keep on writing, man!

Kyera Keenne-Cherot—thank you for opening so many rays of thought to me.

Now, my extended family—Rose Swanson, thank you for always being such a wonderful source of encouragement! And thank you, Rory, for being my first buddy. Joyce Dodd, your radiant smile resonates in everyone's heart that had the pleasure of knowing you. Nancy Taylor Rosenberg—you have been a mentor since the day I met you. Fran Rauch, Peter Simonetta, Patrick Orr and the whole Tuxedo Park crew—you all keep life interesting. Richard Douglas and Pat Kearney—I'm waiting to send Cole down to Florida for that visit you promised.

Shauna Neely Osei-Yaw—thank you for all of the styling and one-of-a-kind jewelry. Cherie Johnson—thank you for always hooking up my hair, girl.

Thank you to the 66th Street and Third Avenue Starbucks for my rent-free office and especially to the crew who never let my caramel macchiato cups go empty—Shawn, Wendy, Damian, Shawnette, Olga, Blossom, Glenda, Herbert, Lupita, Betsy, Monique, Christina, Christopher, and all the rest of you who made me feel right at home.

Thanks to everyone at William Morris, especially our agent, the tenacious and brilliant Suzanne Gluck—you rock! You helped us breathe life into this BIG story. Dave Wirtschafter, thank you for still taking our phone calls even after reading the first script Tonya and I ever wrote. More important, thanks for telling us to keep writing. Emily Nurkin and Christine Price, your assistance is greatly appreciated.

Sandi Gelles-Cole—thank you for helping us iron out such a TIGHT plot line.

Thank you to everyone at Hyperion, especially Ellen Archer for believing and trusting in our characters, our world, and our story. Leslie Wells, as an editor, you have been completely on point! Thank you for helping take *Gotham Diaries* to the next level. Elisa Lee, thank you for always taking care of business.

Satchel and Jackson, you two are wise beyond your years, thank you for always telling it like it is.

Spike—you have been behind Tonya and me from this story's infancy—your support and creative feedback have been invaluable.

Tonya—what a journey! What a pleasure! Working with you has been an honor. You have taught me so much—as a person, as a mother, as a writer. From L.A. to Miami to Martha's Vineyard with children in tow—we multitasked, we worked our butts off, and we got it done!!! I am so proud of what we have created together and I look forward to our next book. Thank you for being an amazing partner, but more than anything, you've been a true friend.

Hello Friend up above—always, always, much love and much respect.

Peace and God Bless.

—C.M.A.

GOTHAM DIARIES
Reading Group Guide

1. Manny Marks comes to New York as a young man who hopes to find a place where he can be himself and fit in. Does he ever achieve that goal and, in fact, do any of the characters in the book ever really fit in? What does it mean to fit into a particular social group?

2. Throughout *Gotham Diaries* Tandy notes that "Times are a-changing." With Tandy and Ed's generation both being first-generation New York socialites, are the times really changing or is it merely Tandy's life that is changing?

3. Lauren constantly resists taking a seat on philanthropic boards in the city because she wants to pursue dreams of her own career. Since she is married to a billionaire and financially secure, is it her responsibility to get involved in charitable organizations or should she pursue her own desires?

4. Lauren had isolated herself from her peers after marrying Ed because she was concerned that people were impressed by his money, but then all the people that she did trust betrayed her. At the end of the novel, she has reached out to new friends. Do you think she will make the same mistake in trusting the wrong people again?

5. At the end of the novel, Lauren is pictured in a magazine in the same way that Tandy suggests she would like to be featured. Does this suggest that Lauren is developing the same selfish traits as Tandy?

6. Manny is pictured in a newspaper carrying Lauren's bag and is referred to as an errand boy to the rich and famous. Did Lauren use Manny in much the same way as Tandy? Or did Lauren truly consider Manny a friend?

7. Was Manny really a bad guy at heart or was he vulnerable to the world of high finance because of his desire to (a) get rich, (b) fit in, or (c) a combination of the two?

8. In the end, did Manny, Tandy, and/or Ed learn a lesson about Lauren and/or life?

9. In the end, Lauren decides she needs to find self-love before she can love anyone else. Does this imply that she will remain with Ed?

10. While Manny's goal in life appears to be that he wants to be a major player in New York real estate, his homosexuality does not seem to be an issue for him. In fact, being gay seems to facilitate his ability to maneuver in this crowd. If *Gotham Diaries* were set in another city, would this remain true?

11. Most of the moneyed black characters in *Gotham Diaries* are self-made people, gaining their footing in this world by attending college and maintaining friendships from school. Are these people living the American dream?

12. *Gotham Diaries* takes place in a world where money is the ticket into society. What is it that people get out of being connected to a society or class that they deem meaningful?

13. What does it mean when, at the end of the novel, Lauren seems to choose artistic, intellectual people over her former friends?

14. Grace, Lauren's mother, seems to be very critical of Lauren's decision to marry Ed and then of her choice to be more creative instead of more business minded. Is there anything that Grace could have done or said to offer Lauren more guidance or did Lauren just have to experience life in her own way?